**The final book in the award-w
ROYAL DRAGONFLY Book /
Finalist in the 2020 KINDLE F
AUTHOR SHOUT Editor's To
Finalist in THE WISHING SHELF AWARDS
'10 out of 10' The Booklife Prize**

'Mielitta's time with bees is beautiful yet tense, and Kermon's adventures "in the walls" prove continually surprising and exciting. Best of all, Gill's characters are convincing and unique… Jean Gill's *Natural Forces* series offer a rich, strange, and alluring adventure that buzzes with intrigue and nature.' *The Booklife Prize 2020*

'A thrilling fantasy adventure YA will love. A FINALIST and highly recommended.' *Wishing Shelf Awards 2019*

'An epic fight for nature...With more backstabbing that the Roman Senate, more deceit than *Game of Thrones* and more paranoia than *The Handmaid's Tale, Queen of the Warrior Bees* is a compelling story with life-like characters and a fast-moving plot.' Deb McEwan, the *Afterlife* series

'Spellbinding! If you liked *The Bees* you'll love this. A brilliantly imagined fantasy with a strong environmental message. Jean Gill writes with a beekeeper's clarity about hive structure, and of 'hive mind' with the heart and passion of a talented author and poet.' Ashley Dyer, *Splinter in the Blood*

'The most original book I've read this year.' Anna Castle, *the Francis Bacon mysteries*

'Perfect gift for young environmental campaigners raised on Harry Potter.' Debbie Young, the *Sophie Sayers Village mysteries*

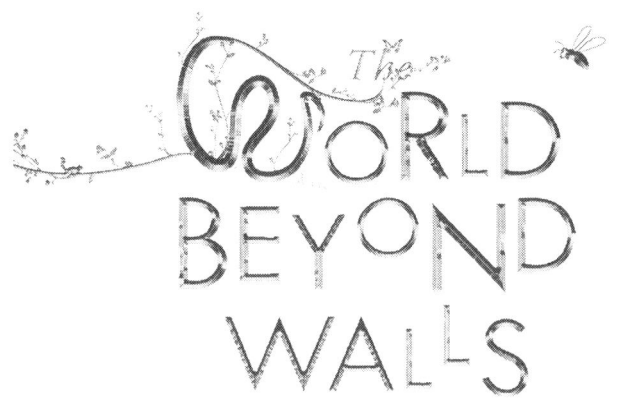

THE WORLD BEYOND WALLS

NATURAL FORCES III

JEAN GILL

© Jean Gill 2021
The 13th Sign
ISBN 979-10-96459-16-2

First published in 2021

All rights reserved. No part of this publication may be reproduced, stored in a retrieval system, or transmitted in any form without prior permission from the publisher.

This is a work of fiction. Names, characters, organisations, places and events are either products of the author's imagination or are used fictitiously.

For Ruth
with love

You are the bows from which your children
as living arrows are sent forth.
Kahlil Gibran

CHAPTER ONE

'Evil lurks in the walls,' they said.

Nobody would listen to her, so why should she listen to them? If she was too young, too stupid *and* a girl, then they were too old, too blind *and* men, so how could they see the truth that was so obvious to her? Arguing with herself, Janette hopped from one foot to the other in front of a stone wall, in the gloomiest corner at the base of the spiral staircase in the Mages' Tower.

She was really arguing with Nathan, who was not there. Usually he was as unobjectionable as a boy could be and he was her only sure way of returning from an excursion into the walls. And he'd said no.

His black spike of hair nodding in agreement, he'd responded to all her irresistible logic with that one word. And she'd let him think he'd won.

Her cheeks grew warm at the memory of his relief, his offer to help her in apprentice work in the forge, which he hated, or in binding her stories into books, which he hated even more. But she had not lied to him. She'd never said she wouldn't go. He'd just assumed she wouldn't dare go without him. And if he'd let her down, then she had no choice but to go alone, did she?

The more she thought about it, the more she realised this was all Nathan's fault. He didn't appreciate how important her work was. He didn't appreciate her gift. He didn't appreciate *her*. He was just like the adult mages who still wouldn't allow girls into the walls. Now they'd even banned *all* apprentices from entering the walls unless under mages' orders and then only one at a time, in the company of Councillor Verity.

She mimicked the pompous tones they used. 'Because evil lurks in the walls.'

Janette had seen Councillor Verity often enough, a girl barely older than her, as waif-like as Janette was solid, as pale-skinned and golden-haired as Janette was dark and haloed in frizz. The Councillor didn't even have any magecraft whereas Janette could levitate Nathan with just a thought-beam. He objected to that, as did their tutor. Mage-Smith Kermon said it was a very clever trick but not respectful to a fellow-mage.

He could talk! Her teacher hadn't even looked at her story, however often she reminded him and said how important it was. Janette didn't need any of them. She'd been into the walls before and she could stand up for herself. She could balance on one leg too: it helped her concentrate.

The story. Telling stories was her special mage gift, just as Mage Kermon was a smith and a soul-reader. But it was as if her gift was cursed. Nobody believed her stories mattered. And this one could shake the Citadel to its foundations.

Was that what she wanted? Oh yes, that was *definitely* what she wanted. When she'd sneaked into the walls with Nathan, back when he'd been a true friend, she'd seen the honey hunter and she'd known in her bones how important the girl was. And she'd *known* she had to go back, to get the whole story. She'd imagined discussing the implications in Council, being a hero for what she'd discovered. Instead the story was languishing on a shelf. Read and dismissed. Or maybe not even read at all.

Calm now, in the ageless certainty of her gift, Janette stepped forward and walked smoothly into the walls.

A shimmering, a shift of the light and, instead of stone walls, stairs and darkness all around, she was now in a leafy green space. Not grassette like in the Citadel but real grass. Dozens of people ran, walked, played ball and not one of them could see her. Nor was she interested in them.

Janette's paces were regular as her heartbeat. She walked through people as if they weren't real – or as if she wasn't. She shivered and continued to picture the honey hunter in her mind's eye until the scene shifted to a village in the mountains, the inhabitants outside their huts, watching a girl argue her cause.

Qwian. Long black hair, flashing eyes and her father's two long bamboo spears in her hands. No woman had ever been a honey hunter and at first the Headman denied her passionate claim. She insisted that her dreams had named her the honey hunter, that her father's sacred role had been passed on to her when he died. Only when the village Shaman spoke on her behalf was Qwian given the chance to prove herself worthy, as judged by the bees themselves.

Janette's story lived and breathed in front of her. Qwian's team of twelve hunters carried bamboo ropes, slats of wood and a wicker basket through the jungle, across the leech-infested river to the sacred clearing above the high cliffs.

When the men at the top lowered her down those sheer cliffs in a basket, Qwian was almost flying herself among the giant bees that streamed out to protect their comb. Vast, glistening slabs of their treasure filled every crevice in the rock face.

Qwian's only protection was a veil around her head as she speared huge chunks of comb through black clouds of enraged insects, sent the severed pieces down the dizzying drop to the men waiting with baskets below. The rhododendron honey so prized in the village was its trading lifeblood. Men craved the heady rush, akin to madness, offered by a single teaspoonful. Those who risked a second helping, learned of its dangers.

As she swung in her basket, amid smoke and bees, doubts and stings, Qwian was smacked in the face by a morsel of comb, before it fell into the waiting basket below. She automatically licked her lips and then deliberately licked again. Qwian tasted the honey as she'd been warned not to do.

Hah! thought Janette, watching her story again. *Someone like me.*

And what Qwian saw during the honey madness was what had brought Janette back here. Not the boy and the kiss waiting in the village. Not the celebration for the first woman honey hunter, at the moment when she came back to the village, victorious.

In that honey-mad moment, swaying in a basket, dizzy from bee-stings and vertigo, Qwian spoke to the bees, thanked them.

And they replied.

We will need you, they told her. *Your hive and ours. Never forget our gifts.*

Through Qwian's eyes, Janette saw the smoke curl into the soft lines of a girl's face, surrounded by bees. The girl running through a forest. A tattoo glittering on her thigh, a queen bee coming alive, flying.

Never forget, the bees buzzed. *We protect our queen. We protect you.*

Born and bred in the Citadel, like generations before her, Janette had never seen living beings that weren't human until she'd made her illicit trip with Nathan into the walls. She knew of such creatures from books in the library and had been brought up to give thanks they'd been exterminated. The Citadel was indeed free of infestation but rumour populated the nearby Forest with all manner of monster, including the defectives in exile from the Citadel.

Like every citizen, Janette had heard the terrifying story of the Citadel freak who'd been infected with Forest. Who communed with bees, could even become one. And who'd been defeated – the stones be thanked! – in the Battle of the Forest, where she now lived in exile.

And then, in the mysterious world through the walls, where the past existed in layers of time, Janette had found the honey hunter and the bees. *What if?* Janette had asked herself ever since she shared Qwian's vision through smoke and the blackness of bees. *What if* the vision had come to pass? What if the girl running through the Forest was the Citadel's enemy, the Queen of the Warrior Bees?

Conquered but alive, she was held as a threat over naughty children by Citadel parents. Bees instead of hair, black eyes filling her face. 'She'll take you off to the Forest if you don't behave. And if you don't obey her every wish, she'll have you stung until you're more full of holes than a hairnet.'

Not that Janette believed such stories any more. Given the number of times she'd misbehaved, she should have been whisked off to the Forest long ago.

What if this was where it began? This communion with bees, a promise and a prophecy? Were Qwian and the boy who loved her parents to the freak? And if the running girl was the Queen of the Warrior Bees, Janette knew something about her that would end her reign. Their queen would not be protected, however many bees were with her, if she was suppressed before her life began, here in the walls.

First, Janette had to follow the story, find out how it led from here to the Citadel side of the wall. Then she could go to the Council of Ten and impress them. Mage-Smith Kermon would be sorry he hadn't taken her story seriously.

'Show me the honey hunter returning with her harvest,' she instructed and, in the manner of the world within the walls, her focus created a destination and the scene shifted around her, until she was once more among the huts of the village, watching Qwian lauded by the Headman, returning triumphant with her two spears and precious baskets of mad honey.

By refining her search terms, she navigated the stages of Qwian's life, willing time to pass ever faster so she watched only key scenes. She saw Qwian and her young man grow older, their children playing hunt-the-honey with wooden sticks. Until the year came when one of the boys knelt in front of the Headman and received his mother's spears as pride lit her eyes.

Not a girl-child, thought Janette. And the other children showed no interest in bees. So the running girl was still in the future. Janette must walk through time, following the story of the bees' promise. Once she was on the scent of a story, she was oblivious to all else and she was happy on the honey trail.

But her presence in the walls had not gone unnoticed and a great evil awoke. Finally, its time had come. And it laughed.

CHAPTER TWO

Janette watched Qwian's family through the span of six generations of honey hunters, four replacements of spears and in the village, a multiplication of huts with new tin roofs. The bees' words to Qwian were passed on with due reverence to each subsequent generation.

A thousand stories of lives lived well or badly, sometimes both, flickered past Janette but as far as she was concerned, she was witnessing a jungle, cliffs and a village where nothing happened.

Boredom whined, 'How much longer?'

One more generation, she told herself. *Just one more. Then I'll go home.*

But her concentration on the honey hunters had been interrupted long enough for more than boredom to pose questions.

One more generation. The words shocked her. How long had she been here, in Citadel time, watching? Nathan had relayed all the warnings the boys had been given. How easy it was to follow one distraction after another, gorging on the rich sensations of past lives, forgetting to nourish the Citadel body and staying too long in this seductive world.

What happened if you stayed too long? Janette's throat went dry and her empty stomach rumbled.

That's just boys' talk, she told herself. Like frightening small children with the Queen of the Warrior Bees. And now she'd seen bees through the mind of a honey hunter, they weren't so frightening at all. If you treated them with respect.

She ignored the inner voice reminding her that the boys had been given all this information because they were allowed to go into the walls. They were trained – and she wasn't.

One more generation, she repeated sternly and at that moment, two things happened. The first was that a stranger walked into the village, a craggy-faced man in dark trousers and jacket, out of place beside the tribesmen in their colourful wrappings. Janette felt the tingle she'd known when she first saw Qwian.

The man was not alone. Behind him were tribal bearers, carrying packs on their heads, and behind *them* were three more men in suits. The outsiders were panting and red-faced from the rugged trek up the mountain to reach the village.

As was proper, a villager fetched the Headman, who kept the visitors waiting long enough to establish his importance. Then he came out of the largest hut, wearing his ceremonial head-dress, always worn when he appointed the new Honey Hunter. In seven generations of honey hunters Janette had seen five headmen and nine changes of head-dress. This one consisted of bright feathers and beaded tresses. The Headman pointed at the strangers' leader to indicate permission to speak.

'You speak trader language?'

The Headman nodded.

'I'm Oliver Dupont and we have travelled far, seeking your Honey Hunter,' said the strangers' leader, as Janette had *known* he would. Her story was unfolding.

Qwian's great-great-great-great-granddaughter Mahamauri duly appeared. Coconut milk was brought to mark the coming of the strangers as a great occasion and, with some discomfort,

Oliver and his companions copied their hosts and sat cross-legged in the dust. They took their turns, sipping from the hairy-shell bowls.

After a polite meander via words of little substance, the Headman said, 'Where are you from?' which was a sign for the real conversation to begin. And for the words to be interpreted by each man according to his hopes and fears.

'From your future,' said Oliver, his expression as sober as his suit.

The Headman didn't so much as pause over his coconut shell but sipped and passed it on again, clockwise around the circle. Curious villagers in their brightly-coloured robes had formed an outer circle. From Janette's bird's eye view, the gathering looked like an exotic flower with rainbow petals. One bold villager passed a coconut shell behind him and so the drink spiralled outwards to the shyest man in the village, hovering on the fringe.

'Then you should speak to our Shaman,' said the Headman, nodding his feathers towards a hut which seemed to gather shadows around its boarded door and shuttered windows. The Shaman had not come out to welcome the visitors.

'No. It is your Honey Hunter I seek. Mahamauri. We too have our shamans and I need Mahamauri's help.' He corrected himself. 'Mahamauri's help can create a force for good. A natural force. Nobody else can do this.' He struggled to find the words. 'Because she knows the bees. We need to do this for the bees. And for people, all people.'

'What do you want Mahamauri to do?

'Come with us. Do the right thing at the right place at the right time. Then she can come home.'

The Headman shook his head. 'We need Mahamauri. Our village cannot survive without our Honey Hunter. She has been chosen by the Shaman and has the trust of the bees. If we have no honey to sell, we can't buy goats or grain, tools or cookpots.'

There was silence.

Then Mahamauri spoke. 'I should do this. I want to see this place, where these people come from. I want to do the right thing.'

The Headman shook his head again. 'You are a good woman but you trust too easily. Be more like the bees. Test people.'

He looked straight at Oliver. 'I do not trust you.'

Oliver looked at Mahamauri instead. 'Remember the bees' promise. Now is the time.'

Mahamauri recalled the words her father had told her, passed down six times from his ancestor Qwian.

'I have to go,' she told the Headman. 'It is my family duty.'

'I won't let you.' The Headman spoke without menace but two of the strongest villagers stood up.

Before they could be given orders, a voice floated from the furthest point of the outer circle, like a contribution from the gods on high.

'I will be your Honey Hunter,' said the shyest man in the village. 'And you will repay me by permitting our marriage when she returns.'

'This is mad honey talk!' said the Headman. 'You are not from the right family, you know nothing of the work and the Shaman has not chosen you.'

'Let the Shaman speak, then let Mahamauri speak,' said the shyest man.

Suddenly all there realised that the Shaman's hut was now in brightest sunshine, the doors and windows blazing with light that came from inside. The figure who emerged was a mere silhouette against the brightness and his shadow made him look twice the height of any normal man. The men in suits shrank back as he passed them to take the place cleared for him beside the Headman. The Shaman stared at the strangers, made noises that were contemptuous in any language.

'Let the suitor prove himself among the bees in the usual way,' the Shaman pronounced. 'Then Mahamauri can go. If he fails, no. If she rejects his terms, no.' Then he made his heavy way back to his hut, took the brightness inside with him and shuttered it into shadow again.

'What do you say, Mahamauri?' asked the Headman.

A path had cleared between the people for the shyest man to walk to the centre of the inner circle and he stood in front of Mahamauri, his eyes cast down. His brown linen robe was gathered over one shoulder and the other glistened, naked.

Mahamauri stood up in one graceful movement, kissed his bare shoulder and said, 'No, Bibek. Not this way. It is too dangerous.'

The shyest man in the village had a name and the villagers gasped at this unsuspected romance in their midst.

'You must go. You said so. Then we will both have honour. I will do as Qwian did and prove myself. Let the bees decide.'

Mahamauri had no answer that would not show disrespect for him and for his family duty but her black eyes were cloudy with misgiving.

Janette remembered the gut-wrenching drop in a basket down mountain cliffs, the cloud of enraged bees stinging Qwian everywhere but her face, which was protected with a net. Her only protection. No wonder Mahamauri was scared for her shy suitor. But she could not forbid him. And no villager needed to ask whether Mahamauri was happy with the terms. The kiss and the look in her eyes said she'd marry him now if she could.

Dupont's triumphant tone cut across the moment. 'That's settled then.' He stood up but was quelled by a gesture from the Headman.

'First Bibek must prove himself.' The pause was heavy as a body falling from a basket among the bee-black cliffs.

'If he does, Mahamauri may go with you to do this right thing you care so much about. Then she must come back to her duties here and honour her word to this man.'

Mahamauri's eyes shone again, black pools of truth; she looked only at the shy man. 'I will return. I will come back for the honey and for you.'

The beauty of these words echoed in Janette's mind, ready-made for the page in the book that spiky-haired Nathan was crafting for her stories. Hadn't Qwian said the same to her black-haired boy when she set off on the trek to the cliff-top, with her team of catchers, carriers and rope-makers?

Surely Mahamauri was the next part of the story. The part which created the Queen of the Warrior Bees and would put the Citadel's enemy in Janette's power. Then she could ask the mages for anything she wanted. Permission to visit the world within the walls, for a start.

Janette was so much enjoying her imagined future status as a hero that she was slow to realise the second important thing happening here, now. One story does not preclude another.

The shadows were deepening around her and she felt a sudden chill, unrelated to the cramps of hunger which crippled her again. The shadows that came from behind her were not from the Shaman's hut and were not created by sunlight. Shadows that moved like a crowd, with multiple hands, heads, boots; rippling ever darker and more concentrated. Cramming darkness into a smaller and smaller space, fitting the imprints of a girl's boots on the ground. Underneath Janette. She could feel the ooze of it, seeping into her flesh, her bones. She stood petrified.

Blackness moved like hands swarming up a rope, writhed up her boots, her borrowed britches and shirt, up the side of her neck and drilled into her forehead. Blackness that had one viscous eye pierced with a bee sting, blinded but all-seeing.

Blackness that whispered inside her head, 'I know who you are and where you're from.'

Janette screamed but nobody heard except the laughing dark.

She filled her mind with directions, the way to navigate the walls, so she could hide.

Follow Mahamauri and Oliver, wherever they go next, up the layers of time to the right thing to do, whenever it might be.

But blackness muddled her magecraft and she couldn't see where she was going so she just imagined herself running. Anywhere, any time period, as long as it was away from *that*.

'Nathan!' she yelled, seeking the connection that would take her back to the Citadel side of the walls. But there was only the rush of strange places and invisible people. She'd told her anchor she didn't need him and now she was lost in the walls, the blackness at her heels.

CHAPTER THREE

'Crumbling stones!' Kermon swore, as the steel he'd been tempering so carefully in the fire flaked and shattered. He dumped the debris on the anvil, nodded to his assistant to clean up and gave his full attention to the apprentice mage who'd interrupted him. No wonder his concentration had lapsed.

'She did what?' he demanded, knowing full well that the tale would grow even more catastrophic when told a second time.

'I think she went into the walls on her own, Mage-Smith Kermon,' stammered Nathan, 'and I don't think she's come back because she wasn't at breakfast and nobody's seen her.'

'On her own!' repeated Kermon stupidly.

The boy looked at him directly for the first time. It didn't take a soul-reader to perceive the worry – and guilt – in those eyes, the pupils huge in the flickering forge light.

'I know. I should have gone with her–'

Kermon cut him short. 'Neither of you should have gone!'

'I tried to stop her but when she gets an idea in her head… And she doesn't think it's fair that the boys can go into the walls, even if it is only one at a time, and accompanied, and she says her stories are just as important as any Councillor's work and that the story she brought back last time could be life or death for the Citadel and that you haven't even…' Nathan gulped and tailed off, perhaps conscious of Kermon's raised eyebrow.

'I don't think *our* priorities are for Janette to decide. Do you?' But the youngsters were right. He had been too concerned with what he considered weighty matters to read the girl's story. And he knew what it was like to be sidelined. Trivial as the story was, it mattered to Janette and he should have acknowledged that. Something else to put right – when the girl was found. He sighed.

Nathan wisely made no response to the rhetorical question. 'Is she… is she dead?' he asked.

How the stones would I know! Kermon stopped himself from saying, knowing full well the dangers in the walls and the reason nobody was permitted to go into them without Verity's protection.

'We have no reason to think so,' he lied, 'but she could be lost and she's been in the walls longer than is good for her.' *Any* time in the walls was longer than was good for her!

'So you'll set up a search party? And you'll find her? I should come with you. I'm her anchor.'

As Verity was Kermon's anchor: his way to return to the Citadel from the four-dimensional labyrinth on the other side of the walls. And now Verity was the only guarantee of safe passage. Impervious to all magecraft, she passed on this protective contagion to anyone she touched – but only while she was touching them.

She knew the evil in the walls intimately. Once, the evil had been Verity's father Rinduran, Chief Mage in the Citadel. After his death, what remained of him within the walls was something which made Kermon shudder but bore an external resemblance to the man Verity had known Daddy. This was why she refused to even talk about it, let alone take action. Which was why he and Verity were the only people who knew what the evil in the walls was. And now their procrastination might cost his student her life.

Kermon's fears made him rough-tongued. 'Then you should have kept her from such a dangerous stunt. If you hadn't taken her into the walls in the first place, none of this would have happened. Janette would be safe and sound, satisfying her curiosity in the library!'

His face ashen, Nathan mumbled, 'I'm sorry.' His voice trembling. he brushed his eyes with the back of his hand and rushed out of the forge before Kermon could put things right.

Never mind the boy for now. What mattered was to find Janette. And he didn't have the faintest idea where, in the vastness of space and time, to start looking. First, he had to tell Verity the bad news.

As a result of this thoroughly unpleasant conversation, Kermon was heading to an emergency meeting of the Council of Ten to discuss what to do about his missing student, or, as Verity had put it in the message sent to all members, 'a matter concerning trespass and treason'.

Kermon didn't care whether Janette was seen as a criminal or as an endangered child as long as she was brought home safely but he knew he would have to bite his tongue and let Verity handle the political debate. He would need every bit of political nous he'd gained during his time on the Council to support her without creating even more enmity around the table.

In the months since Verity had established her authority in a remarkable duel with the green mage Hamel, she had quietly imposed new rules in meetings. As joint Leader of the Council and its Speaker, she had every right to do so but as a non-mage and a girl she had to fight doubly hard for respect. 'Change' was not a word welcomed in Perfect society.

His position as her Right Hand made him the only mage entitled to use magecraft in the Council Chamber and then, only at Verity's bidding. This had not made Kermon popular even though, so far, he had not been called upon to act and the Speaker had maintained firm control over turn-taking and interruptions. Which of course allowed her to speak whenever she wished and for as long as she wanted.

Hostility simmered beneath the surface but Verity kept a lid on it. Her brother Bastien, the other Chief Mage and Leader of the Council, no doubt wished to proceed differently, to judge by his frequently gritted teeth. However, he was hampered by concessions made to the Queen of the Warrior Bees after losing the Battle of the Forest. He must have wished a thousand times that the Citadel had won the battle, as the populace had been led to believe. The treaty was personally binding on Bastien as he'd signed with a mage's blood oath. Any breach of its terms would exact payment from his body, so he had to be extremely careful in thought and deed.

Kermon remembered every demand the Queen of the Warrior Bees had made. He'd been there, enough in the background to claim afterwards that he'd been protecting the children, under duress. But he'd played his part in the victory and the Queen of the Warrior Bees would always be Mielitta to him. He was still playing his part, still protecting the Citadel children, to further Mielitta's dreams of changing Perfect society.

She had been very insistent on Verity being an equal leader of Council and on the rights of Citadel women, mages or not, and however much she hated the Forest, Verity certainly made the most of the treaty's constraints on her brother in that regard. The Council now consisted of five women and five men, all harbouring resentment and discontent for different reasons.

All, that is, but the other non-mage on the Council, Zora, who was inanely contented with her lot. Unfortunately for Verity's championship of non-mages, Zora held only her husband's opinions. She was the Perfect example of a Citadel lady, formed by the system of forging at maturity. A system banned by Mielitta's treaty but regarded with nostalgic affection by some of the Councillors. As Zora's husband, Zeebo, was also on the Council, there were effectively only nine contributions to any debate and agreement.

Not that political matters were ever settled 'for good'. Or even 'for evil'. The Council showed as much unity as Kermon's steel, liable to break under pressure. In temporary alliances, one faction wanted a return to the good old days when only mages could be Councillors; its extremist core wanted a return to the more recent and short-lived days when women couldn't be mages; and yet another group wanted to use the treaty terms as a basis for a different society.

Kermon kept out of the bickering and backbiting as best he could, taking refuge in the forge or in tutoring the magecraft adepts he'd taken under his wing. Not that he'd had any choice but he had accepted the role of Maturity Mage, creating a new test and ceremony to fit the terms of the treaty.

Janette might not like the distinction between boys' opportunities and girls' but the new test *had* created openings for girls as well as boys to develop knowledge of what lay beyond the walls – and to become more discerning about what happened in the name of Perfection. But that aspect of his aims was something Kermon could share with nobody inside the Citadel's walls. Not even Verity. Kermon had his own personal walls and must keep them fortified or fail in his purpose here.

He ran through the terms of the treaty in his head to see whether any of the conditions could help his missing student. If Janette were considered a criminal, then maybe Mielitta's clause to protect those labelled 'freaks' in the Citadel, could be called upon. Bastien had agreed that nobody would be suppressed because of an affinity with the Forest and those who chose to leave the Citadel could do so.

But then they must live in exile, like Mielitta, and Janette didn't want that. She only wanted to leave the Citadel for an adventure into the walls, not go into exile. Nor did being a wilful magecraft student mean having an affinity with the Forest. Kermon sighed and hoped Verity could get what she wanted from the Council.

CHAPTER FOUR

Kermon should never have let Verity insist on discussing Janette's escapade in an Emergency Council Meeting. The two of them could have *found* Janette in the time the Council usually took to decide on voting procedure. But she had insisted on having proper authorisation and debate so here they all were, wrangling instead of doing something.

Whenever Verity gave a Councillor permission to speak, Kermon concentrated on what lay beneath the words as much as on what was said.

'Does it matter? She's merely a girl, albeit with some magecraft. But even that is low quality I'm told, with no useful skill. We'll hardly miss her,' observed Hamel, a Councillor from the previous regime, who'd hoped for a prominent position by now but had been unlucky both in his allegiances and in his attempted assassinations. His skin was as acidic as his comments, tinged with green due to an error made in his forging. He was Verity's open enemy since she'd defeated him in a duel in this very Council Chamber and ended their engagement to be married.

Such an alliance would not have produced the concord Bastien might have hoped for, Kermon thought, listening to Hamel's oblique digs at Verity. She showed no signs of caring but merely signalled permission to the next speaker.

'I think we've established often enough that women mages are every bit as useful as men.' Mage Puggy emphasised the word 'useful' with a wrinkling of her squat nose in the doughy face she chose to present to the world. Her use of magecraft glamour to appear plain was understandable to those who'd seen her true form. Beauty so dazzling as to prevent coherent thought. Except in Kermon, who'd married her from kindness, hoping to return her to her right mind. He'd succeeded, only to find that her right mind was hostile to her new husband, all non-mages and most of her colleagues.

He'd also found out she loved only women. One woman to be precise, executed in a Council uprising, leaving Puggy bereft and bitter. But Kermon had known none of that when he'd married her.

'I never said women weren't useful,' sniggered Hamel in his scratchy voice, his tone an innuendo in itself.

The Speaker let it pass and Kermon's wife-in-name-only also ignored the comment. She continued in the flat-vowelled northern accent she affected in this avatar. 'We need more female mages. Recent events have diminished the supply.'

'Recent events' included Puggy being stripped of her magecraft and forced into marriage with the previous Leader of the Council, Mage Rinduran, now deceased. She had suffered more than most from Rinduran's stringent laws, designed to restore Perfect society to its core values. And there were several mages around the table who shared Rinduran's views even if they no longer dared express them.

When permitted to speak, Zora, the non-mage, expressed her view so softly Kermon had to strain to hear. It was always a surprise when the new female Councillor spoke, which she did with due reference to her husband Zeebo sitting beside her and with an air of permanent apology.

'Just think of that poor girl, how frightened she must be. What would the citizens think if we didn't try to find her?'

Bastien, lean and sharp-faced, barely waited for Verity's signal and spoke with the weight of his status as Leader. 'They'll think whatever we want them to think,' he said curtly. 'And that will depend on what we tell them. If we say nothing, they'll make up their own story about her disappearance.' He shrugged and cracked his interlaced fingers. 'People disappear. It happens.'

It did indeed. Often in this very Council Chamber at the top of the Mages' Tower. Kermon did not want to become one of the disappeared and if the Council mages ever came to know of his other loyalties, they would condemn him on the spot. He kept his expression blank, caught nobody's eye. He knew there would be many blank expressions around the table. If the citizens could believe that the Battle of the Forest was a triumphant victory, then they'd believe anything. Not a critical brain in the populace.

He caught himself short. Now he was thinking like Puggy, lacking humanity. After all, Verity had no magecraft but her political acumen was peerless, honed unintentionally in her childhood sickroom by her brother Bastien and her father Rinduran.

'I agree with Hamel,' Verity began, shocking the silence into deeper silence. 'One girl – or boy,' she added pointedly with a glare at the green mage, 'is irrelevant to the well-being of the Citadel unless she – or he - is so skilled as to be irreplaceable. And that is not the case.'

The mages waited, sensing some verbal trickery was about to change the apparent direction of this judgement.

'So let's consider the well-being of the Citadel, the bigger picture,' she continued. She held up her slim, white hand and ticked off points on her fingers. 'One. We have to meet the terms of the treaty.'

Bastien glowered. The blood oath bound him physically. Any thought of 'interpreting' the treaty 'creatively' caused him pain and he knew the consequence of any breach. His life was the Forest's security though few councillors would mourn his death.

'Two,' his sister continued. 'We have agreed a new Maturity Test, so that our young people may become Adults. They must proceed with their initiation.' Nobody commented on Verity's own youth, of which she seemed unaware.

'Three. Going into the walls is an essential part of that test and we are constrained by the new danger. The idea that I accompany each young person, singly, is a watering-down of the Test and an insult to me. What a waste of my precious time as Leader!' She had no need of the speechcraft used by the mages to reach an audience. Her voice carried easily but, more importantly, so did her conviction. In some ways she was her father's daughter. Only in some ways, Kermon hastily reassured himself.

'Four. If we contain the new danger, we restore sovereignty to our Citadel and control movement on both sides of the walls. Five,' she waggled the last finger. 'This girl has defied the Citadel's laws and should be held up as an example to others, a reminder that all must walk in the ways of Perfection or be sanctioned!' She thumped the table for good measure and in the silence, the noise was startling, despite her slight build.

Bastien was nodding. 'Councillor Verity makes good points. We can't afford to let these two insults pass. This silly girl could infect others with her attitude. Maybe she's already done so! And the danger in the walls is interfering with our plans, with our sovereignty!' He banged the table too but however hard he tried to claim Verity's analysis as his own, he came across as a younger sibling trying to keep up with his elder, instead of the reverse.

'I propose we act on these two issues,' he said. 'We contain the danger once and for all and we get the girl back into the Citadel. Whether she's alive or dead we will make her an example for others. And if she's not found, then we assume her death and make capital out of it.'

'How exactly do you propose to do all of that?' asked Hamel, picking his long, pointed nails.

A hunted expression flitted across Bastien's face and he opened his mouth to speak but Verity rescued him, smoothly.

'Two of us must go into the walls. Me, obviously, because of my… skill.' Nobody had decided what to call Verity's innate shield against magecraft. 'And–'

Bastien interrupted her. 'Me,' he declared.

Verity looked down, frown lines appearing in her forehead as they always did when she was negotiating some tricky business.

'That would be wonderful.' She beamed at her brother. 'How could we fail if we are together?'

Kermon thought quickly. Bastien had no idea what 'the new danger' *was*. As a revenant, Rinduran's last words to Verity had been 'Bring me your brother.' To do this would place everyone in danger. And with no chance of finding Janette. Whether Verity's motive was really punitive or not, Kermon couldn't bear to think of his lively student lost in the walls. He knew what that was like. But he couldn't blurt out that Bastien should not go. He needed a plausible reason, one that flattered the Chief Councillor.

While he was still thinking, Hamel was given the floor.

'Then that's decided.' He smacked his lips. 'And we'll need a Substitute Chief Councillor here while Councillors Bastien and Verity are on their mission. How brave of them to face such danger, knowing that they might not return. In which sad event, we would have to continue with the new Chief Councillor.' There was no doubt who Hamel had in mind.

Bastien and Verity exchanged glances and she looked suddenly upset.

'I'm sorry, brother,' she said. 'That was selfish of me, to think I could have your skills to lean on when the whole Citadel needs you here, especially as I won't be.'

'No, it wouldn't be right,' Bastien agreed, with a show of reluctance. He might not be as manipulative as Verity but he wasn't stupid. Or suicidal.

'Take Kermon,' he ordered. 'he's been before, he knows the girl. He's adequate protection against danger.' Bastien couldn't own up to being clueless as to what this mysterious danger was. The stones alone knew what Verity had told him!

Kermon looked grave, mumbled empty expressions of obedience and loyalty.

The motion went to a vote but the arguments were over and the decision made easily enough in the end.

'Record the decision,' ordered Bastien and the Council, and the Red Book duly complied, covering a page with neat script.

As Kermon made his escape, heading towards the big oaken door and the calm of his forge, Verity stopped him.

'Councillor Verity.' He bowed his head respectfully, then asked the question that had tormented him ever since Nathan broke the news. 'How are we going to find Janette? I don't know where to begin looking.'

Her eyes told him he was an imbecile but he was her imbecile. 'We might try reading that story of hers. Nathan said that's why she went back, to find out more.'

Of course. He was an imbecile.

'Bring the story to the library. Take the time to eat and drink, prepare. We don't know how long we'll be away. When we've read it, we'll go into the walls. And we need to talk about the danger we face.' *Not here obviously,* was what she meant.

She moved gracefully out of the room, her gown swishing, every bit the lady. She was growing up and had been through unofficial Maturity Tests more demanding than any he could devise.

Well played, Verity, he thought. But his smugness vanished when one of his students caught up with him in the corridor.

'It's Nathan,' Mage-Smith Kermon. 'He's disappeared. Kept saying it was all his fault and he was going to put it right. That nobody else should be in danger because of him. He's taken those stupid stories Janette writes all the time and he's gone.'

CHAPTER FIVE

Two missing students and not a clue how to find them. However fiercely Kermon grilled the contrite youngster in front of him, no more information was forthcoming.

'Round up the rest of the group and anybody else Nathan or Janette might have spoken to. I want them all on the Forge greensward by the time I return. And I want to know everything anybody can tell me about Janette's latest story. Go!'

The boy didn't need to be told twice and ran as if the grassette was on fire.

What the stones should he do now, Kermon wondered. Verity would explode when she heard the news, even if he didn't tell her it was his fault. Which it was. He knew he'd upset Nathan and sorting it out 'later' might not be an option.

He drew on his mage's training to calm the fears that stopped him thinking. He and Verity would have to go into the walls anyway and it was highly unlikely he'd ever come back. He'd find Nathan and Janette or die in the attempt. He'd make sure Verity came back. She was the one who mattered. His heart knotted strangely but he had no time to analyse why.

He rushed off to the Citadel kitchens, stuffed the deep pockets of his black robe with packets of tasteless sustenance, white, stringy and labelled 'chicken'. He swigged insipid liquid from a bottle, pink and labelled 'apple juice'.

Chewing the necessary food with as little enthusiasm as if it were paper, he strode along the stone corridors. He told himself, *This might be the last time.* Past the entrance to the Great Hall where so many speeches had been made, where his wedding to Puggy had been celebrated. Past the mages' quarters and his own room, inside which his bed, chair and clothes chest looked exactly the same as in all the other rooms in the Perfect greylight of daytime.

He did not love this place, nor the people in it. His heart thumped in dissent but he ignored it. He had no time for might-have-beens or nostalgia. He'd only felt at home in the forge. He'd tried his best to be a good teacher and this was the result – two students' lives at risk. They were probably already dead. He might as well face the fact. Mielitta had given him a mission and he'd failed. Instead of fostering new ways of thought in the Citadel children, subtly challenging the ways of Perfection, he'd killed two of them.

His feet knew where he needed to go, despite his gloomy thoughts, and he found himself heading downwards to the water gate set into the curtain wall underneath the Citadel. He let his fingers trail on the dripping moss to his right and he heard the rush of water down the sheer drop to his left.

He had come down here with Verity in his arms, one of the hostages they'd taken with them to the Forest on the glorious day he'd helped Mielitta break free. All the children of the Citadel had followed, enjoying what was to them an unprecedented day's outing beyond the walls. Somewhere forbidden. They'd played in the stream, climbed trees and tasted honey, served them by Mielitta's bees. She still believed that taste of honey had stayed with them, would shape a different future.

Kermon didn't know what he believed any more but he'd tried to do as she'd asked. He'd heard nothing from her for months yet he still kept faith. He'd tried to contact her but could never reach her.

He fingered the Damascene arrowhead pendant around his neck, twin to her Steelwing. He pictured Mielitta; long red hair, straight as a waterfall; black eyes and golden skin; a disconcerting halo of bees that appeared or vanished according to her needs or their whim. The way her eyes looked inwards when she communed with her bees.

He must try to contact her one more time. To pass on all the news. And to say goodbye.

Not wanting to go as far as the water gate, he stopped before the end of the path. Too many memories. That was the way he'd come back into the Citadel with all the children, leaving Mielitta with their friends on the other side of the wall. Free in the Forest to be who they really were, to let their second natures blossom. He'd given up so much and it had all been for nothing. The mages still argued and the children would grow up to be just like their parents, despising anybody who was different.

He held his arrowhead. Perfection Unfinished. So it had been named in both curse and blessing. His fingers sensed the patterned waves in the steel, identical to Mielitta's Steelwing, designed from her dreams, crafted with love.

'Mielitta,' he called in the dark, beside the dripping walls, holding the arrowhead, despairing. As had happened for months now, he felt warmth in the steel, the connection, but he saw only white. Flurries and swirls of white.

He spoke to the whiteness, just in case.

'There's been a development.' He swallowed, finding it difficult to speak to a whirling mass of nothing. 'Two of my students have gone into the walls and I have to go after them.' His throat was dry. 'With Verity. We told the Council there was a new danger in the walls. I don't know what she said to Bastien in private but she didn't tell him the truth.' He took a deep breath.

'Rinduran exists there. As some kind of revenant. He still has all his magecraft in that world. And only Verity is immune. Because, well, because she's immune to all magecraft. I think it's because of your bee. The one she killed. That stung her. A gift of sorts.'

The whiteness swirled without comment. Kermon was getting used to it now. Talking to himself was nothing new. He had nobody else.

'So I might not come back.' There. He'd said it. 'And I want you to know I tried. I really did. I've worked with the children to make them think differently. I've created a new kind of Maturity Test, one that encourages the youngsters to think and to be critical of Perfection, not to blindly obey its rules. But two of my best students are lost in the walls. I'm no good at this, at anything except smithcraft.'

The white wafted, drifted, shifted in layers.

'I don't know how to say goodbye to you. It's like saying goodbye to life itself. I always hoped we… but I know you and Jannlou… I know how it is between you.'

He gulped, paused again. 'Jannlou, I know you would have come back instead of me. But this is how it's meant to be and I want you to know I wish only the best for both of you. Truly.'

And then some words for the girl who'd taught him what it was like to go into the walls. 'Drianne. You saved my life. I would never have come back from the walls the first time without your help. That's who we are. We fought together and won. We saved each other's lives. We tried to understand each other even if we didn't always succeed. The four of us. Our ties are deeper than this.' He was pointing down at the water flowing underneath the Citadel, heedless of whether anybody was listening or had any idea what 'this' meant.

'And that's it,' he ended lamely. *Great final words* he thought bitterly.

Then realised that the whiteness was thinning, revealing patches. Was that a wall? Piles of furs? A person? Yes, somebody holding Steelwing. But it wasn't Mielitta.

'Don't you see,' the person's voice was over-precise, youthful but full of authority. 'Your students rebelled. They thought for themselves. You have succeeded beyond what we thought was possible.'

'Where's Mielitta?' snapped Kermon, hoping this stranger had not heard all he'd said. 'What have you done with her?'

The whiteness shimmered, faded and fully revealed a slim youth holding Mielitta's arrowhead, standing in front of a wall. As the last wisps of white cleared, Kermon saw it was not a wall but rough-hewn stone, with dark holes where large tunnels branched off. The back of a cave.

'I'm Arven,' said the speaker, 'son of Tannlei.'

Kermon remembered Tannlei, the Citadel's Archery Mage. The youth had her black eyes and hair, and her golden skin, but his stare challenged and provoked whereas she'd been kind-faced and used questions to push her students to deeper thinking. Always so patient. She was the teacher Kermon tried to emulate with his own students.

'Our Archery Mage who died. May she return to the stones,' he said in a perfunctory manner. He realised how callous he must sound. 'I'm sorry. I'm so immersed in Perfection, I don't know how to react differently, in the Forest way. It's a lot for me to take in that she was your mother.' He was fighting his instinctive distaste at the notion of a female mage having a child. It was a crime against Perfection but then so was everything he, Kermon, did for Mielitta, who was a crime against Perfection in her very essence. He would *not* let Perfection possess his mind.

He tried to express himself better. 'Nobody loved her more than Mielitta did.'

'I did,' was her son's reply, without inflexion.

Kermon flushed, wrong-footed again, feeling the unspoken rebuke. Arven's face was all edges and angles, cheekbones sharp in the cold light. He must be sideways on to the entrance to get such deep blue shadows.

'I can't reach Mielitta. It's been nothing but whiteness until you. There. With Steelwing.'

Arven answered only one of the implied questions. 'It's snow. We've had winter and deep snow.'

Kermon had only seen the Forest in summer, green-gold shimmers in breezes that tickled. There was no weather in the Citadel. Just greylight by day, darklight at night and always the Perfect ambient temperature. Perfect monotony.

He tried to imagine snow. He'd read about winter in the library but words needed imagination to bring them to life. That was what he wanted to bring to the Citadel: the rich variety of experience across time and space. For his students to savour the world beyond their walls. To taste and smell winter. To eat honey and drink milk. That was what his Maturity Test would let them do within the walls. The first steps.

Maybe he hadn't failed after all. If he could only find Janette and Nathan, send them back home even if he remained, trapped.

'She's here,' said Arven, answering another question. 'Look.'

Kermon followed Steelwing's image of the cave as Arven gestured. A pile of furs humped over two bodies. His throat constricted. 'She's dead.'

'No, sleeping.'

Kermon's heart thumped. He knew who the other body was, sleeping beside Mielitta. He didn't ask. His generosity had limits.

'And Drianne?'

'Here too.' Arven walked over to a different part of the cave, startling a white wolf. A frog opened its mouth, blowing soundless bubbles on top of a rainbow-knit blanket and the pile of fur underneath shifted restlessly.

There had been a rainbow shimmering in the water gate when Kermon passed through into the floral meadow and sunshine. All he'd lost. His eyes stung.

'I'm here to wake the sleepers,' Arven said. 'But you have no time. You must go. There is much to say and we will talk again. But you must go now. Find your students.'

'Let me talk to Mielitta.' She was there, stirring underneath the furs, just moments away from the goodbye he needed to say to her.

'I will tell her all you've said.' The vision cut to black.

There was no appeal and Kermon was alone in the dripping darkness.

He drew a deep breath. Yes, it was time to go but he'd changed his mind. There were no rainbows in the Citadel and now he did want to look at the gate one more time, to remember that he *had* been on the other side. To remember why he'd come back here and to strengthen his resolve. To remember the taste of honey.

He walked quickly down to the path's end, heedless of the slippery stone under his feet or the drop on his left to the water's rush. He knew there would be only mud and iron, the gate closed by magecraft, warded against exit or entry, without any password.

So he blinked at what he saw. Maybe he was hallucinating. He wasn't holding his pendant but maybe it was touching his skin, showing strange reflections of the Forest. When he'd last been here, there had been only mud sealing the solid iron gate to its rocky base, the water streaming through, purified and Perfect for Citadel use. The gate had been a barrier so opaque that it was impossible to believe in a world beyond the Citadel wall. Unless you'd been there. If Kermon hadn't seen the stream's origin, he wouldn't have believed there was one.

When he'd last been here... he remembered *why* he'd last come here, months ago. He'd found the seeds in his pocket, a gift from the Forest.

'Moss,' Mielitta had suggested. 'Try putting them in moss from the walls. That might be natural enough for them to grow.'

He'd put the seeds in moss, planted them in his old boots and left them at the rocky base of the gate where natural light might reach them from beyond the walls, though none could be seen.

He'd hoped. He'd come back. There was nothing but mud and decaying boots. He'd despaired. He'd got on with his life, alone, living a double lie. Mielitta was unaware of his link with Verity and nobody in the Citadel knew he was a Forest spy.

And now this. It wasn't an illusion. The iron gate was still a solid barrier but covered in branches, twining and clinging to every inch. And even in the gloom, the green of burgeoning leaves was tinged with rainbow. The seeds he'd planted had grown and forced their way outside.

What if the gateway was open again? Kermon could jump on the rock, hold onto the gate as the water rushed past his feet, pass through the rainbow into the meadow. He'd planted the seeds and his work was done here. He could rejoin his friends in the Forest, work with them to open up this breach in the Citadel's defences.

He hesitated. Pictured the dumb insolence of a rebellious student whose story he hadn't read. And the spiky-haired lad who blamed himself, who was brave enough to rush into the walls to rescue her. And Verity, his anchor. Who trusted him.

His feet leaden in new boots that still pinched, Kermon marched up the dank pathway to keep more promises.

CHAPTER SIX

First there was an icy tingle in his right foot, then his leg and up his torso until his face thawed. Then across his hairline and down the left side of his body until each toe could wriggle and Arven was awake. He looked at the empty rocking-chair and green eyes challenged him from a ruff of ginger fur. Hui maintained his stare, while performing a series of feline contortions that Arven could only envy, as he too stood and stretched.

Winter had lasted only a long sleep for him and Hui, cocooned in the farmhouse while the world turned white. He pulled one hair from his head and measured it against a knitting needle from his bag. He'd grown five months of straight black hair so that's how much measured time had passed since Arven knitted the snowflake pattern of winter into the world of the Forest.

He looked automatically at the clock. The hands marked the time of half-past eight, as they always had. Since Granny cried out on the evening she'd felt her daughter's death and stopped the clock. And told Arven, who believed her but hadn't cried. Not then. Not at half-past eight.

Now Arven knew more about how his mother died, half-past eight presented evidence. It would have been after the evening meal in the Citadel's Great Hall. His mother, Tannlei the Archery Mage, would have made sure she was in her rightful place at the High Table, drawing no suspicion. All the better to sneak off after the meal, cloaked and anonymous. Heading for the water gate and freedom in the Forest to be with her husband and their son, in Granny's homestead among the trees.

But somebody had caught the mage, executed her for crimes against Perfection. Female mages had no right to marry, nor to have children. That's why Arven had grown up here in the homestead, safe with Granny. Who had died with the autumn leaves, fading naturally as her chair rocked to a standstill. So old he'd though her ageless, immortal. Their family's story flowed through her knotted veins and would continue in his own. He wondered whether a natural death would be his lot. Or suppression by the Citadel for treason or age crime, depending on how many decades he lived outside their rule.

While the windows still showed only blinding white, he opened his seer's eyes onto the mists of what might be and what should be. Bee, Bear and Flower. How did he fit into their pattern? And what of their friend in the Citadel, like steel in flames: was he truly tempered and strong or brittle from too much heat?

Arven picked up his knitting and cast off the white fabric with its snowflake patterns, singing softly to himself as he did so. As a lullaby induces sleep so this air nudged wakening, like birdsong on a spring dawn. He buried the white wool deep in his bag and pulled out gold needles and green wool, still singing as he cast on, then he began to work the new fabric. Glints of lemon, lime and sage formed a background on which accents of rose budded randomly.

Hui purred and groomed his deep fur, rasping the length silky. Then, in one bound, the cat leaped onto the dresser and batted a china cup across to Arven, who caught it deftly, his knitting paused. Hui looked disdainfully at Arven, jumped down onto the carpet and stalked his way to the kitchen. His upright tail expressed disappointment in his servant.

What would Granny do? Arven asked himself. He was not only thinking about the cat, who was quickly pacified with preserved anchovies from the well-stocked pantry. The trading journey to market last summer had topped up supplies of dried beans, flour and more exotic supplies, in exchange for honey, meat and eggs.

Honey, thought Arven. *The bees will wake soon. Who will tend them now Granny's gone?*

The words chilled him more than winter had. But he knew what she would have done on waking, whether from a night's sleep or a month's. Hui had reminded him. Arven used a meagre drop of magecraft to fire the range. He put the kettle on the hob, waited for the whistle and made a pot of tea, with due respect as he'd been taught. He thought of those who'd grown and gathered the leaves, the process of drying them and the provenance of the water from the well. This cup of tea was unique and he sipped slowly, thinking of the wise woman who was not there.

But you are, he told her. *In my head and my heart. You, my mother and my father. And the Citadel will know of my existence, sooner, not later. It is time for me to take our work there to its rightful conclusion. But first I must wake the sleepers.*

The trees' music tinkled in icy percussion as nature shrugged off her white coat. As Arven neared the cave, melting snow made duller notes as it dripped and slid onto the Forest floor. The waterfall had been completely frozen and rivulets were only just starting to spurt, rushing joyfully downwards.

The cave entrance was still snowed in and, stooping, Arven heated his body just enough to enter, like a hot poker moving through ice. The scene was as he had left it, the three sleepers on two soft piles of fur. Chests were piled high with all manner of clothing, weapons and tableware, as in a mythic hall. Leather jerkins and britches, fleece coats and cotton shirts. Chain-mail, swords and daggers. Goblets, plates and platters.

The woodland creatures which had kept Drianne company were waking, assessing Arven with their wild eyes. Prey or predator?

He walked over to the pile of furs which covered Mielitta and Jannlou, gently pulled back the top cover and revealed the sleeping occupants, outside time and beyond worry. He hesitated, knowing what he brought them back to do. Mielitta's hand held tightly onto the arrowhead that she wore as a pendant. Steelwing.

When Arven saw the Damascene patterns glow ice-blue, he knew that somebody was trying to make contact through the pendant's twin in the Citadel. He could wake Mielitta but he knew she could not shake off the confusion of sleep quickly enough to cope with a conversation pitted with hidden traps. One wrong word would end their hopes and she needed time to know, to understand what the man in the Citadel faced, to judge what would temper his steel and what would break him.

Gently, Arven prised open Mielitta's fingers, took the arrowhead. He covered the sleepers again and moved away from them. He focused on the pendant, let his mind find the twin arrowhead and the seeker. He could see nothing at first in the dark vision.

The forge? No. As his eyes adjusted, Arven saw the Mage-Smith's face, desperation etched in every line and his eyes shadowed by more than his dreary surroundings. There was stone behind Kermon, oozing water down tufts of moss. Faster water – a stream? – made a rush and gulp in the background as Kermon spoke.

So this was the Citadel, this narrowness in building and in mind. Constraints of stone and Perfection in thought. The place where his grandmother had fallen in love with a non-mage and escaped to the Forest. Where his mother and father had loved and been executed. Murdered. His roots were here and they would crack the Citadel's foundations. He had seen it.

He brought his attention back to Kermon, acknowledging the news of missing students and an undead mage. It was as if Arven recognised the story being told though he could not have predicted what Kermon would say. That was the usual manner of his gift, a form of déjà vu with flashes of possible outcomes. Sometimes he knew the pattern he must knit and sometimes he followed his instincts, trusting to Nature, of which his own nature was but a part.

He gave Kermon all that he could to strengthen the Mage-Smith on this journey only he could make. Everything except what was asked, the chance to speak to Mielitta. When Arven broke the connection, the brutality of his act bruised his own feelings.

'What's the target?' he asked himself softly, drawing on his legacy, his mother's and grandmother's wisdom. He blessed them both in tears, a minute's luxury. He looked at the sleepers, so peaceful before wakening to their ordeals. He thought of the man alone in the Citadel, struggling to keep the evil out of his head.

To protect them all and help them do what they must, Arven answered his mother's question.

Steelwing grew heavier by the second, as if complaining about the usurper abusing its powers; Arven gently returned it to its rightful place around Mielitta's neck.

He sat cross-legged on the cave floor, took the bag from his shoulder and placed it beside him. He started singing the spring song again to the tune of the waterfall nearby. Ice tinkled and broke on the rocks as new melt gushed. Arven took out his needles, added pale blue and white to the greens he'd knitted in the homestead.

As he sang and knitted, one pile of rugs moved. The woodland creatures hopped, skipped and loped towards the entrance, leaving Drianne to yawn as she flicked her fine golden hair back from her face and returned from the dream world. She sat up, blinking and yawning with part of her mouth. Half of her face stayed immobile, held in an asymmetrical cast. Silvered by a web of scars, the young mage's face glittered strangely in the cold light from the entrance. She was wearing the rainbow knit Arven had made her, which rippled and wrapped itself around her neck as a scarf, while she stretched and emerged from her bed.

Then the double furs were thrown off and first Mielitta, then Jannlou, stirred and looked at each other, shy and tender. As if their dreams still wrapped them in honeyed visions. No words were needed. She reached out and combed his black locks into a warrior's queue with her hands, tied it with a strand of her own long red hair.

That tender look and gesture would have dried the words in Kermon's throat, brewed his feelings into a lethal draught and sent him to his doom. Arven had not missed his target, nor had he been unkind, in sparing the Mage-Smith this scene of awakening.

A scout bee hovered over Mielitta then disappeared again.

She wore the look of intense concentration that showed she was communicating with her bees, then she fixed Arven with a black-eyed stare.

'How long have we been asleep?' she asked. 'I'm hungry.'

'Winter is over. You slept through it. And there's food and drink. Help yourself.' Arven pointed to the banquet table at the back of the cave, now piled with fresh and dried fruit, bread, bowls of oats, jugs of milk and juices.

Mielitta's eyes lit up at the sight of the honey pot.

'The bees,' she said, 'in your beehives. They'll be waking now too. Does Qingzhao need help to check they've over-wintered? I can shift shape, go into our home hive and find out. And help her visit the others, from the outside.'

'Qingzhao has passed.' Each word stabbed Arven to the core. He could call her Granny only to himself from now on.

'But who will look after the bees?'

Jannlou and Drianne glared at Mielitta, who stuttered, 'I'm sorry. You must feel…'

'Bereft?' asked Arven coolly. He left no time for further

comments on his loss. 'Qingzhao would have asked the same question. She would want her bees tended.'

'But I–' Mielitta began in protest.

'And her cows, her chickens, her horses, her cat – all the homestead. It's her legacy to Drianne.'

CHAPTER SEVEN

'What?' asked Jannlou, defiant, piling even more raisin muffins onto a precarious tower of food. Balancing the plate already entailed a feat of engineering but, with surprising delicacy, he took a strategic bite out of an apple that restored the equilibrium.

'Mmm,' he grunted with satisfaction.

'That's disgusting,' Mielitta told him cheerfully, putting another spoonful of honey in her yoghurt.

She heard Drianne's voice in her mind. *Men!*

Her bees added their own contempt for Jannlou's second nature. *Bears!*

And Mielitta realised that she was fully back in the waking world, facing more problems than any nightmare could throw at her. Opinionated bees in her head, who hated the bear aspect of the man she'd married in the Forest; Drianne, whose magecraft was as volatile as Arven's was controlling; and Kermon. Their friend in the Citadel had sacrificed everything to do the Forest's work there and he must feel abandoned. There was no chance the Citadel had slept through the winter as had the Forest.

She reached for Steelwing, murmured, 'Kermon.'

Arven put his hand over hers and shook his head.

Knowing his prescience, Mielitta feared the answer but could not leave the question unspoken. Her breakfast churned in her stomach. She was Queen of the Warrior Bees and truth could not be changed by hiding from it.

'He's dead too, isn't he.' Kermon's death would have been no gentle autumn fade but a traitor's execution such as she'd witnessed when Crimvert died. Arven's father. His mind emptied and his body burnt to ashes at the Council table.

'No, he lives!' The solemn youth was quick to correct her. 'I'd have told you straight away if I knew otherwise. I'm sorry. I haven't spoken to anyone other than my – than Qingzhao for so many years, I forget that I have to explain so much.' His grandmother's mannerisms gave his elfin face a quaint dignity. Now she knew his parentage, Mielitta saw that he had his mother's wise eyes, black as her own. She had loved the Archery Mage dearly, still hadn't come to terms with the manner of her death. So how must Arven feel?

Mielitta scanned the cave in the brightening light from the entrance. Sun-rays had broken through the thick winter snow clouds and were hastening the melt outdoors. On the cave floor, the friends' meagre belongings were piled as they'd left them, by the ashes of the fire they hadn't needed. Arven's work. She did not like the high-handed way he used his magecraft without so much as a by-your-leave. Maybe she would have accepted the notion of sleeping the winter away. Maybe she wouldn't. But he should have *asked*.

She sighed. People were so complicated.

Bees aren't, the voices in her head told her. *Just get rid of the bear. He's dangerous.*

She sighed again. 'Bees add complications too.' She must have spoken aloud because the others were looking at her strangely.

'Kermon,' Jannlou said firmly to Arven. 'Tell us.'

After the tale of lost students, rescue missions and the evil in the walls – Rinduran undead! – Mielitta wished she could go back to sleep for a few months more.

'This student, Janette, came across a story that has something to do with me?' she asked Arven.

'So she said to her friend Nathan,' he confirmed. 'But he's taken everything she wrote down into the walls with him, to try and find her. Kermon hadn't got round to reading it so he's in the dark but he's going to ask the other students if they know anything about the story.'

'If only I could go into the walls!' She would give anything to know who her parents were. Why they'd sent her through the walls in a basket to emerge in front of Declan, the Mage-Smith who'd then brought up the foundling. And who'd hated her for being a freak.

She frowned. A queen did not waste time on 'If only'. *What's the target, Mielitta?* Tannlei would have asked. She could choose only one.

'Kermon. We need to help him. We could try to get into the Citadel and Drianne could go through the walls.'

'That's not what Kermon wants,' pointed out Arven.

'As if you care!' Mielitta regretted the words as soon as she'd spoken.

'I know,' she added quickly. 'You're thinking of what's best, for all of us and for the Forest. And so am I.' Arven had been raised as much by the Forest as in it so he'd earned her respect. And she did respect him. If only… stop it! No 'if only'!

'It's not just about Kermon,' she said firmly. 'It's about what he's doing for us. The evil in the walls is *our* responsibility. It's Rinduran, or whatever he has become. Kermon said the thing still has my bee-sting in his eye, still works against our changes in the Citadel, still seeks to kill the Forest. All of this means Kermon is fighting *our* war and we should be at his side.'

She continued. 'That's only one of our responsibilities. We have the bees – all the animals – on the homestead to look after. No, Drianne, it's not just your responsibility.' She gave Arven a stern look. 'We should share our thoughts and help each other. Isn't it your family home, Arven? What do you want?' She tried not to sound accusatory but if there was a suggestion that he should be the one looking after everything, then she couldn't help how she felt.

'But I want to,' Drianne told her, in the silent communication only Mielitta could hear. *'I loved the homestead and every creature in it, from the moment I followed the chickens and met Qingzhao.'*

Arven's face was serene, so like his mother and grandmother. 'Qingzhao did not lay this as a burden on Drianne. She would not have done that. It was a gift, one she felt would be well received and a boon to all. The homestead is a haven and wherever Drianne walks, the Forest creatures walk with her in peace.'

His words rang true. 'I cannot speak for how she feels but you ask about me, my inheritance.' His smile was gentle. 'I am free to go into the Citadel and do whatever must be done there. I've seen this come to pass and I will not let you down. Or the Forest.'

'I'll go with him,' said Jannlou. 'We'll find a way in somehow and once we're in the Citadel, we'll go into the walls.'

Mielitta's stomach had not settled. 'You make it sound like I'm not going with you.' She was conscious of Drianne's studied indifference, her silence, her white face. Of course. Drianne was *not* asking for help but she would need it.

Arven waited, presumably for Mielitta to realise what he already knew. With resignation, she said, 'Drianne needs my help.'

'Bees,' he replied. 'And I'm not leaving you in the lurch. Qingzhao left a notebook with detailed instructions for Drianne and I can interpret anything that's obscure.'

Knowing *that* family, every word would be obscure, thought Mielitta. Philosophy in even the simplest action.

'And I can show you where the tea is kept,' Arven said. This was the nearest he'd ever come to making a joke so Mielitta humoured him and smiled. *Yes, philosophy in every teacup.*

'I'll stay here,' said Jannlou, 'until Arven comes for me.'

There was an awkward silence. Jannlou was banned from the homestead in case his ursine nature took him over while he was there. He had proved unstable on a previous visit and Arven didn't trust Jannlou's self-control – a sore point between them. Although bears could not cross the wards Qingzhao had erected, the creatures on the farm were not protected from a guest who shifted shape.

Mielitta studied his face, familiar as her own heartbeat. Blue eyes startling as ice against the walnut skin, hair drawn severely back in the warrior's queue she'd tied such a short time earlier. A lifetime earlier, when she'd thought only of him.

'But you can control it now!' she told him.

He shook his head. 'I'll be fine here. Besides, I've lost body weight.' He grinned and she loved him so much she ached. 'And a bear has to do some serious eating after hibernating. If you thought that was disgusting, you really shouldn't be here.'

She moved into his arms, knew he was right. They were all of them right. Each must play the role given to them. But she didn't have to like it.

'I'll come back with Arven. We'll go together then.'

Nobody argued with her, which was strange, as if they sensed things would go otherwise.

Bees, insisted the voices in her head. *Need to check on the home hive.*

Mielitta barely had time to kiss Jannlou and tell Drianne she'd meet her at the homestead, when the sigil on her thigh glowed and she was transported through space and time directly into the beehive.

However many times, Mielitta shifted and went into the hive as a bee, she was startled by the way the multitude of furry bodies crowded her, tapping her with antennae, checking she had the right scent.

Suspicion quickly changed to a welcoming buzz, passing the good news throughout the hive.

The Queen Mother is back.

A small group of bees fussed around Mielitta, feeding her nectar in an exchange of food and solidarity. As her vision adjusted to a bee's range, adding the ultraviolets and losing the human reds, she tried to get her bearings.

Was she upside down at the top or standing on the bottom? Or even standing on one of the sides? Thanks to the adhesive pressure exerted by her six legs, she could crawl up or down. Each leg was equipped with double claws that could grip firmly on any rough surface. As a human Mielitta could run and somersault, even backflip and fire arrows at the same time. But as a bee, she could defy gravity –yet always know which way was up.

Acclimatising to her bee self, she knew she was on the base of the hive, beside the wooden wall on the west side. Her sense of direction was so precise she could easily understand other bees' waggle dance, telling her where to find a nectar source, so finding her way around their home was no problem.

She waddled forward, stopped at the first vertical towering above her, a waxed frame of row upon row of octagonal cells, as far as she could see. All empty, with a fragrance of long-gone honey. Her guard of honour accompanied her, making the usual gestures of respect for a queen. They didn't seem worried so neither should Mielitta be.

She waddled forward to the next vertical. The cells were all empty.

And to the next frame. Empty. Now she was worried. Yet many bees had greeted her when she arrived. Where were they now?

She walked to the fourth frame and looked up. The cells nearest her were empty but a dense cluster had formed of bees clinging together, huddled as close as possible. Mielitta had never seen them behave like this. Were they diseased?

When all was well, the worker bees went about their business, tending brood in the nurseries, cleaning the hive and each other, flying out to collect pollen. And of course feeding and paying court to the queen, encouraging her to lay eggs. Of which there was no sign.

Mielitta had seen the hive in trouble, queenless, attacked by beetles and even damaged in the Battle of the Forest by Rinduran himself but this was different. She knew by the smell that the hive was queenright, with a queen who made the workers happy. So where was the brood? The hive needed to renew its population regularly. How could she ask tactfully?

'Is there a meeting?' she asked. 'Is that why all the bees are in one group?' She knew that such a cluster formed outdoors when bees were moving to a new home.

Bee laughter tinkled at her ignorance. *It's what we do in winter.*

That made sense. Like her and Jannlou snuggling together for warmth, multiplied by fifty thousand. That was a *lot* of warmth and could be used to kill. Mielitta herself had once been hotballed by the bees. Luckily they'd recognised her in time but she knew first-hand how much heat they could generate. Her tattoo glowed at the memory.

Of course! Mielitta could question her inner queen and spirit bees, without worrying about diplomacy.

'Where is the brood? Why are there so few bees? Why are they all workers and no males? Where is the queen? Why is nobody working?' The questions tumbled out. She had to find out what the hive needed the beekeeper to do – no longer Qingzhao but Drianne now. And then they'd have to figure out how to do it. With help from Arven and Qingzhao's notebook.

It's winter was the unhelpful response from her bees, with another tinkle of laughter at her ignorance.

An individual bee voice spoke in Mielitta's mind and she sensed her inner queen, taking pity on her ignorance. *The queen is in the centre of the cluster, warm and protected. Winter workers live longer than the summer ones so the queen lays few eggs and the hive conserves its energy, eating honey reserves and waiting for spring.*

'But that's not fair,' said Mielitta. 'Just because you're born at a different time of year, you live longer.' She thought of her friend

Pollen Bee. Mielitta had once assumed a worker's body and been granted a day among the flowers with her, filling the two baskets on her legs, labouring so hard they'd slept in a flower before flying back, weighted down by the golden ingredient for bees' bread. No wonder summer bees only lived six weeks. They worked themselves to death. But would she rather be a winter bee, never knowing the joy of flowers that opened to a bee's long tongue, the taste of nectar?

'Pollen Bee, the one I flew with last summer, is she–?' Mielitta couldn't say the word.

We are the bees and if our hive thrives, what happens to one bee is of no matter. It is pitifully human to become attached. You have been told why there are no drones in winter. They were put outdoors in autumn because they are a waste of resources in winter.

Mielitta had not forgotten. It seemed so cruel, the males desperate to get into the hive and the workers on gate duty preventing them, leaving them outside to die. But she knew she had to think like a bee not a human. And she'd have to teach Drianne that the hive must thrive, not necessarily each tiny being who lived there.

Some bees from the outer layer detached themselves, crawled and flew to another frame, from which other workers returned.

We take turns in feeding. And when we've eaten, we move to an inner layer, so the colony stays fed and warm. And of course her courtiers feed the queen, who comes out of the cluster occasionally to lay some eggs, enough to replenish the colony. It has been so cold for so long that we are careful to go quickly for food and return to maintain body heat. The queen dare not come out now so there are fewer of us to keep the hive warm.

What a delicate balance between food stores, population and the length of the winter! Mielitta watched the latest group of workers returning from their feeding sortie. Their mood seemed less buoyant than when they left the cluster. Another group returned, the mood even more sombre. There was a change of atmosphere throughout the cluster as the bad news was passed on.

Winter's been too long. We've run out of honey stores.

There was no panic among the bees but Mielitta sensed the depression spreading and burrowing like a mite into each bee's sense of purpose.

Why bother? she thought. *There's no food.*

Then her human nature told her to cut out the self-pity and do something.

'That's just bee thinking!' she told her inner queen. 'Show me what is in the hive.'

She waddled further along the base, ignoring the bleak thoughts of the bees above her. The cluster was breaking up. She could see some brood, in a compact pattern, a sign that the queen was healthy and laying well, if still in winter mode. None of the capped cells were the bigger bumps that covered baby drones but that was normal for winter. Spring had not yet come.

Seven verticals along, Mielitta could see that this frame had contained honey and now contained only desperate bees. As bees gave up the will to live, they put their heads into empty cells, taking a last scent of honey, awaiting their death by starvation.

Mielitta continued her slow, methodical progress. There was just enough room for her to walk under each frame – a bee space. Nothing on frames eight and nine. But when she reached the tenth and last frame, she wanted to shout and cheer. A buzz of excitement did not fully express how she felt. The tenth frame was a solid wall of honey, from the bottom up as far as she could see.

Mielitta clambered onto the frame and pierced one capped cell. She sucked a mouthful of honey and savoured the flavours of last summer. Forest honey, made not from nectar but from tree sap sweetened by the aphids who'd eaten it and processed it through their own bodies. She tasted the beech and oak trees around the clearing where she'd first been drawn into the beehive and the sweetness of the trees' relationship with their insect guests. But most of all she tasted home hive, the work of all her fellow bees.

'We have plenty of food!' she told the decreasing band escorting her.

Why bother? There's no food, came the reply, the grisly refrain, paralysing every bee in the hive.

Couldn't they see what was in front of them? wondered Mielitta, frustrated at the bees' suicidal denial. Bee depression had infected the whole hive.

For once, she didn't have to rack her brains as to how she could help them or to argue with the queen bee, whose anguished call was adding to the unbearable misery.

'Drianne!' she called. 'I know what we have to do!'

And as she focused on her bee sigil, shifting shape, she heard Drianne reply.

'I'm glad somebody does,' said the new beekeeper.

CHAPTER EIGHT

Mielitta found herself in human form once more, standing beside the home hive, which stood in a row of twenty on the edge of a grey, slushy field. It was hard to believe that this would become a wildflower meadow but the metamorphosis had already begun. The change from pristine snow to mud to seedlings was taking place with supernatural speed. Arven's work of course, through his singing and knitting.

The ethereal youth came towards her with Drianne, both clad in practical boots and warm clothing, prepared in the human way for the freshness of receding winter. Drianne's scarf peeped above the opening of her cloak. Its colours gave warning of her changing moods and Mielitta was relieved to see seven strong colours, from red to violet. She wondered what her bee vision would make of a rainbow.

Under Drianne's arm was a large book and as she came nearer, Mielitta could see that it was leather-bound, battered and dog-eared, like the most treasured books in the Citadel Library. Arven was carrying some kind of metal jug.

There's a section on what to do in spring but it's in oblique sayings, like poetry. I don't know what it means. Drianne couldn't wait to show her the page, reading aloud.

In springtime when the sun with Taurus rides,
the bees divide their labours 'twixt field and hive.
Some to the first flowers trip and sip while
others clean all that winter's dearth defiled,
prepare the wax for brood and stores a-plenty,
strive to return to crowded house from empty.

'I remember some of what Qingzhao told me. I told Drianne she mustn't use magecraft,' warned Arven. 'The bees are unhappy with artifice of any kind, whether it's artificial material or scents or magecraft – or people.'

But Mielitta was bursting to tell them her news and barely listened to them, focused on the only word in the notebook that mattered. 'Dearth is right!' she said. 'My bees are starving. And they won't eat the honey because it's too far away from them. They're cold and they think they're going to die. You've got to help them now, straight away.'

'Wait,' said Arven, holding up both hands in a stop gesture. 'We can't talk over each other and I can't hear Drianne's words. I only guess them. So I'm getting confused! Mielitta, you know the bees best. Let's start with what you think we should do for your hive and then check we know how to do it!'

Mielitta forced herself to slow down and get to the point. 'We – you – need to move the frame with all the honey so it's right beside the bees, without breaking up their cluster. And I'll get them to eat.' How, she wasn't sure, given the overwhelming misery of their *Why bother*. But she'd think of something.

We'll work with your hive first, then we'll know what to do with the others, said Drianne, looking with apprehension at the row of beehives.

Not one bee was in sight.

Winter, Mielitta told herself. *It's just winter, nothing more.* Already the pale sunshine was risking tentative forays through the clouds. Riding into Taurus, whatever that meant. Perhaps the warmth was imagined but her bees had shown Mielitta the power of negative thinking so she decided she felt warmer. No question about it. And she had a beekeeper to train.

'Usually,' she said, 'the bees would be working and we don't want anything or anybody in our way when we're heading for home. So don't stand in front of the hive. That's our flight path and if you're in our way, we might hit you – and sting you. It doesn't matter in winter if there are no bees out but it's good to get into the right habits.'

They won't sting me. Forest creatures don't hurt me. Do you remember when you sent me your bee?

'I was frightened of what Rinduran and Bastien might do to you. And they did.' Took her voice, arranged her marriage, led her to self-harm.

Drianne took her hand and looked in her eyes with so much tenderness, Mielitta was disconcerted and nearly took a step back. But the young mage had been like a little sister for years, hovering in the archery yard, helping Mielitta with her training and tricks. So she left her hand where it was and gave what she hoped was a reassuring big sister's smile.

You kept me alive and I will never forget it. Drianne's eyes burned with passion and gratitude.

Mielitta covered her embarrassment with a shrug. 'Mage Puggy did more than I did. If she hadn't bequeathed you her magecraft, you wouldn't have been strong enough to resist forging.' She gently freed her hand, returned to practical matters. 'You need to take the roof off the beehive and put it down.'

Mielitta peered into the hive but she was looking at an empty top box, not accessible to the bees. Just insulation, she decided.

'Take the top box off too and then carefully prise up the cover. There will be bees on it when you turn it over.'

I can't said Drianne. *It's stuck.*

'Yes, the bees seal their house with propolis. It's like antiseptic orange goo.'

I remember! You used it on those makeshift shoes to escape from the Citadel.

Arven chipped in. 'Qingzhao's beekeeping tools.'

He fished in his pocket and brought out an object like a metal ruler with one end flat and one end hooked. 'Hive tool.'

Another delve into the pocket. 'Brush.' The brush was flat, with long silky yellow hairs and a wooden handle.

And he brandished the jug. 'Smoker'

'We won't need that,' said Mielitta hastily. She didn't want her bees afraid of fire as well as starvation or she'd never talk them into eating.

Drianne looked at the hive tool and after a bit of experimentation levered the cover off the brood box and immediately there was a hum of bees. A subdued hum. The frames could be seen and the shadow of huddled bees darkened the centre of the box.

'Put the cover upside down on the ground so the bees are on the top and can fly back into the hive,' Mielitta instructed but they just clung there with their *Why bother* attitude.

'And *that,*' she continued, 'is the frame full of honey. If you pull it out, you can put it back in right beside the bees, near the centre.'

Drianne obediently freed up the end frame and gave it to Arven to hold so she could look into the hive. *I can't see any bees on the next two frames.*

'Try lifting each one and if there's nothing on it, move it to the end.'

But what if I squidge a bee?

Mielitta's spirit bees offered her no wisdom that she could pass on. In fact, they'd been suspiciously quiet for some time. All she found was a sleepy *Why bother?* so she grasped the nettle firmly without their aid.

'It can't be helped. What matters is the whole colony, not one bee. They know that.'

Oh. Drianne's expression was bleak at the thought.

'But this time, I can help you. I'm going into the hive. I'll tell you where to put the frame with honey and I'll move the bees if they're in your way. I'll make sure the queen is safe. And then I have to get them to eat.'

Dianne's expression brightened.

'Gently does it,' Mielitta said as the bee sigil glowed and then she was back in the hive, looking upwards at the sky instead of a roof. She scuttled along the base until she found the space between second and third frames. Nothing on the third frame.

'Move the next frame into the space,' she told Drianne, using their telepathic link to communicate. The third frame gave a little jerk as Drianne used the hive tool to free it, then move it upwards.

'Gently,' reminded Mielitta, 'and try to keep to the middle of the space just in case any bees are wandering around. The buzz had diminished to a whine without the smallest reaction to losing their roof and being invaded by hands that shifted their home like an earthquake. The poor souls were either crammed in cells or clinging to each other in despair.

'Wait!' Mielitta told Drianne to stop the frame moving, halfway up. She crawled up the fourth frame, nudging bees aside as she went, with a bare *bzzz* of an apology. She flew between the frames and kicked a small group of bees to dislodge them from the third frame. They put up no resistance but fell to the floor of the hive, safely, not squidged at all.

'Carry on!' Mielitta ordered. The frame rose smoothly up the rest of the way and came back down further along.

Even more carefully, Drianne lowered the frame laden with honey into the space Mielitta told her was right, beside the outer ring of the bee cluster.

'You can put the top box and the roof back on,' Mielitta told her friends. 'I'll make them eat.'

If Drianne had never been rendered mute, their communication today would not be possible. How could such wonderful possibilities arise from the evil acts of men like Rinduran?

Because people like Drianne and herself fought back!

She nudged the nearest bee.

Why bother?

Oh for the stones' sake! How did you get depressed bees to eat? Mielitta thought back to her previous visits into the beehive. Get the queen bee to set the tone? But she didn't need to eat. She was fed by her courtiers and would be the last one to starve. And anyway, Mielitta couldn't fight her way through to the centre of the cluster. Not until it was so tiny all hope would be lost.

All that life-giving honey within reach and yet the bees were starving to death. They'd never have let her starve when she'd been their queen. She remembered her courtiers' incessant offerings of nectar and honey.

Being fed. That was the answer! She scurried up the honey frame, drilled through the wax cap into the cell and, instead of gulping it all down, she stored the honey in her crop. Then she clambered over to the bees in the outer ring.

She ignored the *Why bother* that greeted her and forced her long tongue down the other bee's throat. By sheer reflex, the feeding began, as this was what foraging bees always did when they returned to the hive and gave succour to those working at home. Honey was even better than nectar, the refined product!

Mielitta watched with satisfaction as the multi-faceted lenses of the other bee's large eyes regained their gleam.

'Work,' instructed Mielitta. She didn't need to dance the direction of the food source as the frame of honey was only a bee space away but she gave a nudge in the right direction. Now that her spirits had lifted, the bee could smell the honey from the cell Mielitta had uncapped and she didn't need to be told twice.

Work, she agreed, moving onto the honey frame.

'Feed ten bees and tell them to feed ten more,' Mielitta told the revived bee, then she continued to the next of her ten bees. By the time her tenth bee was invigorated by a slurp of honey, the cluster had broken up and bees were taking their fill, then warming the hive with their wings and bodies. They still crowded together but were no longer huddling. No longer depressed. The change was so fast Mielitta couldn't believe her own success.

Is it working? Drianne asked, her voice quivering.

'Yes!' Mielitta replied, as a group of bees passed her, tightly packed around their precious charge, heading for the honey frame. From the automatic gestures of respect by all the bees, Mielitta recognised the courtiers, with the queen safe and warm in the middle of the group. They too gorged and then fed the queen.

Then home truly became a hive of organisation.

The call to work completely replaced *Why bother* and the scent of open honey cells flooded the hive, irresistible, as motivating as the sudden warmth of spring.

Bees flew to their allocated duties: feeding the grubs in their nursery cells; weatherproofing the hive with propolis; cleaning; dragging dead bees and hapless ants to the entrance and dropping them off the platform into the greening grass below. Some workers went foraging, to see what was available and to report back. A source of water was as vital as food.

Now that they could extract the sugar from honey to make wax, repairs could be carried out on old frames and new wax built on frames which hadn't been worked, ready for the spring boom in brood and food. To support the wax-making process, a festoon of bees linked legs in a lacy net between two frames. Replete with honey, they processed the sugar to make flakes of wax from their abdomens. Fellow workers then collected the flakes, softened them by chewing, and used the result to construct the precise hexagons of their home honeycomb.

The queen was working too, laying egg after egg in neat, concentric circles in the middle of an empty frame. There was no question as to what her target was. Mielitta remembered the urgency with which she'd laid eggs to save the hive when it was queenless and she knew that the queen would choose the right time to lay drones rather than workers. Not yet but soon.

She indulged in one moment more, soaking up the happy buzz and the honey smell, then she shifted back to human form. There was so much to tell Drianne about beekeeping.

CHAPTER NINE

'We have to tell the bees.' Arven was reading a section in the notebook, his bag of knitting slung over one shoulder as Mielitta's bow was over hers.

Both are weapons in their own way, thought Drianne, as she stood beside the beehive and held out her arms in a welcoming gesture. Several bees were walking around the landscape her body offered.

That tickles, she said, watching a bee on her open palm. *And the buzz vibrates down through its feet, right into my body.*

'Her feet,' corrected Mielitta. 'All the worker bees are female and this year's drones haven't been born yet. They don't go out scouting or foraging. The only work the males do in the beehive is keeping it warm, which is useful near the nurseries. But their sole purpose is mating and that happens outside the hive, when a new queen flies. On just one occasion.'

Inwardly, Drianne sighed. Her friend could be so… so factual. Another bee explored her hand with its long tongue and antennae. What did she see? Not the circles of a flower in ultraviolet that Mielitta had described from her pollen-gathering. And yet the bee was treating her as a flower, sipping gently at her palm.

Qingzhao had called her Mielitta's flower and that was as good a description of their love as any. Love. Drianne sighed again. Mielitta offered her sisterly pats and gruff affection while Jannlou received the full blaze of her passion.

A bee crawled up onto the rainbow scarf, weaving in and out of the patterned holes in the knitted fabric. Drianne didn't have to look at Arven's gift to know that each colour glowed, equally vibrant. She could sense her equilibrium.

Despite what's between Jannlou and Mielitta, she thought, proud of what she gave them and of hiding the cost. Like a flower.

The bee's little antennae appeared up through a tiny space between blue and indigo yarn, followed by its big eyes and body, in the same way it would come through a wax cell on a frame in the beehive. It tickled but she didn't mind being an extension of their home.

She looked at the beehives in a row against the trees, all waiting for her attention. She could do this.

Affinity, she told Mielitta. *Affinity is my special mage talent. With all living creatures. That's why Qingzhao chose me.*

Arven was insistent. 'We have to tell the bees.'

Drianne glanced at the slanted green writing in the notebook and understood why he couldn't explain himself fully.

Mielitta was not as perceptive.

'Tell them what?' she asked.

Arven's throat moved in a gulp but his voice showed no sign of his turmoil. 'That their beekeeper has died. And that they have a new one.'

Dianne took the notebook from Arven and read:

TELLING THE BEES

Nothing is too trivial to tell your bees for they understand the importance of small things and how these make up the whole.

Whisper, gurgle, chant, hum, sing and share your joys and sorrows. The bees will learn the honeyed tone of your voice. For each of us is composed of unique flavours, blended from time, terrain and life's blos-

soms. Share all of yourself with the bees and they will share their honey with you. You will never taste finer fare.

Should you forget to tell the bees something trivial, this will be as the death of one bee, unimportant among so many of their kind. But should you forget to tell the bees of a weighty matter, the hive will droop and fail.

The weightiest matter of all is the loss of the beekeeper. Should you come across neglected hives, you should sit beside each one and tell the bees what has come to pass so that they wait no longer for she who will not come again.

Drianne had a lump in her throat, picturing Qingzhao, a wizened lady with a wise sparkle in her black eyes, the sadness in her heart covered by years preparing her grandson for the future. How could Arven read this and his face stay set as marble?

WHEN THE BEEKEEPER HAS DIED

Sit by each hive in still contemplation and speak this rhyme and name her. Thus the bees will thrive again and accept their new beekeeper as they accept a new queen when the old one dies.

Your keeper ___ has left this world
in the solitary flight of the soul.
May she be home by nightfall.
In your keeper's name who loved you well
greet the one she chose with care
to tend to you and with you share.

The beekeeper (name) is dead.
Long live the beekeeper (name)!

Then shall you speak of the beekeeper, what manner of person she was and all that made up her life. Then you shall let go of that little life, into the big stream of life itself.

By the time she'd finished reading this aloud for Mielitta, Drianne's face was wet. Even her friend's composure had crumpled and she spoke with an effort, looking at Arven.

'Yes, we need to tell the bees. I can help. Qingzhao deserves this. And your mother, Tannlei. And your father, Crimvert. Let us name them all and call the bees to witness the greatness of these lives lost to you and to us. And the greatness of your heritage.'

She bowed her head in respect to the youth. 'And your inheritance.' She bowed to Drianne too. Never had she looked so regal, her long red hair thrown back, eyes gleaming from the tears she fought, wreathed in a halo of bees.

'If you two carry out the ceremony and read the lines, the bees shall also tell the bees. This is for my Archery Mage, may the walls receive her spirit. For Tannlei!'

Mielitta nocked an arrow and wailed an unearthly cry that seemed to vanish beyond human hearing while her mouth was still open. The bow twanged and the arrow flew high above them and in an instant, Mielitta was merely one bee among many. The swarm followed the arrow in an impossible vertical flight which grew blacker and blacker with bees as the other colonies joined the cortège.

When the sky was black with a million bees, they clustered in a gigantic cloud above the beehives.

'Your keeper Qingzhao has left this world,' intoned Arven and Drianne, repeating the verse beside each beehive. Half of Drianne's mouth moved though her voice was silent as Mielitta's final scream. She thought the bees could hear her, in their fashion.

Her eyes were on the sky throughout and she barely had time to wonder whether the arrow might fall back to earth and wound one of them when the cluster of bees burst open and a fireball burned bright where the arrow had been.

Qingzhao. Tannlei. Crimvert, thought Drianne, instinctively focusing her magecraft into the fiery heart hanging above her. For one glorious moment, the names of the dead mages were written in fire across the sky.

As the sparks faded, Mielitta wrote the names again, in the black of a million flying bees, over and over.

Then Arven began to weep, sitting beside the last beehive. Tears washed his cheeks, poured down into the bag beside him on the ground. He sobbed loud and unashamed, a winter of grief. Drianne didn't know whether to touch him or let him cry unimpeded, so strange were his ways to her.

May the walls keep her spirit, thought Drianne. And the memories came. The oldest woman she'd ever seen welcoming her chickens back from the Forest, and Drianne with them. As if she was family, like the horses, goats, cows, cat – and bees.

A ceremonial tea drink in a bone china cup. The same cup Drianne had smashed in a storm of wild magecraft while Qingzhao watched patiently, with understanding in her wise black eyes. Her face that was echoed in younger faces.

Her daughter Tannlei, so much loved by Mielitta, had been Drianne's archery teacher too. Now her friend and mentor was Arven, Qingzhao's grandson, orphaned by the Citadel mages without them knowing he existed. Qingzhao had borne all this and still fed her chickens, tended her bees and loved Arven. She had never lost hope for the future. Her death was a loss and a fulfilment, after a life well lived.

Drianne watched a bee settle on the first flower of Arven's speedy springtime. A creamy-yellow crocus, purpled with fine lines and with a golden heart, its scent exuding the essence of fresh starts. She did not pick it and could not lay it on a grave but offered it to Qingzhao all the same, in love and thanks and remembrance. She promised she would try to live up to this strange inheritance.

As the skies above cleared to the pale cold blue of spring and the bees returned to their various hives and enmities, Arven reached for his knitting. Soaked with tears, the wool hung grey and heavy from the needles yet he lifted his work as others would an axe, with workmanlike strength and purpose.

The tears continued to roll and he knitted their silvery sheen into fabric that rippled like a broad stream. By the time Mielitta was human once more and looking down on Drianne and Arven as they sat by the hive, a garment had been knitted. No shifting rainbow scarf-waistcoat this time but a shimmering suit that could have been cobwebs or armour, so silken but impenetrable it was. As strong as teardrops.

'We should go now,' he told Mielitta, who looked away from his red eyes and streaky face. 'Jannlou is waiting for us.'

She nodded, adjusted her quiver, gave Drianne a bluff, sisterly hug and kiss. Told her, 'You'll be fine.'

Drianne was still staring after them when they vanished across the boundary between the homestead and the Forest. On their way to the cave. And to the Citadel. Yes, she would be fine. But would they?

CHAPTER TEN

Jannlou yawned and stretched. How could waking up be so tiring after a winter's sleep? Was his human nature responsible or the bear in him? Whichever it was, his stomach rumbled and his flesh hung slack over muscles that lacked exercise.

He stretched again, gorged once more at the table in the cave. Fruit, hams, cheese – he ate as much as he could. You could never tell when the food or the table would vanish as strangely into the cave wall as it had appeared.

Then, overcome by lassitude, he slept. Not the fitful sleep of hibernation but the deep plunge into an icy dark, that replenished his soul. And this time when he woke, he was ready for a different kind of icy plunge.

Assuming his bear form, he scratched at the patches where fur hung dull and winter-loose, felt a different kind of hunger and padded out of the cave entrance down the path to the rocky pools at the foot of the cascade.

He stopped to eat the greens spiking up in the accelerated growth induced by Arven's magecraft.

Then he thumped across the stones into the pool, a chilling

wake-up call to his system. He splashed through the turquoise rills, where snow caps had melted to free white froth.

Having wintered underneath the frozen surface in the deeper pools, fish were wriggling, enticing, but although he had a bear's reflexes Jannlou found it tiring to catch even one silvery tease, so he left the waterfall to look for easier pickings in the Forest.

Alert for competitors in stripes, spots or even brown fur, he ate the choice parts of a deer's carcase and trotted on, still hazy from the torpor of the last few months. There was enough dead meat around now for all the Forest carnivores but, like him, they would be possessive and bad-tempered about their meal. Starvation was a poor teacher of manners, in man or beast.

Jannlou dug and enlarged a burrow, curled up and napped again. He could never explain to Mielitta that day sleeps were a joy. He thought it politic not to explain to her that the solitude of a male bear could also be restorative. The thought of crowding into a hive with thousands of bees made him want to rub his back against a tree-trunk to get rid of the itch but Mielitta accepted the communal living along with the communal thinking. They were so different, bee and bear.

He stopped short. Better not to follow that train of thought. He and Mielitta were first and foremost humans, with control over their own destinies – and instincts.

When he was a bear, he would live his second nature to the full, alone. No creature in this Forest was his superior although some might test whether they were his equal, especially if protecting food or young. He thought briefly of young, knowing that no creature feared him more than a female bear with her winter-born cubs. Even should those cubs be his. He didn't want to follow that train of thought either although he knew Mielitta had bee offspring. And he did not like it.

His instinct told him that the season was not come for a male bear to seek a mate and that females would not emerge from their dens yet, not until their cubs were bigger, better equipped to climb trees and escape their fathers.

Jannlou swiped casually at a tree, scoring deep marks across the bark and licking the sap, seeking insects. Not bees. Never bees. He had promised Mielitta. And he would prove Arven wrong in his stupid ban on a bear entering the homestead.

Solitude and freedom, Jannlou told himself. He stood on his hind legs and roared. Listened to the instant silence, spreading outwards from his shout, like a ripple from a stone in a pool. This was power. He might not have magecraft but he was King of the Forest.

He wondered when Mielitta and Arven would return. In the Forest, time was not of bells, meals or greylight and it trod its own measures of wake, eat and sleep. And he was sleepy again. Maybe he'd go back to the cave and nap until his friends returned. Until it was time to force entry to the Citadel.

Something roused Jannlou from the depths of his bear torpor to that state of awareness necessary for defence. He looked around for the danger, screwing up his eyes in the darkness of the cave. A bear's eyesight was never his most acute sense and he used his nose instead, flaring his sensitive nostrils. The food had gone from the table but the chests still overflowed with their treasure store of piled weapons, armour and precious tableware.

Which must belong to somebody, thought Jannlou, as his nose confirmed the change in atmosphere, a sudden chill and almost dusty, rather than damp. He sneezed.

Figures appeared as if from the cave wall at the back, wavering and then solid, a line of warriors striding towards the chests, where they sifted through the armour and weapons. Broadsword and double-edged blade, knife, axe, hammer and spear, each went to a man who slotted the weapon into its accustomed place.

Jannlou named them in his mind according to his first impressions.

Towering above the others, a man trailing broken chains that swung like flails, was Man-Mountain. Fur-Hat wore a leather padded jacket and trews and a bonnet with fur flaps dangling either side of his wide, flat face. Two wore skirts, composed of leather strips, over protective gartered leggings. As one of these looked like a statue come to life, he became Marble-Skinned, and the other Leather-Skirt.

Only the metal clanking could be heard as men girded on bucklers and hauberks, sheathed swords into scabbards, with the wince of steel Jannlou knew so well. Some warriors ignored the blades. Redbeard's weapon of choice was an axe and Jannlou named another man White-Hammer, white being the colour of his long hair and even longer beard.

A small man with jet-black hair under a plumed head-dress took a hollow tube from beneath his heavy robes and put it to his lips, testing. The others ducked in alarm and he smiled but hid his weapon. Death-Pipe.

One left a watery trail as he walked, his long hair dripping without cease down his hauberk, sword-belt and leather trousers, as if he wore a raincloud on his head instead of a helmet. Lake-Born.

Eagle-Shield and Winged-Helm were followed by Curved-Sword, worn by a swarthy turbaned individual, clad in ballooning trousers below a robe. The garb looked too lightweight for battle but the sword looked deadly. The cross-piece curved like a new moon and mystic symbols were etched into the long grip, while an engraved ball decorated the golden pommel.

Heavy-headed, in half-sleep, Jannlou accepted the vision as dream and he lay there watchful but without fear. He scented no harm from these men and he felt curious rather than threatened.

Warriors all, in full battle apparel from helm to boots, they circled Jannlou in slow procession before walking back to the wall and stepping through it.

The last warrior paused. The Jewelled King. His black helmet was encircled by a gold crown that glinted green and red from bloodstones set into the band. Two ravens emerged from the walls, circled and landed on his padded shoulders. They cocked their heads, as if considering whether Jannlou was carrion or not but they drew in their wings at the earth-shaking rumble of their master's voice.

'Tell the seer he awoke *all* the sleepers. We heard the call and the ravens will circle the mountains once more.' The voice was earthy, ancient, noble as the circlet around his helm. He wore a fur cloak over his long mail hauberk, a short sword and a long sword sheathed in his belt. The jagged edges to his hauberk hung like teeth, snapping at his knees.

More god than man, yet he paused to speak to Jannlou.

'Join us,' said the king. 'You are better than you know, man and bear, our berserker. Follow us. Then lead us.'

Berserker, thought Jannlou. A term spoken with respect, as if his kind were known and valued, not despised and shamed.

The king offered his sword to Jannlou, a ceremonial gesture to which the bear could not reply and the man would have found himself lost for words. From the fine point to the cross-piece, the steel patterns caught the light, moving like the sea and given depth by the central ridge.

Like Mielitta's Steelwing, he thought, and no doubt imbued with magecraft.

'Sound the hunting horn three times when battle begins,' the king said. Then the cave darkened as the sword was sheathed once more.

The king paced steadily towards and into the wall, looking around once and repeating, 'Join us, follow us, lead us,' before he disappeared.

Jannlou slipped back into his restless sleep, until his nose warned him of more intruders in the cave, living humans this time, not ghostly visitors. His hackles rose at this second disturbance and he growled, warning the intruders that a bear's sleep was not to be interrupted without consequences. He rolled onto his four paws, reared up and staggered. Half-blinded from sleep and the light from the entrance, he saw a cloud of insects and swatted at them with his front paw, claws extended.

'It's me!' Mielitta shouted at him, her human form visible where he'd only seen bees at first. She stepped back, eyeing him as she had when they'd fought, so long ago. 'Your eyes are brown,' she said, accusing him of something but of what, he wasn't sure.

Then somebody stood between them. Arven. Nobody should stand between Jannlou and Mielitta. The bear roared and lashed out again, raking Arven's clothes with his claws.

But instead of ripped fabric there was no sign of Jannlou's assault. Arven's silver garments gleamed, intact. And seconds later, Jannlou howled with pain as his claws burned to the quick, as if he'd stuck them in forge fires.

'His eyes are blue again,' observed Arven dispassionately, as Jannlou felt his body change, assume his warrior's form. His head cleared and he knew exactly what was meant by his eyes being brown. He'd gone too far into his bear nature. Again. His face burned, though his dark skin and the cave light hid his shame.

'He can't be trusted,' Arven told Mielitta as if Jannlou wasn't there. Understandably.

'You should have let me deal with it.' Mielitta stepped around Arven, hugged Jannlou fiercely. 'We startled him when he was sleeping. And I should have kept my bees hidden. It's my fault.'

'No,' Jannlou said quietly. He licked his sore fingers, which were cooling already. One of Arven's lessons. Humiliating. Deserved. 'He's right. I'm trying but I'm not there yet. I have… lapses.'

'We all do,' Mielitta said, still holding him. 'We just have to be more careful.' She moved away, light-footed as always, despite the uneven cave floor. She shrugged and changed the subject.

'Arven has a plan for getting into the Citadel, by reopening the water gate.'

Jannlou shook his head. 'We don't need it.' He hesitated. Would they believe him? 'I saw something.' He told them about the warriors, describing each one. He cut short some of the detail of their weapons, sensing Mielitta's impatience, and he omitted what mattered most to him. He didn't tell them how he'd felt, being praised for being a *berserker*.

'We have to follow them, into the cave walls. Perhaps this is a way into the Citadel or perhaps we'll be inside the walls and we can find Kermon but this is our way. I know it.' He pleaded with them silently. *Please believe me.*

'I don't know,' said Arven in broken tones.

'But you always know!' Mielitta couldn't keep the frustration out of her voice.

'No, that's not what it's like,' said their seer. 'And I can't see the paths at all now.'

'Then,' said Mielitta, 'it's simple. Let's follow these–' she glanced at Jannlou, '–mythical warriors into the cave wall. We know how it's done, from Kermon and Drianne, and Jannlou watched the warriors go through, so it should be easy enough. If we don't want to be there, we can retrace our steps, come back here and try Arven's idea with the water gate. What do you think?'

'Yes,' said Jannlou. 'but it might be dangerous. You should stay here. Drianne will need your help.'

Mielitta laughed at him, her eyes flashing with scorn. 'I won't dignify that with a reply.'

'Yes,' said Arven slowly. 'Maybe my sight will return as we travel. It always comes in glimpses and possibilities, not with certainty.'

They took each other's hands, Arven between Mielitta and Jannlou, who wondered whether this was another lesson but accepted it. If so, Jannlou accepted it without so much as an imagined swipe with a paw.

Once connected physically, they concentrated on the world beyond the walls, on what they could not see but knew they could reach. Jannlou took a step forward, pushed through the frontier where the cave wall should be and found himself in a dark passageway, walls on both sides. Arven shimmered into solidity beside him. And they waited.

And waited.

His heart pounding, Jannlou said, 'This is a trap! I'm going back for Mielitta!'

He focused on the cave interior, on Mielitta's face just the other side of an imaginary barrier and he stepped forward, whispering, 'My anchor. Nothing can come between us. I won't let it.'

And he was blocked again.

As Mielitta must be blocked on her side. The walls had played one of their tricks.

'I think you were right.' Arven's cool voice broke into Jannlou's anguished attempt to break through the wall. 'The cave wall connects somehow. I've seen this in dreams. We're inside the Citadel.'

CHAPTER ELEVEN

Hitting walls and swearing at them was a lesson in futility that left Mielitta with knuckles and pride equally bruised. First Jannlou, then Arven, showing how easy it was, wavering, half with her and half beyond the cave wall, then gone. She still felt the tingle of Arven's hand holding hers – and the smack as her fingers hit stone.

'Why did you let them through and not me?' Her question echoed through the tunnels at the back of the cave, as if in mockery.

Emotions still raw from Qingzhao's memorial flight, she wondered if she'd ever see Jannlou again. They'd wasted their time together in a winter's sleep. Curse Arven, curse his obsession with destiny and most of call curse the walls! She should have told Jannlou how much she loved him, not held back.

What had her last words been? Something stupid like, 'You go first,' probably. She couldn't even remember. What if those were the last words between them ever? And she hadn't even been holding his hand but Arven's when they'd been separated.

She waited an aeon of seconds, counting each one. Jannlou would come back. He'd never continue without her, destiny notwithstanding.

Time passed and he didn't come. Which meant he *couldn't* come. The walls had put worlds between them. Why?

She would not cry. She crouched in the dirt, cradled her head in her arms. Alone in a dark cave.

Not alone, piped up her bees, flitting around her anxiously. *We're better off without the bear. He nearly ate us.*

'No he didn't,' Mielitta snapped. 'He didn't recognise us, just for a second after he'd woken up, that's all. Don't *you* need time to come to your senses when you wake up?'

She felt the bees' puzzlement and she tried to share her experience of a grumpy wakening, picturing it as a mind map where she started with sleep, then fog, before the directions to the nectar source were clear.

Sleep, the bees agreed happily. *Then work.*

'Sleep then grumpy,' insisted Mielitta. How to explain grumpy? When were bees grumpy? Ah yes. She pictured a wild wind, knocking foraging bees off-course when they returned to the hive, threatening every nook and cranny with draughts and whistles. She buzzed the bees' feelings.

'Grumpy,' she told them.

Her bees considered this. *Not grumpy because we wake up.* They were emphatic. *We wake up then we go to work.*

Mielitta sighed. *She* understood grumpy waking up completely. Maybe humans had more in common with bears than with bees. But she felt less desolate from the contact.

Why had the walls treated her differently?

They always did, she realised. On her side or against her, she couldn't tell.

She stood up and felt the cave wall, gently this time, observing. Clammy, leaving traces of cold moisture on her fingers. Rough but not sharp, worn smooth in places, polished by water and time. She ran her fingers horizontally along the wall and found strata, seams of different rock. Hewn by nature, unlike the Citadel walls which had been constructed stone upon stone.

What if Jannlou was right and the walls were linked? Perhaps the Citadel was built from the same stone. She held her hand flat against the wall as she had against his chest to feel his heartbeat. But the life in the walls lay beyond her reach.

The walls gave. And then they took it away.

According to her foster-father, they'd given birth to her. She'd shimmered into existence in the Citadel, a baby in a basket, with her name-tag. Mielitta. A foundling, parents unknown, somewhere on the other side of the walls. Now they'd parted her from Jannlou too.

And yet, when the Council of Mages wiped her memory, the walls had saved her mind, stored and returned every precious particle of what she'd witnessed: Crimvert's courage and death, dark treasures to pass on to his son.

Like an impartial tutor, letting her figure out what it meant, they'd shown her a second Council meeting and more murders: Jannlou's father and his Right Hand, Mage Shenagra, who'd loved him. Mielitta had watched Rinduran come to power and the manner of it, the blood of the previous Chief Mage still wet as he claimed the vacant seat.

Yet Rinduran was the expert in wallcraft, the mage who had accompanied and tutored others into the walls and who existed there now, after his death. Why did the walls tolerate such a man and shut her out? Favouring her one minute and refusing her the next? What did it all mean?

Jannlou said that warriors had come through the walls and claimed what was rightfully theirs from the chests piled high with weapons and treasure trove. She'd seen the table laden with food, appearing through the wall as once a baby in a basket had done. Now all that was left on the table was a piece of paper with green scrawl upon it.

She didn't have to read it as she knew it by heart and it gave no clue as to the walls' behaviour. The prophecy left by Qingzhao was merely a reminder that there was a higher purpose and Mielitta was sick of portentous mysteries.

Hah! thought Mielitta. Qingzhao's green scrawl had been on that other note, the one that arrived in her chamber in the Citadel on her 18th birthday. She'd meant to ask Qingzhao so many questions and now it was too late. The wise old lady must have known of the link between the walls, must have used it to send the note and perfume to Mielitta on her eighteenth birthday. How long ago that seemed, the start of all this. The start of living with bees.

Go to your flower, urged the bees. *Be happy with her. Visit the hives together. Wait at the homestead, safe'*

Maybe they were right. Drianne would be happy if Mielitta joined in the farm life. Throwing grain to chickens, collecting eggs, milking goats and cows, and caring for their young. Pouring tea into china cups with roses on them. She picked up Qingzhao's last message, folded it and tucked it into a pocket, as a memento.

She headed out of the cave, down by the waterfall and into the dark shade of the Forest, towards the homestead, her thoughts as gloomy as the path she walked. She lost everybody she loved and now her hopes of answers about her origins had gone too. Qingzhao was dear to her for Tannlei's sake as well as her own and there was nothing left of either of them but Arven, and now he was gone too. If only the Archery Mage had left some last words for her student.

What's the target, Mielitta? rang clear in her mind.

Without thinking, she replied, 'To reach Jannlou.'

Her own words caught her by surprise and she repeated them slowly. 'To reach Jannlou. And Kermon. And even Arven. And fight beside them against Perfection. Drianne doesn't need me.'

Her thoughts raced, freed from the overwhelming despair of having Jannlou ripped from her side.

If Jannlou was in the Citadel, she didn't need to go into the cave wall. She needed to get into the Citadel. And Arven had suggested another way, by trying to open the old water gate route.

Mielitta couldn't walk through solid stone but if anybody could get through the tiniest space between magical wards and a gate, she could. The bee sigil on her thigh glowed and she started to change shape. She would fly into the Citadel and join Jannlou.

No! buzzed her bees in a frenzy. *Not safe.*

Despite their protests, they had no option but to fly with her. They were one hive and she was their warrior queen.

Mielitta accessed the hive mind map that directed her to the clearing in the woods where she had first seen home hive. From there, she would follow the route the bees had danced to show where the sunflowers were in the field beyond the Forest, near the Citadel.

For once, Mielitta ignored the fun of flying, diverging from her beeline only to avoid trees or winged threats that dived and snapped, too slow to catch her. Arrow-straight to her target she flew, thinking only, 'Jannlou'.

Until the rain began. Pattering, soft spring rain, misting the earth fertile. A mere tickle to a human. And fatal to bees who didn't shelter.

Hide, urged her bees. *Or change. Or you'll die.*

Already Mielitta's fur was weighing her down, dragging her earthwards and she knew she had no choice. Heart heavier than her soaked body, she shifted back into human form. Her spirit bees had taken their own advice and hidden so deep in her mind she couldn't feel so much as a flutter.

She was blocked again and must wait until the rain stopped.

CHAPTER TWELVE

The shadow at her heels, Janette kept running. She must not lead the evil towards her true story so she didn't think once about the honey hunter or the man in the suit. Her thoughts were spinning but she had to focus to move in this world.

Honeybees, she ordered and the world obliged, taking her from one beekeeping scene to another as fast as she could bring it into focus and then run to the next one.

Dizzy with lack of food and drink, her heart pounding – from running, she told herself – she still couldn't help lingering for some of the stories.

An old man, honey-brown and wrinkled, showed his grandchildren the miracle that lived with him, both curse and blessing.

'I've moved three times to different villages,' he said, loud enough to be heard over the buzz from a black mass in the corner of his hut. 'But they followed me and I must accept a life with bees.'

He shrugged. 'Your grandmother and your parents lived with me and never lacked for honey. But their friends and the neighbours were afraid so they never came here. It can be a lonely life. Apart from the bees.'

The grandchildren shuffled their bare feet, torn between curiosity and fear.

'Will they sting me?' asked the littlest boy.

The grandfather turned big, sad eyes on him. 'If you're scared, then they might. But they never sting me.'

Then four of the grandchildren sheepishly backed out of the hut and ran to their bee-free homes, never to visit grandfather again. But the littlest one stood his ground.

The grandfather nodded. 'Yes,' was all he said, more to himself than the boy, who settled down in a crouch on the mud floor.

'How do they make honey?' he asked.

Crouching beside him, the grandfather took a stick and started to explain, drawing in the dust.

The mud floor darkened. Shapes that weren't drawings in mud sharpened into noses that lengthened and sniffed, shadows that tracked somebody.

Jolted out of the story, Janette ran again.

Honeybees, she instructed.

And found herself on a farm, where a man in a red and black checked shirt wept and spoke in a guttural accent, words which she understood on some level beyond language. As if all was translated within the walls.

'Bears again,' the man said. 'Unless we shoot them all, we must give up.'

'No,' said the taller man. 'There must be a way we can live together.'

'We've tried everything, Len, but they come back! Tonight, I will wait with this.' He lifted his rifle.

'One last attempt,' the other man pleaded. 'We move the hives.'

'Those that are left,' was the bitter comment. Checked-shirt man kicked at a pile of broken hive parts on the ground.

'And we put up the electric fencing around the hives but this time we hang strips of meat from the fence. The bear will try to eat the meat and will get the shock through its muzzle, where it hurts, instead of rushing the fence.'

A shadow had crept up on the shattered wooden frames nearest Janette, was lengthening, sending out fingers that reached for her – and clutched at thin air.

Honeybees! she shrieked and ran again.

Almond blossom whitened the orchards as far as the eye could see. And beehives were being placed at regular intervals, carried by dozens of beekeepers and farmhands, staggering as they shifted their live cargo from the mechanical monster that was stacked with box upon box of bees, its headlights blazing in the soft purple of dawn.

Janette lost count after calculating there must be more than a thousand such boxes on the vehicle. What would the grandfather say to this business of bees? The scale of the operation took her breath away.

Men's voices drifted across to her as money changed hands.

The seller returned some of the bills, magnanimous. 'Discount the twenty dead hives. Can't offer replacements – they're all spoken for. Not so easy these days keeping the stock alive.'

A grunt of assent and a handshake.

The seller spoke again. 'Be back in two weeks to collect them. They're wanted for the orchards out east so that's another long haul. Bees don't travel too well, even on a flatbed truck.' He shook his head. 'I've told Joe he'd lose fewer hives if he didn't play country and western on the road. It kills me too.' He laughed, loud and nasty. 'But he just fires back about other truckers losing the whole load. Accidents do happen.'

The farmer was already walking away, giving instructions, keen to make the most of his rented pollinators.

The trucker in charge of the operation turned to Joe and lowered his voice. 'Nice work. No sign he was suspicious.'

'Why should he be? We've been running this business for years now. Totally legit apart from where we get the bees. There's enough miles between here and the fields we lifted them from. Who's to recognise a bee, right? And they're our boxes.'

An unpleasant laugh. 'Yeah. Imagine those dumb suckers.' He put on a squeaky voice. 'Officer, somebody done come in the night and stole hundreds of my beehives. You gotta find them.'

He played the officer's reply in a deep voice, 'I need some dee-tails. What do they look like?'

Squeaky voice again. 'Kinda little and stripey, in black and yellow.'

Both men laughed.

'Nope. They won't be finding us in a hurry.'

'Burn 'em Joe.' The man indicated the twenty boxes set to one side. 'And try to keep more alive for the next drop? You're bleeding money.'

'I'll turn the volume down,' joked Joe as he lit a match and dropped it onto the discarded hives. They didn't stop to watch the pyre burn out but jumped into the truck and hit the road.

Janette felt the smoke sear her throat, wondered how many bees had died, would die. After what kind of a life. She gulped back tears and sensed a sudden taste. Honey.

And she remembered one bee bringing her honey fresh from the hive. She was sitting with her schoolmates in the Forest. Not in this world. She was sure of it. In the other world beyond the Citadel walls, when Mielitta kidnapped them all and held them to ransom. Only it had been fun. They'd played in the stream, seen trees and birds and sunshine. And a bee had served her with honey. She was sure of it. What a story that would make when she returned to the Citadel.

She'd been too absorbed in her thoughts to notice that the rising sun seemed slow in reaching her, the shadows deep, one lengthening from somebody standing behind her.

'No,' she shouted but she was grabbed from behind before she could run to the next honeybees scene.

At least she hadn't led the evil to the honey hunter and the man in a suit and nothing would make her!

'Janette! It's me!' said a familiar voice as she was released.

She whirled around, then relaxed. She had thrown the evil off her track after all. But not her best friend.

'Nathan,' she said. 'How did you find me?'

'Thank the stones I did!' He pulled sustenance and a bottle of water out of his pack and she barely thanked him before she guzzled the lot.

'I knew where to start looking because of your story,' he said, brandishing her notebook before returning it to his pack, 'and then some instinct led me after that. Because we're friends and I know how you think, probably.'

Janette watched the deepening shadows. Fingers of dark matter lengthened, uncurled, reached out. She stood up, grabbed Nathan's hand, yelled, 'Honeybees!'

And nothing happened.

From the black centre of the deepest shadows, a shape materialised as a mage's cloak, hooded over a face she could barely see bar one milky eye, pierced with a bee-sting.

'So much easier if we all travel together,' said the revenant who had been Chief Mage Rinduran. 'Until we part, that is.'

His instructions were every bit as clear as Janette's had been. 'The honey hunter and the man in the suit.'

As if he'd plucked the words from her mind, Janette pictured them both.

And the world obliged.

CHAPTER THIRTEEN

The silence between worlds deafened him but Jannlou could not appeal against the walls' verdict. Mielitta was on the other side and he was back in the Citadel. The place where he'd lived a privileged life as the Chief Mage's son and peerless warrior, where all assumed he'd inherited his father's magecraft. But he hadn't. His outer confidence had been a cloak to hide his second nature, which grew in his awareness each day that Bastien covered for him in magecraft lessons, in all innocence. Poor Bastien, his best friend and his victim. Jannlou flexed his hands as if unsheathing the claws that had killed Bastien's father – in this world at least.

'I see only walls,' murmured Arven. 'And danger.'

Jannlou laughed, mocking himself more than his companion. 'It takes no seer to have such a vision.'

He remembered that Arven had never been into the Citadel and knew it only from tales told by his grandmother and his parents, or from his dreams. He, however, knew the place like the lines on his own hand, from the forge to the Maturity Barn; from the Great Hall to the Archery Yard; and past the schoolrooms to the Mages' Quarters and Tower, with the Council Chamber at the top. Not to mention every passage down which he'd chased

Mielitta, every nook and cranny where a girl might hide from boys who chased her in their ambiguous bullying. The dark hid his shame.

He also knew the ways of Perfection and the specific dangers they courted, marked as intruders by Arven's alien apparel and his own tatters. Citizens of Perfection blended in, women in long gowns, mages in cloaks that covered warriors' or artisans' garb. A knight wore a leatherette jerkin and britches, sword and boots. As he did. But his clothes were scratched and weathered by life in the Forest. Here there was no weather, just optimal greylight by day and darklight by night.

Dark, he thought, realising.

'It's night here,' he told Arven, whose face turned towards him, seeking explanations. 'They're all in their chambers, sleeping. The lights go dim.'

'What about candles or moonlight?' Arven asked. Then he too realised. Even in the dark of the passageway, Jannlou saw the expression on the luminous face shift like clouds across the moon as he struggled to understand what life in Perfection meant. That his family had lived in this place. He who knew only the freedom of the Forest, the safety of the homestead and the superiority of his magecraft.

'None.' Stating the obvious might be the way he convinced himself of the truth. 'No candles. No moon. The canopy above the Citadel blocks out the sky, the sun and moon, the weather.'

'Keeps the citizens safe.' Jannlou's tone dripped irony. He thought aloud. 'We can try to go into the walls. From the usual place, at the bottom of the Mages' Tower.' He glanced around him. 'That's not where we are now. There's too much passageway ahead and behind. Perhaps the walls could take us back to Mielitta.' Hope surged.

'Or,' he continued as Arven seemed uncharacteristically silent, 'the walls could take us into their world, to Kermon.' *And his fight against Rinduran. That's where we should be.*

'How would we find Kermon?' asked Arven. He'd clearly dismissed the possibility that they could return to the cave.

Jannlou's heart constricted. *Mielitta,* he thought.

'I don't know,' he admitted. If only he could go to the forge, talk to Kermon, make a battle plan. If Kermon were only here and they could go through the walls together, fight side by side as knights should. Magecraft and might.

The sudden pang of nostalgia brought his friend to life in front of him: Kermon's earnest nobility as he took on the burden of his mission in the Citadel. The same courage as he'd shown when he took Declan's evil from Mielitta's arrowhead pendant into his own soul, cleansed it for her at whatever cost to himself.

'By the stones, Kermon, you shall not fight Rinduran alone,' swore Jannlou.

Arven waited, still said nothing.

The forge, thought Jannlou. 'If Kermon is inside the walls, the forge will be empty. I can lead us there and we should be able to find clothes that let us walk the Citadel passages unquestioned. We might hear news of the lost students and of Kermon. Then we can find them. And act together.'

The luminous face nodded. 'Mielitta will find a way to you,' Arven said.

Prophecy or an attempt at reassurance?

'I can see better as a bear,' Jannlou told Arven.

He felt his body surrounding itself in fur like a nut in a case, his snout grew and added to the information of his night vision, as he sniffed the air and recognised every turn of the passageway ahead.

One advantage of Perfection's rigid ways was that there was little chance of a citizen sneaking about the Citadel or even peeking out from a doorway and spotting them. Anybody who did, would have more sense than to report a bear lumbering along with a silvery male intruder behind it – he'd forfeit his life as much for lying to the Council as for breaking curfew.

Left again, then out the door and across the greensward to the shelter of the forge. Jannlou hoped the door was open as usual, as he shifted back to human form to turn the handle.

Stones be praised! The door opened without a creak. Good smith that he was, Kermon would never have left a knife or door gasping for oil.

'Grassette,' Jannlou told Arven, who had bent to touch the ground. 'Fake grass. If the mages activate it, you'll be imprisoned by its tendrils, unable to move. There's fake flooring too, woodette. Man-made sustenance and drink, fabrics, everything.'

'As if nature is the enemy,' murmured Arven. 'I didn't really believe it could be so.' He clutched his knitting bag tightly.

They entered the forge, breathed in its scent of ashes, oil and sweat, overlaid with a metallic tang that smelled like blood but must surely be from heating and cooling steel or working iron. He felt Kermon even more present in absence than when he was about his craft, bronzed by the flames he mastered, instructing his assistants. This was Kermon's domain.

Arven lit a knitting needle and it glowed like a torch as he walked about the forge. He looked at the anvil and tools, raw blades laid out ready for tempering and wooden handles at various stages of readiness.

'Woodette?' he asked Jannlou.

'No. Kermon said some artisans had access to real wood from forays into the Forest. But that was before the Battle.'

He remembered something Mielitta had told him. 'Your father, Crimvert, led parties of lumberjacks to collect wood. He was supposed to wipe the men's minds clean afterwards but I wonder whether he did? He spoke of his love for the Forest.'

'Yet he cut down trees,' Arven pointed out, holding the cut wooden shape that would become a knife handle.

'And Tannlei loved her bow of real wood.' He held the thought, turned it over in his bear memories as well as his human. 'Maybe, without realising, we prize wood for what it was as well as what it is. It connects us to the Forest.'

Arven had found a row of clothes pegs on the wall. 'Will these help?'

Spare mages' cloaks for the Mage-Smith, one with the braiding of a Councillor and two workaday black ones, all hooded and shapeless. One size fits all. Arven would be well-hidden and could easily pass for a minor mage. Nobody remembered all their names or faces.

There was a leather apron, spare pair of britches, shirt and gloves, all a bit small for Jannlou's bulkier frame. The workclothes for the assistants were better for size but he realised he might as well wander the Citadel in bear form as try to pass for an assistant of any kind. He was far too well known by all in the Citadel and would be rumbled in minutes.

No, he must stay in the forge but Arven could be coached enough to go into the Citadel and seek the information they needed. Kermon's magecraft students would be in need of a tutor and tomorrow they would have one.

CHAPTER FOURTEEN

Arven refused to part with his knitting bag.

'Would you leave your sword behind?' he asked Jannlou.

'My sword won't attract attention! It's my face that will trigger an alarm.'

Arven slung his bag over one shoulder and donned a black mage's cloak over the offending article.

'Will that do?'

Jannlou pursed his lips, critical. 'You look deformed. And nobody in the Citadel is defective.'

Arven could imagine why not. His grandmother had explained that Perfection dictated the suppression of anyone 'old', at an age which was continually lowered and was now set at below sixty. She could have been eighty, ninety or a hundred when she died, given the vagaries of time in the Forest. So he could well imagine the Citadel's attitude to defective bodies – or minds – and the solution. He knew only too well how Perfection was maintained.

'Exactly,' he responded with cool logic. 'As nobody is deformed, no Citizen will think anything other than that I carry weapons, tools, material, whatever I like under my cloak! And it does not strike me as un-magelike to keep my affairs to myself.'

Jannlou grunted. 'Good job Kermon's cloak is big enough to wrap around you twice.'

That was his way of conceding and Arven knew it, so ceased arguing. Instead he repeated Jannlou's instructions. 'I'm to call any boy I see wearing brown – they're all servants. I order enough sustenance and drink for five people to be brought to the forge, straight away.'

'Give no reason and don't be polite – give orders. You're a mage and he's a page boy.'

'Five people.' Arven raised an eyebrow.

'I'm still recovering from winter.' Jannlou grinned. 'But some is for you. And when the boy delivers the food, I'll stay out of sight. And just to be on the safe side, wipe his mind. That's what mages do to avoid unwanted gossip – and we don't want speculation concerning a meeting in the forge.'

Arven left a pause before he spoke but it wasn't so he could speak. It was so he could be calm. 'No,' he said.

'I'm sure you could do it. All the mages can.'

'No doubt,' said Arven drily. 'But I won't. I might wear this cloak from expedience but I will never don Citadel values. Forcing somebody's mind is never acceptable.'

'If we die, worse than that will happen. And I don't mean to us.'

'The risk to us is small and the assault on the boy is an infringement of human rights. It's a matter of principle.'

Jannlou shrugged. 'Not in Perfection, it's not. If you're heard talking like that…' he stopped short.

'I know,' said Arven. 'And I won't.'

Jannlou need not have worried. Arven's Citadel manners were barely tested on this occasion as the moment he stepped through the door from the greensward to the Citadel passageway, he identified a kitchen boy by the empty tray he carried. The servant barely looked at Arven as he memorised and repeated the order for sustenance. Then he scurried off without a backward look.

Arven had barely time to recount the detail of his first sortie to Jannlou when there was a rap on the forge door. His mission had been successful and breakfast was duly delivered. Hunger dictated they paid full attention to eating and Jannlou had not overestimated the quantities he'd require.

'It has no taste,' observed Arven, carefully chewing the last crumbs of what purported to be cereal and fruit. He sipped the 'tea'. 'Nor does this.'

'No,' agreed Jannlou, 'but it will keep you alive. Kermon has this idea that you can imagine the taste it *should* have, if you've experienced it second-hand in the walls.'

'I grew up in the Forest. And *this* has no taste.' Arven's cloak swung up where his arm must be and a white hand waved to cut off Jannlou's words. 'No, don't say it. You're going to tell me to pretend. It's another way I'll reveal that I'm an outsider and get us killed.'

Jannlou didn't bother replying.

'I must be going to work,' Arven told him cheerfully. 'May the stones be with you.'

'And with you!'

Jannlou's fervour did not express much faith in Arven but this made no impact on the latter's determination. His grandmother had told him to make the most of every aspect of the person he was, not the person he wasn't. She'd told him that people would underestimate him and scoff at his knitting. And that both these things were his weapons. As Jannlou had found to his cost already, without fully heeding the lesson.

But the warrior did know the Citadel's ways and Arven could not afford complacence.

'Ignore the servants,' Jannlou told him. 'Walk as if you can pass through them. They will get out of your way. Swirl the cloak a little to look assertive. If knights and ladies come your way, move to the right with politeness but no deference. There is no need to speak to them. They will be equally courteous and incurious. Curiosity is rude, especially towards a mage going about his business. You have more status than they do.

'Should a mage come towards you, pass him on the right, with even pace and without curiosity. Should he greet you, perhaps say, 'May the stones favour your work this day,' echo the greeting and keep walking. 'And yours,' or 'And you,' will be the correct response in most cases.

'If a mage tries to engage you in conversation, this is either an attempt to plot or because he suspects you. In either case say, 'The stones call me to work. I must hurry,' and walk on, at an even pace.'

'So, summarised Arven, 'in the Forest, all the little creatures hide at the approach of striped, furred and feathered predators and here the little creatures hide from those who are gowned, armoured or cloaked. And they survive another day.'

'Something like that,' Jannlou replied, 'but with more rules. If the mage's cloak has braid, this is a member of the Council and you must show respect. Answer if asked your business, say you're going to take Mage-Smith Kermon's place in the schoolroom.

'If the braid is gold, the mage is Chief Mage Bastien. Be sure to use his title if you have to speak to him. You are a minor mage.'

'So minor nobody remembers ever seeing me before.' Arven laughed but there was no humour.

'And if you are unmasked–' Jannlou didn't finish, merely met Arven's eyes. They both knew the risks.

'I'll fight, in my manner.'

'Or flee,' Jannlou said. 'At the foot of the Mages' Tower, in the dark beside the spiral staircase, is the way used by mages to go into the walls. Go there and save yourself. Maybe you can find Kermon.'

Hunched and cloaked, Arven crossed the greensward, repeating the warrior's directions as he walked. Through the door, along the passageway. Swirl the cloak, walk through the servants, pass the knight. No bowing, no change of pace.

'The stones bless your day, mage,' murmured a bold lass in a rose gown.

Should she have spoken? How did mages meet women? There was so much that Arven didn't know.

'And yours,' he replied in deep reproving tones, suggesting she was impertinent.

He heard her giggling with her friends behind him. A dare, he suspected. Pulling a tiger's tail.

He reached the school without further adventure, passed through the entrance and found himself in an internal quadrangle surrounded by an arched pathway, through which he could see doors to classrooms. The sound of children chanting reached him.

He went to the first classroom, knocked – should he have done so? – and walked in. The teacher was standing in front of her class and paused mid-explanation.

Arven threw back his hood. Surely mages didn't go around with hoods up all the time.

'I've been sent to tutor the group of youngsters with mage-craft, instead of Mage-Smith Kermon,' he said.

The teacher smiled. 'You're in the wrong class. Honesty will take you to Lady Fidelity's classroom.'

A girl wearing what seemed to be the standard child's uniform of tabard over short britches responded to her name, received and repeated her instructions and solemnly escorted Arven to the older children's classroom.

He knocked again and this time the teacher came to the door before he had time to enter. He repeated his purpose and she looked at him, puzzled, before her face cleared.

'They'll be a little overwhelmed,' she warned him. 'Chief Mage Bastien is with them already but I expect you planned that.'

No, thought Arven. *We did not.*

CHAPTER FIFTEEN

Bastien looked at Kermon's students as he led them back to the quadrangle. The remaining five students of Kermon's special group, eager and a little apprehensive. Because the Chief Mage was asking them questions or because they were worried about the schoolfriends lost in the walls? Both, probably.

He'd gleaned as much as he could about Nathan, Janette and her cursed story. He'd already asked them to tell him everything they'd told Mage-Smith Kermon, so he could guess where Verity and Kermon would have begun looking for the youngsters. Some girl in a tribal village had taken Janette's fancy, it seemed.

But what was the point of further action? He'd already sent Verity and Kermon to rectify matters. Sending more mages after them would be a futile gamble, losing ever higher stakes. For the sake of two replaceable small beings, he'd already lost two valuable citizens.

Verity could marry and produce an heir once she got over her foolish notions and the Citadel needed its Mage-Smith, not to mention Kermon's skills as a soul-reader. He should never have let them go. He looked with some distaste at the small beings in front of him.

Children! May the stones turn them into adults quickly! When

Kermon returned, Bastien was going to speak to him about the new Maturity Test, insist that there was a built-in fail for disobedience. If only they could go back to Perfection as it used to be, to all his father had worked towards.

One hand spasmed in warning. Curse the treaty he'd been forced to make with the Freak! He couldn't even *wish* for any way of life outside their agreement. If he'd realised what a constraint the blood oath would be, he'd have cut his hands off rather than agree. Now, it was too late. The oath was in his blood.

If only Verity would act on his behalf, but no. She had these modern notions of being an equal, as if she'd been turned against Perfection when held hostage in the Forest. She spoke well enough about Perfect society – too well in fact – but her very presence as Chief Councillor was an abomination.

That was a child who'd grown up *too* fast! He missed the little sister who had worshipped him, who'd hung on his every word when he'd visited her sickroom. He didn't recognise her in the smooth-talking politician who somehow subverted the Council into making decisions which countered his own. Sometimes she even made *him* feel the outcome was for the best. Until he thought about it afterwards and realised what his father would have said. Bastien had been dreaming of his father even more recently. And of the bear that savaged him to death.

'Are they going to die in the walls?' A clear voice interrupted Bastien's dark musing. A halo of brown curls in red ribbons framed a golden face. The girl's eyes were huge with the importance of her question.

'Of course not,' he snapped and the children jerked backwards instinctively, then controlled themselves. as did he, softening his tone as when speaking to the stupid women on the Council – and the women Councillors were all stupid.

'My mages do not allow anything to happen to citizens which they do not deserve,' he explained. *My mages* had a good ring to it. And he had allowed room for a suitable explanation in the future for the permanent disappearance of the two missing students. They would have been punished for their misdemeanours. And there was no need to invent their crimes, which were clear enough.

The children flinched and he smoothed his expression, smiled. Lost their attention to an intrusion.

Their teacher approached, accompanied by a mage he didn't recognise, wearing a cloak so oversized he was obviously carrying a bow and quiver underneath it. Bastien congratulated himself on his powers of observation, noted the mage's fine bones, youth and earnest expression, and he relaxed. Some new mage, appointed during the flurry of changes and replacements after the Battle of the Forest. Bastien had more important things to do than keep up with such trivia.

As was proper, the young mage spoke and the teacher held her tongue.

'Excuse me for the interruption, Chief Mage Bastien. I can wait or return later to work with the magecraft students. I've been sent to replace Mage-Smith Kermon during his brief absence.' There was no inflection, no lingering on the word 'brief' but its very carefulness surprised Bastien. His mages were rarely so diplomatic, old or young.

'What is your name? And your specialism?'

'I'm Mage Hui.' The tone suggested pride in his name, his heritage and his magecraft. 'My pa–' he stumbled for the first time. 'My pater was a mage. He passed to the stones some years ago, and I am recently come into my power. Like him, I'm an artisan mage.'

'I don't suppose you've trained in smithcraft?' asked Bastien hopefully, while the children's eyes moved between the two speakers like an audience watching a game of bat-the-ball.

Hui shook his head. 'I have some minor skill in archery,' he offered, 'enough to teach the children the rudiments, in addition to the foundations of magecraft, which I'm told Mage-Smith Kermon was teaching them.'

Bastien smiled at this confirmation of his own astuteness. Yes, a bow and quiver underneath that voluminous cloak.

'You'd have to ask permission from the Archery Mage,' he told Hui. 'The yard is his domain. You'll find him there all morning so you can catch him before midday meal. My business is finished here and I'm expected elsewhere.' He always said that whether he was or not. It stressed his importance. 'I wish you joy of your charges.'

Without any acknowledgement of the small beings who would grow up to be his citizens, Bastien gave a curt nod that would pass as farewell to the teacher and left the quadrangle.

He'd walked part way to his own quarters when he wondered *who* had sent Hui in Kermon's place. And *why*. Hamel or Puggy were the usual ringleaders in any plots against him – or of course against each other.

The green mage knew well the terms of the blood oath which bound Bastien. What if this Hui had been instructed to break those terms and by that means assassinate Bastien, with no evidence left behind? What could Hui do with the magecraft students that would spill Bastien's blood?

He reviewed the terms of the treaty as he walked the familiar pathways. If one of the students was infected with Forest, like the Freak, and Hui suppressed her, would that break the blood oath? Even if Bastien hadn't condoned it? His hands spasmed and he swore. All such defectives were to leave the Citadel if they so wished. And he had vowed no harm would come to them.

Yes, that must be it. He became increasingly certain. If there was no plot against him, then he would have been told of this Hui replacing Kermon. 'For a brief period' indeed! None of the mages thought Kermon would return, which left Hui in the ideal position to carry out his mission. How ironic that Bastien would be killed by somebody instigating the very policies he approved but could not allow.

But what if it was Puggy? She too would happily see Bastien dead and she was not without ambition on her own behalf. And there was something freakish about her nature that would no doubt be encouraged if she gained control over the Council. There were salacious rumours about her, he remembered, despite her marriage first to his father and then to Kermon! Rumours suggested she was drawn to women. As if such a thing could be physically possible. It was almost laughable. But an abhorrence to Perfection.

Bastien considered his options. He could set a soul-reader onto Hui, force his mind open. But the mage seemed so naive he probably didn't even know he was being used. He would have to be suppressed after such an excruciating experience even if he was innocent and Bastien disliked waste.

Especially when there was a more effective way to find out all he needed to know. And then he could set the soul-reader onto whichever mage was behind this plot.

He sent out a thin stream of summoning power with a name attached and within minutes a servant appeared, one of the older boys who'd done errands for Bastien before. He was reliable and especially easy to wipe clean and re-use, which meant he was trustworthy.

'Go to the schoolroom. Find and follow the mage with the big lopsided cloak, who is working with the group of magecraft students. Follow him everywhere he goes, without being noticed.'

As if a mage would notice a servant! They were indistinguishable and went everywhere with messages and chores. 'At darklight, report back to me.'

By nightfall Bastien would know who was behind this assassination attempt and tomorrow, so would the Council. Then he would be one enemy fewer.

And if Kermon and Verity did not return? What did Verity always say after she'd manipulated the Council? 'I know it's not what you wanted but there are advantages.' *Yes, I can see the advantages, little sister, if you don't come back at all.*

He smiled. Not such a bad day after all.

CHAPTER SIXTEEN

Arven looked down at the earnest faces regarding him intently. The children sat cross-legged on the greensward that formed a pristine grassette rectangle inside the cloister. Not one flower or insect. No scent. No shafts of sunlight or shadows. Just monotonous greylight. He felt he was fading already after less than a day here. How had Kermon held up for so many months? How had his friends lived in Perfection for so many years and kept their souls?

Five pairs of bright eyes reminded him of Kermon's mission. Hope for the future was sitting in front of him, waiting for the lesson to begin.

'You already know I'm Mage Hui.' *May the cat forgive me.* 'And I'm an artisan mage. I'll show you my skills later in the lesson.' That caught their attention.

'You know each other already. So let's go around the circle starting with–?' Arven looked at the curly-haired girl.

'Ceri,' she said. 'Those two are new in the group but we do know them. Lady Fidelity said they might as well be here as with her.' She pointed with disdain at two of the boys and Arven had a strong suspicion their contribution would not be positive.

'Ceri,' Arven tasted the flavour of naming and how it made somebody a person.

Even servants, he thought, remembering Jannlou's dismissal of the anonymous staff. Mielitta had been a servant, long after her childhood should have ended. He would learn these children's names and teach them what he could, as he had taught Drianne and Jannlou. Was still teaching Jannlou, whether he realised it or not.

'Ceri, I want you to tell me the name of the student on your left and tell me one good thing about him. Then we'll go round the circle widdershins until everybody has been introduced to me.'

So Arven learned that Brendon was kind, that Loyalty could move objects by waggling her ears and that Serenity always shared her birthday sustenance in class. The exercise made them self-conscious and the statements were more childish than their years. Honest compliments were often simply phrased and none the worse for that, he thought.

Had he ever been as young as this? It was possible he was little older than his students in years but he had ceased to be a child when his parents were murdered. The Forest had been his Maturity Test and his grandmother had nurtured him, body and soul. Now it was his turn to nurture.

'If you understand *why* you should control your magecraft, *how* is only a question of practice.'

'Mage-Smith Kermon says we will get too tired if we use magecraft for everything,' Brendon explained with the confidence of repeating word for word what he'd been told.

'Mage-Smith Kermon taught you well,' Arven told him. 'But I bet you've all broken the rules and used your powers without permission and without any emergency. To save you work or to play a trick on someone.' He dropped his voice to a confidential whisper and the students all leaned towards him, agog.

'When I was your age, I made a cushion squeak at a–' he

remembered in time not to say *cat* '–a playmate, to give him a fright.'

The children giggled.

'What was your friend called?'

'Was he a mage too? Did he get you back?' they asked eagerly.

'He was called Arven. No, he wasn't a mage but he was very skilled at leaping and catching. He was a gymnast.' That part was true enough. Leaping off bookshelves and catching mice were indeed among Hui's skills. And it was only fair to Hui to offer an identity in exchange for the one stolen. Arven could picture the disdain in Hui's green eyes at such tomfoolery.

'I turned my water into beer so I could find out what it was like to get drunk,' Kind Brendon volunteered.

'What was it like?' asked Curly Ceri, wide-eyed.

Brendon made a face. 'Tasted like sick, twice. Once going down and once coming back up.'

The students' faces showed their disappointment.

'Maybe you didn't do it right?' Ceri asked, seeking a glimmer of hope.

Brendon shook his head. 'I don't think that was it.'

Thinking of the tasteless sustenance and liquid that maintained life in the Citadel, Arven doubted whether Brendon had crafted anything like beer but the message was clear enough regardless.

'Would you do it again?' he asked Brendon, who shook his head energetically.

'So,' Arven said, 'maybe one reason why we use magecraft carefully is because we have to be sure of the consequences. Maybe some of you did something that felt wonderful at the time – not like Brendon's beer – but led to something bad…'

The floodgates opened and the students turned confession into a competition, discussing their misuse of their powers with much laughter. And the costs. With a mix of shame and understanding. It was so much easier to judge somebody else and excuse your own actions.

Arven let the why and why not discussion flow around him, thinking of the two students not present. Who might pay dearly for their breach of regulations.

When he judged the time was right, Arven called their attention back. 'Now you have more personal reasons to control your magic, you can practise how.

'First, imagine yourself in that situation you've told me about, or another one that you can imagine, one that's tempting you, where you want to use your magecraft.

'Now think of the reasons why you won't. Why you need to control yourself. And now you can choose your favourite way of mind control. I know Mage-Smith Kermon taught you some, so you can practise the one you like best.'

The silence of concentration was explosive, filled with leashed power.

Yes, thought Arven, *that is the moment on which destiny turns. The moment before anything happens. And the power to hold back is the greatest of all. If only Jannlou could learn this.*

Gently, he said, 'Well done. Now, I'll show you my magecraft.'

His cloak swung wildly as he extricated his bag and set it down on the fake grass. He felt suddenly shy, exposed, as he saw himself through the students' reactions.

Anticipation at the prospect of a mage demonstrating his powers.

Admiration. They'd seen the silvery flicker of his teardrop suit as the cloak swirled.

Disappointment. A weather-beaten bag that looked like leatherette or sackcloth was hunched on the ground like a beggar. Only there were no beggars in the Citadel. And Arven's bag was so much more than it seemed. As was he. Being underestimated had its advantages.

He sat down beside the bag in the middle of his students, cross-legged like them, cloak tucked firmly around the more exciting garments underneath.

He dipped his hand into the bag and pulled out knitting-needles.

The disappointment deepened to boredom.

He could have knitted his weather patterns, drawing down lightning or sunrays, both equally terrifying to those who lived under the Citadel canopy. He could have thrown scarves towards the canopy, cut them as they landed with the speed of his needles, his weapons of choice. He could have challenged his students to fight him, all at the same time, with swords, arrows, daggers *and* magecraft, and he could have pricked them all with his needles, remaining unscathed himself until they surrendered.

He did none of those things. This was not an act of self-aggrandizement.

'My grandmother taught me to knit,' he told them, pulling a ball of wool out of the bag. Multi-coloured. Yes, it would be.

Boredom sneered its way to contempt, especially from the boys. They'd no doubt noticed his fine bones, small hands, delicate features. His lack of manliness.

'I wanted to be a warrior like my father.' He twisted the yarn into a loop and put the first stitch onto one needle.

'But I learned that my skills are different.'

One of the two newcomers, Philip, sniggered and whispered in Brendon's ear. Arven could well imagine how Citadel males would translate 'different'.

'That's not magecraft,' observed Ceri, 'I can do that.'

'You can make the next stitch.' Arven quietly passed her the wool and needles.

'See!' She was as good as her word, dismissed the activity as pointless and was passing the knitting back to Arven, when he stopped her.

'Pass it on so each of you can make a new stitch.'

Slight increase of interest – and anxiety, especially among the boys. Should they say they couldn't do it and be mocked or, worse, show they *could* do it and be mocked? Arven hid a smile.

Loyalty saved them some red faces by taking the knitting from Ceri and saying, 'Well I can't do it. Can you show me?'

Ceri looked at her in blank amazement. 'I thought everybody could. Is there anybody else who can't?'

All the boys and two of the girls looked uneasy.

Brendon said, 'I don't think boys usually learn it – knitting's for girls. Is that what you meant, Mage Hui? That it was shaming to be taught by your grandmother?'

'I found out that it was a privilege,' Arven replied, hoping his voice didn't betray his emotion. 'Ceri, can you show how it's done and then everybody can add a stitch.'

Proud of her new status, earned from such a simple activity, Ceri took her role seriously, standing up and exaggerating the movements as she explained.

One by one, the students added a stitch, a different colour each time and then Arven worked one stitch on the first row and passed the knitting to Ceri.

'This has four movements, easy-peasy to remember,' she said. 'Just say this while you do it.' She grimaced and suited each movement to the words. 'Stab it, strangle it, scoop out the guts, and toss it off the cliff.'

'And your mother taught you this?' he asked.

'I think we all say it, don't we?'

Some of the girls nodded.

'I say it in my head,' said Loyalty and then she blushed. 'Because it sounds a bit vi-oh-lent.' She rolled the word around her mouth slowly, savouring it and her eyes shone.

Each student dutifully followed suit, mouthing the vi-oh-lent instructions or in silence, whatever they might be doing in their heads.

'Mine's always blue!' said Loyalty. How does the wool know my colour?'

Arven smiled. 'Magecraft. I express my power through the yarn and let your colour tint the wool for your stitch.'

A little interest. Not awe but a flicker of curiosity. Arven added a last stitch to the row with a different mood in mind so there were seven different colours.

Then he cast off one stitch and again the students followed suit. He held up the thin band of stripey fabric and gave it to Philip.

Tear it apart,' he told him sternly. 'Cut it, break it, gnaw it with your teeth. Use your hands, a knife or your magecraft. But break it.'

His voice grew deeper, grimmer, louder. 'Destroy it!'

CHAPTER SEVENTEEN

Philip hesitated.
Ceri whimpered, 'No.'
And then the boy jerked the frail bit of knitting savagely, one end in each hand. It should have fallen apart but instead it held firm and the act jarred Philip's arms so much he gave an involuntary squeal.

He dropped the knitted band as if it had bitten him, then picked it up again, the light of battle in his eyes.

'Can I really do anything to it? Even use magecraft?' he asked.

Arven nodded. 'Anything you like. I picked you because you're probably the strongest. We really want to test what we've made.'

Now the excitement was growing as Philip did his worst.

Horror, disbelief and amazement but no boredom. Chewed, sliced, tied to a pillar and pulled – the band showed no damage at all.

Finally, Philip set fire to their work, pouring all his power into the flames, so tense with the effort he was more likely to snap than the band.

Arven reached into the flames and plucked out the band, as unmarked as his hand.

'Thank you, Philip,' he said. 'Truly great work and good judgement of your self-control.'

The warning was enough and Philip feigned insouciance as he cut off the stream of fire. He nearly fell over in doing so but his fellow-students were looking at the knitted band, taking turns to hold it. No one was inclined to mock.

'You all saw Philip try his best to destroy this little band and yet, here it is.' Arven held it up, each colour clearly defined in the pattern.

'Why couldn't I?' asked Philip, taking the band again, examining it.

'Because it is stronger than it looks. There is a binding spell in the yarn and we brought it to life by collaborating with each other.'

Like bees clinging leg to leg, he thought as he looked at the stitchwork. 'Each of us put work into its making and this band shows how strong our group is. We can be different colours but stronger together.'

'Can I keep it?' Philip asked, his eyes glowing.

'Yes,' said Arven.

Disappointment again, among the others.

'And we will make eight bands so each of us can have one to remind us how strong we are. For days when we don't feel strong at all.'

'But there are only five of us,' protested Ceri.

'One is for me,' replied Arven and let them make of that what they would. 'And the other two are for Nathan and Janette.' *To take with me and keep them strong when we find them.* Now he'd met their schoolfriends, it was personal.

'Can we make them into wristbands?' asked Ceri, inspecting her multi-coloured strip of fabric.

'Try,' Arven told her.

'You can't make it do anything,' Philip warned her. 'I really tried everything.'

'No and I'm not as strong as you,' she told him. 'So I'm not going to make it do anything. I'm going to ask it nicely.'

She screwed up her face with the effort of focusing her magecraft and chanted, while holding the band against her left wrist.

'Little band of coloured wool
please shape yourself to hug my wrist.
Fit and knit!'

Gasps came as the stripey wristband adjusted its size and the open ends knitted themselves into a seamless circle.

Soon every student was wearing a snugly-fitting stripey wristband, which chose to highlight a different colour for each of them. When they put their hands on the ground, palms down, five colours stood out in a circle.

When he dismissed them, they raced off to show off their magical wristbands to their other friends.

After his morning's work, Arven did call at the Archery Yard but he did not seek out the new Archery Mage. He sought the old one, his mother, Tannlei. This was where she'd taught Mielitta and Drianne, Jannlou and Bastien.

What's the target, Arven? He heard the words in his head, in his grandmother's voice. Because he'd been so young when his mother died, he barely remembered how she looked, never mind how she sounded. A softness, a special way of saying his name and his father's name. *Crimvert. Darling.*

He watched the youths firing arrows at the circular targets, while the Archery Mage rattled off instructions about stance and technique. Demanding the appearance of skill, not bringing forth the essence in his students. Not like Arven's mother.

Mielitta would have understood how he felt. She had grieved for Tannlei as if for the mother she'd never known. Had learned so much more than archery on this very training ground.

As the youths vied for success in hitting the bull's eye, two girls waited shyly in the shadows for their turn. They weren't watching the boys but were talking with animation, their hands describing the angle of a bow, the flight of an arrow, the possibility of setting their own challenges by helping each other. Or so he imagined, picturing Mielitta and Drianne helping each other in this very yard, his mother instructing them.

When thinking happens deep inside you and does not seem like thinking, it shows the true quality of your mind. That too is archery.

It was shallow thinking that Arven found difficult and he too often tuned out the babble that humans used to connect to each other. The idea that Perfect citizens had been forged at maturity, blocked forever from their deep thinking and condemned to a lifetime of babble, filled him with horror.

As if invisible in his mage's cloak, Arven walked the perimeter of the archery yard. Here, his mother had stored all the spare material for new students, bows and strings in different shapes and sizes. Here, she talked to her students and she listened to them, just as he had that morning. Challenged their assumptions, made assets of their differences. Helped them become their best selves.

He wanted to keep every detail of his mother's workplace in his mind's eye and some instinct made him look up at the woodette side of the storage barn. A broken arrow was embedded just below the roof, as if somebody had tried to shoot it right over the top of the building but it had fallen short. As if she was aiming beyond the Citadel walls, for the Forest itself, but her strength was failing. And then the shaft had broken off. He saw the archer, knew her.

Was it here, at half-past eight, that his mother was suppressed by Council order? Which had they considered her greater crime? Love or treason? And if they'd known of her baby, his life would have been forfeit too. The offspring of a female mage. Dangerous. Seditious. A threat to Perfection.

He hoped to be all of those things.

Slow and stealthy, Arven extracted one needle from his bag, tied wool to it and threw it with all of his mother's expertise to circle the broken arrow and fall back into his hand.

He jiggled the two ends of wool until the arrow was dislodged and it too fell into his grasp. Dull and heavy, as much unlike the gleaming twins of Damascene steel forged by Kermon as a toad to dragonflies, it was nevertheless *his* arrowhead.

He studied it closely and saw a word roughly engraved on each of the two convex sides. His heart thumped and he knew the words before he confirmed each letter. Tannlei. Crimvert.

He considered for some time what justice was due for murder. And whether there might be a time when it was right for a mage to unloose his magecraft to the last particle of his being.

'Your father killed mine,' he had told Jannlou.

'And I killed Bastien's. When will it all end?' Jannlou had replied.

And Arven had vowed to find his mother's murderer. Would that end it? Or merely add more blood to the future pattern?

He had not reached a conclusion when he found himself crossing the greensward to the forge, slipping through the door Jannlou opened and shut as quickly as possible.

Unnoticed by the young mage who wore a black cloak over his teardrop armour, an anonymous servant withdrew from his snooping-cranny in the doorway overlooking the greensward and the path to the forge. Everyone knew Mage Kermon was away in the walls and the forge empty. Only now it wasn't. Chief Mage Bastien was sure to reward him well for this report.

CHAPTER EIGHTEEN

B astien watched the forge as if it were a monster lurking in the depths of the castle. In *his* Citadel. How dare they!

His magecraft bubbled like acid in his stomach, ready to erupt. Two of them, the servant had reported. Not a bow and quiver but women's craft in the lump under the cloak. Used for party tricks with the children. Mere glitter and vanity like the silvery clothing glimpsed beneath the cloak.

Bastien was annoyed at being wrong, even if nobody else knew he'd jumped to the wrong conclusions. But at least it meant Mage Hui was easy pickings, a posturing weakling, who'd even lied about his archery skills. He'd not once picked up a bow and arrows in the archery yard, merely stolen a broken arrow. To reuse the metal, no doubt!

But who was the second man? Taller and broader than the mage. Not cloaked. Furtive. These were the only details the servant could recall, so fast had the door been closed.

And *why* was there a second man? Could he be the mage behind the plot? The description fitted neither Puggy nor Hamel but could be the Archery Mage. But then Hui would have spoken to him in the yard or avoided the place altogether in case it gave him away. And the new Councillor was a follower not a leader in the political games of the Chamber.

No. Hamel or Puggy was the likely culprit but why put two lackeys in the forge?

Bastien might have been wrong about what Hui carried under his cloak but that just reinforced his faith in his other deductions. If Hui was finding out the children's secrets, as seemed likely from the servant's account of confessions and silliness, then he'd made the first steps towards breaking Bastien's blood oath by suppressing one or more for their differences.

Who knew how many freaks were in the Citadel, their second natures hidden? He certainly wasn't going to encourage such abnormality. His hand twinged. Even if he must tolerate it. But he wasn't going to die because another mage carried out Perfection's demands. What chafed his spirit most was that the actions were righteous but the motive was mere ambition. Whereas he would have purged the student population for the purest of reasons.

Another warning twinge, which he ignored.

If *he* were that mage, why would he employ a second man?

'Put yourself in your rival's shoes and you'll always outwit him,' his father had told him.

Back-up, he concluded. Somebody with the courage to follow through. If Hui used his womanish tricks to learn which children were defective, this second man would be the one to suppress them. Somebody taller, stronger and more masculine. Of course!

Which took him back to the question of what to do. Much as he wanted to storm into the forge, to unleash his powers on the scum cowering within, he needed to know who was behind this.

Watching in the dark would gain him nothing. Nobody in the Citadel would go outside in darklight – except him. He carried Perfection in his own person and could do as he chose but the men in the forge showed no sign of breaking Citadel laws in this regard. The blind eyes of the shuttered windows and wooden door gave him not a glimpse of the people within.

He sighed. Time to go to bed. Tomorrow, he could set two servants to watch the forge and follow both Hui and his partner.

Then the forge door opened. And out lumbered the creature of Bastien's recurring nightmares. The bear. It stood on its hind legs, nostrils flaring, beady eyes glowing red with night-sight. And it was staring at him.

Bastien's magecraft quivered into useless jelly, making his whole body shake uncontrollably. If he'd spoken, the words would have vibrated too much to make sense.

He was back there, in the Forest, reliving the attack, screaming 'Father!' as he ran through the trees at the beast. He tried not to see the bloody remains dropped by the bear as it faced the new assault but he couldn't forget the raw smell of foul breath, singed fur and death. He'd rushed at the bear in a red fog of rage, prepared to kill or die. And had met contempt. Been made a laughing-stock. The mage spared by a bear.

The creature had gripped Bastien in arms stronger than grassette shackles, crushed his face against the stench of blood and beast, against matted fur. He spat at the memory. He'd sent spikes of power to consume the bear in a ball of flames but he'd been so drained by battle they'd puttered out like a child's tantrum. Torn apart by his own impotence, not by the bear, the final humiliation had been one word.

'Bastien.' The beast had spoken his name, low and guttural, but unmistakeably his name. Then it had fled. To haunt his nightmares, leave him shaking with the fear he'd not known in the Forest. Fear had come afterwards. Paralysing, sweating, delusional fear.

'Bastien,' said the bear now, standing on two legs, glaring at him in the night as it had after ripping his father to shreds.

Unable to move or speak, trapped by his own nightmare, Bastien could only watch as the bear took a few steps towards him. And then shimmered, shifting into something other.

Bastien shut his eyes. Waited. No claws raked him. No furred hulk slammed him to the ground. No sound but ragged breathing. His own? The bear's?

He opened his eyes.

Jannlou was standing in front of him, his warrior's garb somewhat the worse for weather, his sword sheathed. He was speaking but his words pounded in Bastien's head, making no sense.

'Blood brothers… wouldn't harm you… haven't forgotten… kept my oath to you… Opposite sides… Rinduran had to be stopped…'

At the mention of his father's name, magecraft started once more coursing through Bastien's body. He could feel its return like circulation after the numbness of pins and needles. Powerful. In front of his worst enemy, double traitor, murderer. He gathered himself to strike.

'My second nature…' his one-time friend was babbling. 'Citadel kills us…'

Bastien found his voice, low and dangerous. He wanted Jannlou to know what was coming. 'Yes,' he said. 'It does. I'm glad you came back.'

'Listen to me,' Jannlou pleaded. 'We can be allies this time. Arven and I want to go into the walls, help destroy the evil there, rescue Kermon and the missing children.'

Bastien scented more treachery. 'How do you know any of that?' Somebody communicating with the Forest. Another traitor in their midst. And who was Arven?

Jannlou sounded flustered. 'It doesn't matter. But we can help. The walls can be open again if the evil is gone.'

'My mages can suppress the evil without help from freaks. You're like her, aren't you. Defective. A beast.' Bastien laughed at the idea of such aid, growing more confident now his nightmare had a name and was merely a traitor with no magecraft.

'But…' Jannlou hesitated. 'Even though he's… what he is now… a revenant, some mages will still rally to…'

What was the matter with the Freak? He seemed unable to string a sentence together. And Verity had never said the evil was a revenant. Bastien had never been interested but now he thought about it, she and Kermon had been rather vague

Jannlou gulped and strung his words together more coherently. 'Some mages will still rally to Rinduran's aid. So you might find our help useful. Please Bastien, for all those years we were friends, let us face this together. I know how hard it must be for you to accept what your father has become.'

Then the full force of his rage hit Bastien's guts. His sister's betrayal, his friend's betrayal, his stupidity. All rose up in a tidal wave of power, higher and stronger, ready…

'Run, Jannlou!' yelled a voice from inside the forge. 'Go into the walls – they let you in once. They know the need. I'll meet you there! Go!'

CHAPTER NINETEEN

When Arven shouted his warning, Jannlou dropped to all fours while shifting instantly to bear. He felt the rush of Bastien's strike like a storm wind shrieking above his head but he didn't stop to look back. Charging for the door, he made the most of a bear's running gait. Two left legs, then two right legs, pumping at superhuman speed.

No need to watch out for people. All good citizens were in bed.

No need to watch out for other creatures. There were none.

Pounding up the long passageway, past the Great Hall, the school, the mages' quarters, to the Mages' Tower.

Jannlou rushed through the tower door then paused for breath at the foot of the spiral staircase, in front of the section of wall used by mages to visit the world beyond.

He shifted back into human form, his front paws curling into clenched fists. When he'd entered the walls as an apprentice, a fake mage, Bastien had surreptitiously taken his hand, hidden by the long sleeves of their cloaks, and they'd crossed the barrier between worlds, together. Without Bastien covering for him, Jannlou would have known a childhood as bad as Mielitta's, if he'd survived.

The world within the walls had been disappointing. Rinduran, at that time the Citadel's Wall Mage, herded the small group of students from one dry, depressing moment in the past to another. Weather, war and pandemics on a global scale; dysfunctional relationships, unemployment and high numbers of suicides, on a personal level. All to highlight how lucky they were to live in more civilised times. The stones be praised for giving birth to Perfection, their sustainable society, free from all such horrors.

Rinduran had lectured them on the evils of any society other than Perfection, threatened them with suppression if they broke any of its laws, harangued them about keeping company with defectives and stressed how Perfect citizens must excise these cankers for the sake of the body politic.

And yet Jannlou remembered the visit into the walls as fun. He and Bastien had giggled like schoolboys at unintended double-meanings in Rinduran's homilies. They played pranks on a couple of their regular victims, laughing when they got away it and the poor innocents were lectured on their appalling behaviour. He knew what Mielitta would say, and she was right, but he'd be a liar if he said he hadn't enjoyed strutting about and abusing power with Bastien for company.

He'd grown up with the glamour of being Chief Mage's son and Bastien had played the wily subordinate. Whereas, in truth, Jannlou had been a sham, hiding from his second nature, and Bastien's magecraft was so strong nobody had suspected he was using it for both of them.

Now Jannlou's only status in the Citadel was that of traitor. Bastien was Chief Mage and when he'd used his power, he'd meant to kill. When they met again, there would be no attempt to recall an old friendship. *If* they met again. Jannlou did not expect to return through the walls.

He focused on the world beyond the walls, on the barrier being an illusion and he stepped forward, his hand stretched out. To meet all too solid stone wall.

Not again. His frustration grew snout and claws , shifting his body into bear once more, without any intention on his part. It was bad enough being separated from Mielitta but this second prank by the capricious walls was too much.

He threw himself at the indifferent stone, roared and scraped ten long scratches down the surface, superficial tracks that merely roused dust. Futile.

With no idea what to do next, he stood, panting, then became aware that the dust was increasing even though he'd stopped scrabbling at the walls. And it was coming from behind him, not in front. Then he realised that it wasn't dust but white tendrils, billowing through the open door, wrapping the stairwell in mystery. Their chill moisture jolted him back into human form and mind.

Arven, he thought. He hoped it *was* Arven's work, knowing all too well Bastien's power.

Ashamed of his bestial outburst, he determined to get through the cursed walls whether they willed or not. He'd been through before easily enough, when he was training as a mage, without asking permission. What made the difference?

Bastien's hand. A mage's touch allowed access to the walls. Rinduran had taken the volunteers into the walls, Drianne among them, before her magecraft manifested itself. Kermon had taken Verity with him. All he needed was a mage.

The fog was so thick now that Jannlou could barely see his own hands. If this was Arven's work, he was still alive but engaged in battle with Bastien. There was no telling when he would be able to join his friend and he'd instructed Jannlou to go into the walls, wait for him there. When the seer spoke, it was wise to listen. Not to scratch at walls. He'd said he'd come so he would.

Over Bastien's dead body.

Jannlou's stomach clenched. Despite everything, he could not wish his boyhood friend dead. What if he'd stayed at the forge, been forced to decide between Bastien and Arven – his old friend and his new one?

He shook the choice from his mind. He hadn't. He didn't. And he needed a mage to get him through the wall.

This time his shift to bear form was deliberate. Immediately, he could sniff his way through the fog, although his night vision was limited by the swirling white. He lumbered cautiously along the passageway towards the mages' quarters.

The chambers in the Citadel were all warded so only their occupants could open the doors. Maybe he could pretend to have an urgent message for one of the mages? But which one? What could be urgent? And he'd have to remember the right room. He racked his brains but met another stone wall, mental this time.

Was there another way?

No good citizen would be abroad at night. But Bastien had been.

And then Jannlou could smell her. Roses and blood.

'Who's out there? Bastien, is that you? I can't see a thing. What's the meaning of this malfunction in the canopy? And what's being done to fix it?' A blunt northern accent and bitterness by the shovelful lost little of their edge in the fog.

'Bastien, is that you? Do something! I can't even produce enough magecraft these days to light my own way through this blasted greyness, never mind sort the Citadel's problems.'

Jannlou regained his human form. He only had to retrace his steps to find the Mages' Tower and he could do that without his heightened senses. His nose had already lost the capacity to distinguish each element of her scent but he recognised her. Drianne's saviour, Kermon's wife.

'Mage Puggy,' he said aloud. Surely she wouldn't recognise his voice? He deepened it anyway. 'I'm Mage Arven and Chief Mage Bastien asked me to escort you to the Mages' Tower and into the walls. He said a female mage would be required.'

'What the stones is going on?'

Jannlou said nothing but reached out until he found Puggy's arm and firmly urged her to walk alongside him, hoping his warrior's raiment wouldn't arouse her suspicions.

He needn't have worried. Between the fog and her puzzlement over why she was needed within the walls, Puggy had no interest in her companion. Her muttering was entirely for herself.

'It must be to do with that lost student. She's been found and there's some terrible thing happened to her so a woman will be needed to comfort her. Well, I'm not one for comforting people but I do know what women suffer, who better! Or maybe it's Verity something's happened to. That would be it. That's why Bastien wants it hushed up. Well, he can think again. He'll owe me a favour and I'll call it in when it suits me.'

With such ruminations, she tottered along beside Jannlou. He felt along the wall until he found the doorway and through they went.

'Let's get on with it then,' said Puggy. Still arm-in-arm, they walked to the wall and stepped right through.

Into a park and bright daylight, where Puggy looked at him with horror.

'I know you. You're Magaram's son. The traitor. Infected with Forest.'

CHAPTER TWENTY

Grass so well mown it could have been Citadel greensward, alternated with play areas, where balls thunked and clacked on bats and rackets. Those playing shouted their glee or disappointment, ignored by the park visitors who circulated on paved paths, walking through Jannlou as he had through the wall. He shivered at the notion. Ghosts everywhere.

What had Kermon told them about this world? The park was an entry point from a comparatively recent time period and below it were historical layers through which you could navigate ever downwards, deeper and deeper into the past. Where was Kermon now?

Jannlou looked at the enigma Kermon had married. Pudding-plain by choice, using glamour to disguise her true form. But she couldn't hide her scent from his heightened senses. Dangerous, voluptuous, consumed by some passionate hatred for him that he didn't understand. More personal than her Perfect disgust at his second nature.

But he had to try. 'We can put our differences aside. We both care about Kermon and I'm here to find him, to fight against–' Jannlou didn't want to make the same mistake twice. Presumably Puggy had no idea of what – or rather who – lurked within the walls. Especially as Perfection might judge her to be Rinduran's wife still. No, he wasn't testing that quicksand until he was sure of his own ground. He finished, '–against the evil in the walls.'

Puggy screwed up her doughy face in an effort that clearly achieved nothing. Kermon was right about magecraft being disarmed within the walls.

She blinked raisin eyes at him. 'Why in the stones' name would I care whether that blundering oaf lives or dies? Or the so-called Chief Councillor who thinks she's as good as a mage? The evil can have 'em both, along with the defective children. And you along with them. I've no intention of stopping here any longer if there's no leverage in it. And there isn't. You're no more a messenger from Bastien than I'm the Citadel Fool, so I'll waste no more time.

'But you're welcome to stay. You carry on with your little suicide mission. Maybe Bastien will be interested to know Magaram's son was snooping around the Citadel and is in the walls.'

Her eyes narrowed. 'Here to help Kermon, he says. And I wonder why that might be. I think Bastien might be interested after all.' Her face brightened. 'But I think I'll tell Hamel instead. That should rid me of an unwanted husband. Who'd have thought, eh? And Verity was the guarantor of his loyalty. Well, well. Should land her in the net too if we throw it carefully.'

Jannlou reached out to grab her but she wavered out of sight, as insubstantial as the two women who walked through him, talking about their children. Or was it he who had no corporeal form? Whatever the physical laws within the walls, he'd have no enlightenment about them from Puggy. Thanks to him, she'd gone back to the Citadel with the news that Kermon was a traitor.

What should he do? If he followed Puggy back into the Citadel, he might never get into the walls again. And what good could he do there? Fight the whole Council tooth and claw? He was no mage. The damage to Kermon's reputation was done and all Jannlou could do in reparation was to find his friend as soon as possible. Arven would no doubt catch up with them when he could.

A man wearing straight britches and a shirt that was too tight to sleep in and certainly too embarrassing for public viewing, walked through Jannlou, talking to another man dressed in similar attire. As if they'd walked straight out of a history book in the Citadel library.

Jannlou shuddered, hearing snatches of their conversation as the ghosts turned the next bend.

'Gilt securities fund…'

'Competitive interest rates…'

Without a lexicon to this foreign language, Jannlou couldn't comprehend a single word he heard. Maybe he should have studied history more and forest creatures less during his schooldays.

In this world, history offered him all her secrets but he felt no connection with these beings from another time. Yet Kermon had talked about them as if they were fellow-humans. Perhaps that was because he read souls, was accustomed to the mystical plane and connections.

Jannlou needed to feel another's heartbeat, blood and bone. Maybe *he* was the ghost here and nobody would ever touch him again. If so, he might as well live as a bear, revel in being solitary.

'Mielitta, where are you?' he roared.

Nothing. He sensed nothing but the walls keeping them apart.

There was no pause in the chatter burbling around him, indifferent as the sky and grass. The shades smiled, frowned, limped, ran, in pairs or groups, families or friends, in the pattern of their alien lives.

The hand on his back made him jump, so lost had he been in reveries. And so sure he was alone among these hundreds of non-people.

The words in a girl's voice seemed an answer, however cryptic and Arven-like. 'You are here. All is as it should be.'

Jannlou whirled around to confront someone most definitely

human, dressed in a Citadel boy's garb of britches, shirt and jerkin. She only came up to his chest but her gaze was dark and steady in a face framed by a frizz of black curls.

Her companion, a boy with spikey black hair and a solemn face, was taller. He seemed content for her to take the lead and remained silent.

There couldn't be two such students lost in the walls.

'Janette!' Jannlou named her and she nodded, shaking her curls like a restless horse.

'This is Nathan,' she told him. 'He's mute.' She gave Jannlou a sly glance, as if to judge his reaction.

He nodded, acknowledging the boy, who stared blankly at him. Of course, neither of them knew who he was.

'I'm Jannlou,' he said. 'A friend of Kermon's. I came to find him, to help find you–'

Then it struck him. 'How did you find me?'

Janette waved an arm magisterially, indicating the park. 'This is the usual entry point.'

She caught herself short, lost focus as if she were listening to some internal dialogue. Then she chewed a fingernail, the first sign of her youth, and sounded less sure of herself. 'We didn't know who we'd find here of course.'

There was no *of course* about it, thought Jannlou.

'You and Nathan? He can communicate with you?' he asked, remembering Drianne's telepathy with Mielitta.

'No, silly.' Janette almost giggled. 'That would be weird. I told you, he can't speak. I meant I didn't know who'd be here. Nathan just follows me.' She made him sound like one of the dogs Jannlou could see fetching a ball from behind a shrub.

'If you could come here, you could go back through the walls, into the Citadel. Everybody there is worried.'

Her eyes measured him, shrewd, deceitful. 'But we – I – don't want to go back yet. There's a story you'll want to see. Mielitta's story.' She pronounced the name carefully as if it were a beetle in her mouth that she was chewing for his sake.

Kermon had said the girl was obsessed by stories, that storytelling was her mage's gift, and so it seemed. This wasn't what was supposed to happen but what other options did he have? Could he force them both back through the walls? As mages, they were his exit pass. But they looked well, seemed in no danger. He could hardly go back to Mielitta and say he'd missed the chance to discover her history. He knew how much it mattered to her.

Those strangely old eyes mocked him, as if Janette could read his thoughts.

'Follow me, Magaram's son. First we will watch *the creation*.' She'd emphasised the words, a direction to navigate the walls no doubt, but her tone made Jannlou's hackles rise. Something was wrong. And why had the students found him so easily but not Kermon and Verity?

He shrugged his broad shoulders. He was becoming paranoid. He'd spent enough time with a seer to accept Arven's strange ways and Janette was clearly another such. Anyway, who was he to worry about what was strange?

With such comforting thoughts, he walked behind Janette through the whirring layers of time and place. To a council chamber with ten men sitting at a table. This was a situation with which he *was* familiar, in any time period.

CHAPTER TWENTY-ONE

Jannlou blinked. It could have been the Citadel Council Chamber of Rinduran's day, with the Chief Mage presenting his plan and nine other men carefully not expressing the wrong opinions. But this was the past and the plan had already been put into effect – or not.

Why had Janette called it 'the creation'? He glanced at her. As she listened to the leader's speech, she wore a rapt expression, like a flower opening to the sun.

In contrast, Nathan's blankness had turned surly, the clouds threatening to spoil her day. He looked at Jannlou as if he wanted to speak to him, his mouth working. A little drool escaped but no sound emerged.

Jannlou gave what he hoped was a reassuring smile and hid his instinctive distaste. Then he remembered that the boy wasn't deaf and that the Councillors might as well be, so he whispered conspiratorially, 'We'll go back through the walls as soon as Janette has seen her story. Let's indulge her.'

The leader of the council edged his voice with the gravity required for tragic news. 'As this elect group knows only too well, we've accepted the unthinkable. Our world is probably doomed and our society is certainly doomed.'

The leader's broad, flat face and small eyes gave an expression of perennial cheer at odds with his apocalyptic statement. He wore the uniform of his day, the shirt and trousers to which Jannlou was already becoming accustomed.

'And we have followed the science to find a solution.' He paused. He'd no doubt rehearsed this speech and would recycle it when he could.

'A solution that is sustainable. That will create the Perfect society for our children and for their children.'

A girl's voice echoed his every word and Jannlou's glance at Janette confirmed that she was repeating the speech word for word, at the same time as the leader.

'People are ill from making choices. What job to do, where to live, who to live with. Choices are proliferating like a cancer. People even have to choose their gender! In Perfection, there will be no choices. Every citizen will know his role or her role. Boys will grow up to behave as men should and girls will grow up to be the women men want. That way there will be no suicides.'

One man shifted nervously.

The leader fixed him with a stare that did not suggest geniality, whatever his default facial expression. 'We have had all the discussions and the facts speak for themselves. When women pursue this hypothetical notion of equality, domestic violence increases and there are more women raped, more women murdered. Who suffers most in a society where women assume men's roles?'

'Women,' murmured a couple of the men dutifully.

'We must protect them,' agreed the leader. 'For their own good.'

Janette's voice echoed every word, the childish sweetness turning the manifesto into a risible fantasy. But nobody at the table was laughing.

'And we have ever higher numbers of suicides because of choice and the consequent self-questioning! We will have no suicides.'

Jannlou had as much trouble with the concept of suicide as Mielitta's bees would have with the notion of choice. Why would anybody kill himself?

Then he laughed bitterly as the irony struck him. In the Citadel as he knew it, anybody capable of such a thought would be suppressed.

'Shush!' Janette reproved him. 'I want to listen.'

'Our social scientists have analysed various social structures and are agreed that a medieval lifestyle offers the perfect way of fixing occupations, relationships and demands on the living environment, buildings, materials and so forth.'

Medieval. Jannlou rolled the word in his mouth, wondering if it meant the same to these councillors. To him it conjured up the warriors who'd donned armour in the cave and come into the walls.

The king's words echoed in Jannlou's mind. *Join us. You are better than you know, man and bear, our berserker. Follow us. Then lead us.*

'What if somebody doesn't fit in?' asked the one man wearing a suit, more relaxed despite the constraints of his jacket than anyone there in shirtsleeves.

The constraints we choose define us, thought Jannlou. Something Arven had said that, like the warriors, popped into his mind now.

Choice. Could there be too much choice? He had no idea, having grown up condemned for who he was. His second nature was not a choice. Accepting it was. *Berserker,* the king had called him, as if it were a noble title.

'That won't be possible. Children will be prepared in schools for Perfect society. We have details of the curriculum, the child care…' He waved some papers but nobody asked for further information. This was nothing new.

'This is our gift to our children's children and *their* children. They will live in total security. Free of the threats we face.' He held up a finger to indicate the first threat. 'No climate variations and no weather. Thanks to the canopy.'

'Will it work?' asked a bald-headed man wearing eyeglasses.

'Anders?' The leader looked to the oldest man at the table, his thin white hair combed over a shiny pate.

'Yes, Mr Khan, it will work.' Anders replied directly to the man who'd put the question. 'We've created large-scale microclimates for decades now, to grow plants. It's a small step to enclose a community.'

The leader beamed his approval. 'Thanks to our scientists, we can provide sustenance and materials for daily life without recourse to nature whatsoever. We can replace everything natural with man-made substances, from grass to roast beef, preventing disease and waste.'

He barely waited for the expected buzz of approval to die down. 'Nature sends pandemics and tsunamis, and filthy beasts competing for our living space, contaminating our lives. Nature proliferates in change and choice. We can defeat Nature and eliminate all of these threats!'

Frowning, Khan asked, 'But how will there even be scientists in a medieval community?'

The leader's beam transformed his face into a full moon, golden and benevolent. 'There will be mages,' he said. 'And we will rule.'

Approval purred in the atmosphere.

'Such elevation for us. From an elected group to *the* elect, thanks to our leader. The future will indeed be predictable,' declared the man in the suit. His tone was congratulatory but his words could be held guilty of irony.

Jannlou gasped at such effrontery, expecting the man's immediate suppression, but he needn't have worried. The leader's bonhomie doubled as he nodded, accepting the compliment.

'Yes, yes, Mr Dupont,' he agreed, 'safe and predictable. And we have perfected the management of the populace. You all know how politics works. Slogans and table-thumping. Assert our perfection at all times and ignore contradictory evidence should anybody be rash enough to present it. Say "Let's move on to what's important now," and make detractors look like nagging housewives.

'Be strong and manly. When you lie, do so heroically, with verve and metaphor, with humour and total self-confidence. Everybody expects a liar to have a tell, some sign of shame. Ergo, if you have no tell and no shame, you can't be lying.

'Attack is the best form of defence, especially if you accuse your enemies of the errors you are supposed to have made. And then render those enemies ineffective. You know the drill.'

Apparently, they did. And were concerned with what was important now.

'Mr Brown, can you tell us how long will it take? To build it?' asked a man whose bulk hung over its allotted seat. His deep gravelly voice reminded Jannlou of his father.

Again, the leader, Mr Brown, deferred to Anders, who pursed his mouth and blinked as he calculated. 'Nineteen years with an error margin of five, Mr Rolle. We can only factor in weather vagaries approximately in the initial stages but once the canopy is functional, work will proceed optimally and as you so rightly say–' a nod to the man in the suit '–predictably.'

The man in the suit, Mr Dupont, raised an eyebrow, looked at Anders and repeated, 'Nineteen years?'

The scientist replied to the question not asked. 'Of course you are considering my age and suitability. It is statistically unlikely that I personally will oversee the completion of the Citadel but I am training three appropriate successors so you can select the most adept. As you will select the citizens themselves.'

Nobody raised an eyebrow. This was old ground being harrowed one last time before the seeds were planted. Like on the homestead. Jannlou felt a wave of homesickness for the sanctuary Qingzhao had created, which he'd only seen once. Drianne would surely welcome him, regardless of his bear nature. If he survived.

But this council had a different kind of sanctuary in mind. Jannlou pictured grassette, self-cleaning, a trap for their prisoners when the mages called on its green tendrils to bind and clamp.

Yes, grassette was what the ground was being prepared for in this council chamber.

So this was the moment of creation. Perfection's birth. The words spoken here had shaped the fabric of life in the Citadel for hundreds of years. Had shaped his own childhood. Until he'd shifted into his own dual shape.

'Glorious, isn't it?' Janette turned to him, her eyes shining. 'To witness Perfection's birth and to renew our vows to preserve its ways. Every time I hear these words, I know where my duty lies. The Citadel will be Perfect again. Mark my words!'

Nathan stepped closer to her and her expression was lost in the shadows he created but her voice struck a sudden chill, as when she'd named Jannlou Magaram's son.

Every time she heard the words? How many times had Janette trespassed into the walls? Or had she 'seen' this moment as Arven 'saw' things?

'Come,' she ordered. 'We follow the man in the suit. He is the key.'

Jannlou and Nathan followed her orders. It did not feel at all like indulging a child.

CHAPTER TWENTY-TWO

'We have to face it – him – or citizens are in danger every time they visit the walls. We've been avoiding the issue for months,' Kermon told Verity, for the umpteenth time.

He guessed why she might not want to tell Bastien that some vestige of their father was still alive within the walls but that meant the two of them were the only ones who knew about Rinduran. Apart from the Forest dwellers. And he couldn't mention them to Verity without sparking a diatribe on how she intended to have them killed. He was so tired of leading two lives.

'You mean suppress him.' Verity's tone was colourless but he knew her too well to be misled.

'I don't know, Verity,' he confessed. 'I have no idea how we can end his dominion here. Even if I wanted to destroy him–' her eyes flashed and he spoke carefully '–I don't have the means. You know what happened last time.'

Constant head pains and blackouts as Rinduran's righteous anger triumphed, fuelled by Kermon's self-hatred at his double life. His mind within Rinduran's control, replacing his very thoughts with fundamental Perfectionism. Verity had only witnessed the final humiliation and that was enough to make his cheeks burn. He couldn't tell anyone how it had felt to be a puppet in his own body and mind.

But Verity had saved him. The revenant's power had increased within the walls, where other mages were disarmed. Only her capacity to shield him and her anger at being treated by her father as irrelevant had saved Kermon. And now she shielded him still. When he was with her, he felt grounded, purposeful.

The longer he was back in the Citadel, the more *What's the point?* replaced Tannlei's perennial question *What's the target?* When he was with Verity, that dark sense of futility had no purchase on his soul. And she too had been humiliated.

'Fetch your brother,' Rinduran had said. Oh, yes. Kermon could well imagine why Verity was reluctant to put this weapon in her brother's hand. But also reluctant to kill what was left of her father. If she was capable of killing him. A shield was not a weapon.

'I need time to think about it.'

Verity was ducking the question once more.

'Then why did you tell the Council we'd eliminate the evil within the walls?' Frustration made his words an accusation.

'Expedience.' Verity's reply was clipped. 'You want to rescue your students. Nobody else cares about them. I got the authorisation, which is all that matters. Let's not talk about my father any more. We should find these children and return to the Citadel. We can postpone deciding what to do about… him.'

Her expression brightened. 'In time,' she said, 'he would come round. Realise what I am, what I'm achieving. We could negotiate, agree boundaries.'

Delusional procrastination. Kermon just shook his head. He would need the help of another stubborn girl to resolve the Rinduran problem. And a bear. But that was not something to share with Verity.

Barely more than a child herself in years, she was a veteran in political nous and sharp as one of his knives. After years of confinement, her skin still had the luminescence of white mushrooms at night, drawing attention to her soulful brown eyes. No longer dull with endurance, they sparkled in response to challenges. How could anyone, much less her father, look at the Chief Councillor without a tinge of awe at her abilities?

Kermon stopped short of reading her soul. He would never intrude on a fellow being in such a way, knew only too well the duties his predecessor Shenagra had performed for Jannlou's father. He would never let the Council force him to interrogate a citizen in such a manner. He knew what such an invasion felt like. He shuddered at the memory and found it easier to keep to the term 'evil in the wall' than to name the man who personified that evil. He too would rather procrastinate. Though he knew it was wrong.

He was distracted by a ball curving towards them. It passed right through Verity, as did the grubby boy who pounded after it. He flinched but Verity seemed oblivious to the teeming life around them in the park, able to shut out the conversations that dragged his attention in so many directions. Another disadvantage of being a soul-reader, no doubt.

'You know the girl's story was about a honey hunter so let's follow that lead. She thought the story was important and she wanted to know more so we should do likewise. I don't see why... he... would be interested in us even if he senses our presence. He knows I can block him completely from affecting either of us. So let's just get on with it.'

Kermon sighed but had no better ideas.

'The honey hunter,' he instructed, ignoring all the tempting diversions which were on offer. And the world beyond the walls obliged.

And they watched, hoping this honey hunter *was* Janette's story because there were no other ways to find her. Verity vaguely remembered her father telling her how to navigate in the walls, bedtime stories for a sick daughter. A search term's most frequented path would be the first choice presented to a mage visiting so he would create simple paths for training his young students.

That dovetailed with Kermon's memory of his induction to the walls, during one carefully-managed visit. Mage Rinduran, the walls expert, gave the students the illusion of choice as they all focused on 'Citadel history' and all followed the same path of dry scenarios. One homily after another, by shades wearing the fancy dress of bygone eras. A practical lesson so boring that none of them had been tempted to visit the walls again.

Unlike Janette. Their only hope was that she had been here before them.

The park overlay another scene, faded and was gone. In its place they saw a village of ramshackle huts. Some kind of ceremony and a girl's initiation into a role that was meant for men played out in front of them. Kermon could see why such a story would attract his rebellious student but he couldn't understand why she thought it so important to the Citadel. Or why she needed to come back for more information.

The story led them to dizzying cliffs and the honey hunter dangling in a basket, clouds of bees blinding her.

'I feel sick,' said Verity in a small voice, sinking to the ground in a miserable crouch, her head between her knees.

'Do you want to go back? Is it allergy?' Kermon cursed himself for an idiot, putting another child in danger. It was so easy to forget how young Verity was and see her as the equal she thought herself to be. 'Do you think you're having a relapse?'

'No, I'll be fine. It's vertigo, I think. And those… creatures. Their noise gets inside my head.' Her words were muffled by her sleeve. 'Tell me when this bit's over. You can let me know if anything important happens.'

Kermon took her at her word, caught up in the drama of the girl in the basket. She speared another chunk of honeycomb, loosening it from the cliff, dropping it to the catchers with the basket below. A shout came up through the thin mountain air.

They've got it!

Kermon felt the girl's rush of pride and he couldn't help reaching out, letting her joy spill into him. He needed some joy.

Her thoughts brushed his mind, delicate as bee's wings. *Mustn't eat the honey. Mad honey.*

Again the stab with a spear and a blackness of enraged bees. A smack of honeycomb and the taste, rhododendron sweet fire, dizzying.

A vision. A girl running through a Forest, her bees with her. Not against her, *with* her.

At once, Kermon knew what Janette had seen and what she'd understood. He snapped the connection with the honey hunter but his empathy merely reached out gently in another direction, to his companion, hunched beside him. Her fear of bees was a black cloud in his head, blotting out all sense. He was swaying with her in trees as high as cliffs. Only one still point steadied them, stopped them falling into an abyss; her friend, loyal Kermon.

He doubled up in pain. But was skilled enough to withdraw from his soul-reading, to practise detachment. The compassion remained.

'The park,' he instructed, reaching down to lift the girl in his arms. Just as he had when they'd kidnapped her as a hostage. What damage had they done to such a frail being?

He set her down gently, still hunched up. He stroked the top of her head.

'It's over,' he said.

She looked up at him, no barriers between them. Only trust. 'You know what she saw. Where to go next to find her.'

He couldn't do it any longer. He couldn't lie to her.

'Yes,' he said. 'I think it's the story of the Queen of the Warrior Bees. How she came into existence.' He told Verity everything he'd seen. And she drew the same conclusion he had but with pleasure instead of fear.

'We can intervene. Stop the Freak from coming to the Citadel in the first place. Prevent the Battle of the Forest. Go back to when my father was himself. To when he loved me.'

To when you were a prisoner in a sickroom. Kermon thought, but he couldn't say the words. 'I think that's what Janette hoped.'

'I need to go back to the Citadel, talk to Bastien and the Council. We need to tell them.'

'Yes,' said Kermon gently. 'You do.'

'You should come too. You're not safe here.'

'I need to follow the honey hunter's story, as Janette did, as Nathan must have done, to find them as soon as possible. I'll be watchful for… him. I know his ways now.'

'When you've found them, then you'll come back to the Citadel. I want you to be the one to kill the Freak. You promised you would.'

Had he? He might have promised anything to stay alive and fulfil his mission. Or the evil within him might have, whether he blamed that on Rinduran or on himself.

'I will tell you the next bits of the honey hunter's story when we see each other again. Be careful and go quickly,' he told her.

Before she could press him further, he articulated clearly, 'The honey hunter returning to the village.'

Verity's mouth moved but he heard nothing.

The park faded and he could see huts, tribespeople, the Headman greeting the triumphant honey hunter. Qwian her name was.

But Kermon's thoughts were still with Verity. More last words that he'd botched in the forging. He reached for his arrowhead pendant, stroking the patterns in the steel, seeking comfort. Perfection Unfinished, his best work, as good as its twin, Steelwing. *May I be remembered for this.*

He tried to contact Mielitta but there was no tingle of a response. Only his soul-reading worked within the wall. He was alone with two missions instead of one and he must indeed go carefully and quickly. He would find his students and send them back safely. And he would hide Mielitta's past beyond the reach of the Citadel.

He could not fight the evil in the walls alone and he felt his doom moving ever closer. Verity was no longer his shield.

CHAPTER TWENTY-THREE

Verity lay on the bed, a prisoner in her childhood sickroom, wishing Kermon dead, wishing her brother dead, wishing she would wake up and find this nightmare was only that.

But she knew it was the truth. Kermon was a traitor. She didn't need the Council's judgement, nor the pack of lies on which it was founded. Hamel's testimony had been a travesty of justice, alleging that the Mage-Smith had corrupted her, abusing her in ways which made her redden now to recall – not because she was embarrassed but because she was so angry she thought she'd explode.

How dare they belittle her, assume that because she was young and female, she was putty in a man's hands? The very idea that Kermon had manipulated the Council with her as a mouthpiece was ludicrous. That every act taken by the Council at her instigation had really been at Kermon's bidding. Such a monstrous perversion of the truth.

Not one person around the table had spoken up for her and she'd been denied the right to speak for herself. Bastien had shouted over her words and sent her to her room as if she were a naughty little girl. To her locked room. If he'd been able to use magecraft on her to stop her mouth, he would have. For the first time, she wondered about that girl he'd been engaged to, whether she'd always been mute or whether her brother had found silence pleasing in a woman. Her brother – or her father on his behalf.

Now Bastien knew that their father had an existence within the walls because one of the freaks had let it slip. And he knew she'd kept it from him. So Kermon *was* a traitor. Nobody else could have told the freaks about Rinduran. Not only was he double-crossing the Citadel, he was blabbing *her* secrets. He'd lied, betrayed her, made a fool of her, laughed at her naivety with his friends. He was probably laughing now, waiting for the freaks to meet up with him.

Silly little Verity, falling for it. Falling for him.

If Bastien knew what his little sister felt for Kermon and how little was childish about it, he'd suppress her on the spot. She could not forget being in the Mage-Smith's arms. The way he'd carried her into the Forest as if she were precious and fragile, not as if she were a trading item. She'd felt safe, despite being kidnapped. Safer in his arms than locked in her sickroom by her brother.

And Kermon had understood her anguish straight away on the cliff-top, whisked her off to the park, tender and thoughtful. Her Right Hand.

A traitor.

She gulped back the tears, afraid of listeners outside the door, of someone entering. Of Bastien exulting in her misery because he too had been made to look a fool. Through the transparent partition she could see the other half of the chamber, a mirror image of hers, with separate locked door. Where her mother had died of allergy. Where the freak had been imprisoned, briefly. Was this to be her view for the rest of her life?

She gave in to the sobs, turned her face against the pillow to muffle the noise and cried until she choked.

Finally, drained of tears and numb, she faced facts. Her father had caged her in this room for all her childhood. 'To protect her from allergy,' he'd said and she'd believed him, loved him. But she was healthy now, despite contact with the Forest, despite going without the pills her father had insisted kept her alive. He was more alive now, a shade in the walls, than he'd allowed her to be! What if he was responsible for her sickness, him and the pills? A Perfect way to control a girl-child.

Her cheeks burned as she remembered telling Kermon her hope that her father would appreciate her if she eliminated the Citadel's greatest enemy. She'd been clinging to an illusion. She knew all he cared about was Bastien, who would get the credit for anything she did, just as Kermon had been blamed for *her* actions in Council meetings.

Four walls and a door locked from the outside clarified a person's priorities. She would get out of this cursed room and win her Citadel back. Love was for fools. It made you vulnerable.

Her father, Bastien, Kermon. Why should she care if they lived or died? They'd shown no such concern for her. All that mattered now was whether they were useful to her.

She wondered what Bastien would do next. Or Hamel, for his cloak was next in line for the gold braid of a Chief Mage.

With cold objectivity, she replayed the meeting in which she'd been condemned and she analysed the implications. Hamel had waited his moment to cast the net and catch her, throwing aspersions on Bastien's competence at the same time. First, he let her speak to the Council about the honey hunter, the vision and its significance.

She'd explained that they could defeat their enemy in the Forest by destroying her roots within the walls. That Bastien would then be free of the blood oath and the Citadel free of the cursed treaty. She'd urged speed in returning to the walls, where Kermon was tracking the story and the students, which would lead to their goal too.

And then Hamel had pounced. 'So, on Mage-Smith Kermon's interpretation of a wall peasant's thoughts, we are led a merry dance in the walls, leaving the Citadel open to the enemy.' He had directed a significant glance at Bastien, who nodded grimly. A glance Verity only understood later.

Hamel had shaken his green pointed head and eyed her with the same gleam she remembered accompanying his assertion that they would marry. 'Lady Verity,' he'd begun.

Not 'Chief Councillor', nor 'Speaker', she noted, despite all the work she'd put into gaining respect from these people.

'Lady Verity has been shamefully abused, physically and mentally, manipulated by the man we accepted as a peer. Mage-Smith Kermon is a traitor.'

While Verity reeled in shock, the accusations piled into a heap large enough to bury a man. Accusations that were mostly false but only she knew that and her word had been rendered counterfeit.

Hamel worked his subtle undermining on Bastien too, depicting him as a poor young man who'd stepped perforce into his father's shoes and been bamboozled. Unlike Hamel himself. Those present would remember how he'd challenged the Mage-Smith's appointment, been reluctant to train him in wallcraft and been vocal in his criticism of the new Maturity Test.

'Proposed, as it turns out, by somebody whose relationships with children are wholly inappropriate. Didn't you feel his need to save his students was… excessive? Now, we know why! No, Lady Verity, don't speak. No female should utter the words you would have to say. We can all imagine the detail.'

Hamel could dwell on a word and imply disgusting possibilities that word had never known before. *Excessive*.

Such a cunning way to remove not only her role as Speaker but even her capacity to speak. Verity had known then, in her gut, though she couldn't say so. *Traitor, yes. But not that. Never that.*

Even now, hating Kermon with all the inverted passion of her unspoken love, she knew he'd been vilified falsely. As had she. And Bastien believed it all! Every filthy implication. He would never forgive her for the acts she'd not committed. Hamel had spun his net to perfection.

Then Puggy testified that Magaram's traitor son had infiltrated the Citadel, abducting her to get him through the walls.

'He has no magecraft,' she told them, as if there hadn't been enough shocks for one meeting. 'But he can assume the form of a beast.'

Bastien confirmed this, ashen-faced, no doubt ashamed of his past association. 'He was here with a rogue mage, who has vanished.'

Further questions had no doubt been asked and evaded in Council but Verity had been excluded, escorted from the Chamber and down the spiral staircase. She cast a look of longing at the walls in the shadows at the bottom but was forced onwards, out of the Mages' Tower, along the passageway and into her old room. Her old prison.

How long had she been here since then? She was still disorientated by wall time and vertigo, revelations and regrets. A long time, she thought. Very long.

She remembered her mother lying in the other bed, visible through the screen that separated the twin sickrooms and kept each sterile. Only her father and brother visited the occupants but they could talk to each other, hear each other cough. See the blood on the pillows as the allergy progressed. How strange to call it progress.

Until the day her mother lay silent and then Verity was alone in this room, suffering her abandonment. Her mother had been the first to betray her.

How she'd loved her brother and father. How she'd loved Kermon. She had no love left now. But she was not a little girl any more. She rolled onto her back, gazed at the greylit ceiling and waited. Whatever she had to do, she would do. However unsavoury the alliances necessary, she would make them.

The sound of the door wards being unlocked by magecraft was not unexpected but the visitor was.

'You're in a bit of a fix, aren't you,' said Puggy. 'But we might be able to help each other.'

She plonked herself down on the bed. Her legs were too short to reach the floor so her legs dangled awkwardly.

'I don't mind being underestimated.' She gave Verity a shrewd glance. 'That's the point of looking like this. But I do mind being handicapped. I want my power back, all of it. Never would have given any to that girl if I hadn't thought my time had come.'

'But,' she shrugged, 'I'm still alive and I want to fight back when they attack us women.'

Verity knew the attempt to cosy up for what it was. She'd heard Puggy's views on the inferiority of non-mages often enough. But if there was a way out of these four walls, she was listening.

'Go on,' she said.

'You want her dead, don't you?' asked Puggy. 'The Queen of the Warrior Bees.' Her sarcastic tone turned the title to an insult.

Verity nodded. *The Freak. Kermon's true lady. He promised to kill her and never meant it.* Duty and spurned passion melded nicely into an aim. She would prove she was more than her brother's equal by dealing with Mielitta in this world before he could attack her beyond the walls. Much more satisfying than waiting for Bastien to change events. She shied away from the question of *why* she needed to prove herself.

'Well dearie, you come with me then. We're going to the Forest. We'll find the pair of them and get what we want. I can use magecraft on the Freak and finish her. You can shield me from her friend, who'll be using my own powers against me.' Her outrage was palpable. 'And I'll claim back what's mine. Then we'll see what happens in the Council Chamber!'

'Get me out,' said Verity.

It was surprisingly easy for the two Councillors to walk through the Citadel, down deep underneath the living quarters to the water gate, the traditional exit towards the Forest in the old days for those few who had permission to go that way. No doubt the Council was still sitting and less important citizens would only learn of events in the Great Hall at evening meal, depending on what the Council chose to tell them.

The only hiccup was at the gate itself. All Verity could see was an extravagance of greenery, some abomination of Nature invading what must be a gap in the wall. Alien, dangerous, breaking through from outside.

Puggy tut-tutted. 'The gate must be there somewhere, underneath all that filthy stuff. We just have to walk through it. Wrap your cloak tight and follow me.' She jumped onto a flat stone, water racing past her, and suited action to words.

But it was Verity's scream that nearly ended the escape bid.

'Bees,' she yelled, lashing out frantically above her head, eyes closed. Thousands of bees divided into two streams to avoid Puggy as they zoomed from the world outside over Verity and into the Citadel.

'Never you mind them,' Puggy told her, then Verity felt her arm wrenched and she was hauled across the gap onto the stone and through the gate.

She screamed again and was rewarded with a stinging slap across the cheek.

'Now shut up and let me concentrate,' Puggy snapped. 'I need a seeking spell, then we can get on with the job. It's all such hard work these days,' she complained, as she screwed up her face, muttering.

Verity blinked in the sunlight, frightened of its dazzle. Last time she'd been in this meadow, strong arms had protected her. She too screwed up her face. She would *not* cry. She'd trusted him. She hated him.

CHAPTER TWENTY-FOUR

The rain had stopped but something held Mielitta back from shifting and trying to enter the Citadel in bee form. She could see the walls, towering above the surrounding meadows. She ached to take her rightful place, to fight beside Jannlou, Kermon and Arven, but an opposing instinct was telling her to wait.

Her sigil glowed golden, hummed in anticipation of some moment to come. Her bees sang the same song, over and over. *Wait. They are coming.* But they wouldn't answer her questions.

The queen bee tattoo vibrated without cease. *You know what's happening. Bees always know. Let yourself feel.*

Mielitta tried. She was as hungry as a bear after winter, a thought which only made her miss Jannlou more. But evidence that spring was well advanced bloomed everywhere, quickened by Arven's weather magecraft and the soft whispering rain. Why should she feel that she must gorge on honey?

She was restless. She felt the need to prepare for action. Was that bee connection or human?

What was happening in the home hive? Should she worry, go back there? She focused, scented the activity or rather inactivity. So strange not to hear the chorus *Work!*

She could see the hive interior in her mind's eye. The queen bee had stopped laying and the nursery workers were idle, ready to fly. All the spare cells were filled to the brim with honey and the adult population was so dense it was overflowing from the hive. But why? No answers came.

Just *Wait*.

And her own gut feeling that the bees were right. Nothing was wrong.

She took out her frustrations on tree trunks and wild game, practising her archery and bagging a guinea-fowl and a rabbit for her cook-fire. The twang of bowstrings, the slip from conscious technique to unconscious connection with her bow and her target honed her body and focused her mind.

'What's the target?,' Mielitta asked herself.

Dinner, distraction, exercise, were the easy answers.

To be with Jannlou popped into her mind and she considered it as if it were a clump of strange mushrooms that had grown overnight on a tree-stump she no longer recognised.

She identified the strange thought and filed it on her mental shelf under 'Personal'. Her Citadel librarian's habits lingered still and 'Personal' was a category that must defer to a higher shelf.

To fight beside Jannlou, Kermon and Arven was not really a target, she decided. *Why* they were fighting was what mattered.

To eliminate the evil that was Rinduran. Yes, that was part of it. She'd removed him from the Citadel but maybe that wasn't enough. Qingzhao and Arven thought she had been born for a reason.

To save the Citadel from itself.

I've tried, she thought. The battle, the treaty, the taste of honey given to the kidnapped children. She'd let her best friend walk into the Citadel to nurture the seeds of a better future. She'd done her part. Wasn't it up to destiny to do the rest? For the children to change their own world as they grew into adults?

Wasn't her higher target now to get Kermon out safely, with Jannlou and Arven, to return to Drianne's haven and live there happily ever after? She quashed the internal voice judging this as belonging on the 'Personal Shelf.'

Now! We're swarming!

As the bees' shout filled her senses, the golden bee sigil thrummed and Mielitta was instantly a bee in flight among a multitude of others. Workers and drones all flying together and in the heart of the swarm, protected by her cadre of bodyguards, the queen, exuding the scent that united them and gave them purpose.

'The whole hive is here,' she observed.

Scout bees streaked above, directed the swarm and then dipped back underneath to let their fellows take on the task. So many bees around her warmed the air and carried her in their momentum, faster and faster. Towards the water gate and the Citadel. Her own purpose was echoed in the direction of the swarm

A third of the colony, corrected her spirit bees, *and the old queen. We seek a new home, while one of her daughters takes over home hive with a strong population to support her.*

Mielitta remembered her time as caretaker queen, strengthening the feeble hive until a peanut-shaped queen cup hatched into her chosen replacement, the only queen remaining after Mielitta had dispatched all the rivals.

And now the young queen was the old queen.

'That's generous of her, being the one to take all the risks, leave home hive.'

Bee laughter tinkled as they considered what *generous* meant.

Mielitta shared a picture of bees grooming and feeding each other.

Yes, generous, they agreed, buzzing happy understanding. *She knows her role and the right time for each change, as do we. Make more hives.*

Mielitta gave up trying to explain. Without selfishness, generosity could not exist. A bee would never understand the notion of individual priorities. Bees had no Personal Shelf.

Then they reached the water gate, or the place it must be. Mielitta followed the mass, slowed down by the waving violet stems and leaves. She wove in and out the twining plants, through the metal bars and the rainbow which showed the place of the barrier they'd crossed between worlds.

This was the first time she'd crossed as a bee and the colour shifts of her vision gave her two distinct shades of ultraviolet in place of the missing red.

She barely had time to dodge dark blue human shapes, a giant purple face with open mouth shrieking and then she was chasing up the passageway beside the dank wall.

It was her turn to shout, 'Wait!'

The bees ignored her.

Then she remembered what mattered to them and she danced in the air, passionate in her directions.

The worker bees nearest her took up her dance with so much enthusiasm that it was passed along the swarm to the front and, as one, the bees wheeled around, clustered around the queen and took shelter in a cleft in the wall. Where Mielitta's directions had led them.

'Danger,' she told her spirit bees. 'Tell them all to wait here.'

While you scout for a new home? they asked hopefully.

Her heart sank. There was no home for bees in the Citadel. Grassette offered no food and the only water was in the kitchens.

Then she realised how stupid she was. Water was all around, dripping down the walls and rushing into the Citadel past the water gate. They could fly to the stone and sip, without risk of drowning.

Food was a different matter. They'd stocked up on honey before swarming but she didn't know how long that would last them. She could try to persuade them to fly back through the water gate to somewhere more hospitable but she had a feeling they would not copy her dance with such fervour if it meant going back. She could feel their excitement at finding new territory, spreading their wings. But they would die here.

'Yes, I need to scout,' she told them. 'You can drink there.' She danced the directions to the stone by the water gate. 'Fly carefully.'

She shifted back to human shape, walked back to the stone and smiled to see the striped queues hovering over the tiny dips filled with water, taking their turn to drink. What a miracle to see natural forces at work within the Citadel. If only…

'Mielitta!'

She jumped as Arven dropped from the stone wall of the passageway like an angel sent from heaven. Or like an irritating mage seer who could perform unnatural acrobatics.

'I had to move out of the way of two women who came down here. One in a mage's cloak, one wearing a striped cloak. They went through the water gate.'

Mielitta chewed her lip then shrugged. 'If they don't get lost or eaten, Drianne can cope. Her magecraft is very strong.'

'I know,' Arven said quietly. 'When she hasn't drained it or lost control.'

Mielitta flushed. Why did he always make her feel like a student? But she knew why. Because he was Tannlei's son and she loved him for that. Even when she resented his manner.

So she swallowed her pride and said, 'I'm not sure what to do next. The bees can't last for more than a couple of weeks on water alone. I want to go to Kermon.' She carefully mentioned him first but was convinced that Arven saw through her. 'And Jannlou. Where is he? What do you think we should do?'

Arven looked down, fidgeted with a knitted bracelet around his wrist.

'I told Jannlou to wait for me within the walls,' he told her. Then met her gaze with the full weight of those black eyes, so like those of his mother and grandmother. 'I hope he managed to get there.'

CHAPTER TWENTY-FIVE

'I need to settle the bees somewhere safe.' Mielitta was adamant. 'I'm sure they only came here because I influenced their direction. I could think of nothing but getting into the Citadel and my obsession must have spilled over into the swarm's agitation.'

'Can't they stay in the crevice?' asked Arven. 'Until we get back from the walls?'

'Too damp. Let me think.' She knew the Citadel passages and chambers, halls, towers and ateliers, like the back of her hand. She'd hidden here as a servant, worked in the library, been a prisoner and escaped. Surely she could think of a corner where bees could build comb and stay safe. *And* forage *and* eat *and* drink. It was no good. Her mind remained blank.

'I need to *be* a scout to find a home,' she told Arven. 'To see the options from a different perspective. Then we can go to Jannlou and Kermon.'

The seer crouched on the path, leaned against the rocky wall and shut his eyes. 'Go,' he said. Then his head dropped onto his chest and, apparently untroubled by the trickling water or the rumbling bees, he fell asleep.

How long since he last slept? wondered Mielitta, marvelling at

Arven's poise, perfectly balanced even with his whole body relaxed.

Then she focused on her bee sigil and shifted into a worker's body.

At last! buzzed her spirit bees, flying up the passageway with her towards the inhabited areas of the Citadel.

Mielitta knew that the sighting of even one insect would trigger a full-scale alarm throughout Perfection. A danger for her and another complication in siting the swarm.

She stopped short of the junction where the water gate passage turned onto a human thoroughfare, applied pressure to clamp her six feet onto the wall. Then she dug in her claws and considered her surroundings.

If the bees could access this passageway from their home, unseen, they could reach water and go through the water gate to forage. If she turned left, she would get to the door that led to the greensward and the forge. Maybe there would be a dry crevice in the wall in the next passageway?

But the bees would be heard and seen.

Where would they be invisible?

She thought of Arven hiding. Up high!

Up she flew so that she and her coterie of bees were as high above any citizens passing below as the ceilings would allow. Dark and shadowed, beyond the reach of the light-spheres on the walls, the top of the passage was high enough for her purpose and the rocky crannies distorted sound.

But in the short distance to the door leading out to the forge, there was no hole in the wall big enough to home the swarm. Mielitta could try flying in the other direction but those locations became ever more frequented: chambers, the Great Hall, the school, the mages' quarters and the Mages' Tower.

What about the archery yard?

No, too far away from food and water.

She looked longingly at the door to the greensward. She'd rushed through this door so many times, so keen to reach the forge and her work there. Until her stepfather had chosen Kermon to be his apprentice and condemned her to the mindless life of a citadel lady.

If only bees could open doors. There would be somewhere they could lodge on the forge exterior if they could reach it. Or maybe higher, on one of the other buildings.

She crawled over the door handle but bees had no musclepower. They couldn't even move grass blades growing in front of their hive. She flew back to the other side of the passageway to look at the door.

Its brown wood was dark blue to her bee sight, not an attractive flower-blue and with no ultraviolet circles to show a forager where to land and collect nectar or pollen. A thin whitish rectangle outlined the door.

How strange. She didn't remember there being any other colour edging the door and she'd walked through it often enough. Had it been painted?

Then she realised. Greylight was showing between the door and its frame. Enough space for a bee to fly through?

Easily! She found herself on the other side of the door, looping triumphant loops over the greensward in front of the forge. Carried away by the sheer joy of flight and the good news she could take back to the colony, she flew right over the forge.

Below her, the Maturity Barn looked like an innocent rustic outbuilding, hiding in its disused interior the ashes of those who'd been suppressed there. No, that was no place for the joyful work of bees.

She scanned the walls until she found what she was looking for. Crumbling masonry, a narrow entry and a cavity in the stone behind it. Plenty of room for a swarm in the thickness of the wall. And they could fly back the way she'd come, keeping to the top of the door and high in the passageway, to reach the water gate and the meadow beyond. Perfect, for the time it would take Mielitta to do what must be done in the walls and to return to her bees.

How different the Citadel looked when she could fly. The

Canopy curved grey above her, a solid barrier. Below it, the Mages' Tower soared above the Citadel walls. And she could reach it from here. What if there was a meeting in the Council Chamber? If she could gather the latest information? Arven would be as happy as the bees.

The temptation was too much for Mielitta and she flew up to an ornamental ledge at the top of the Mages' Tower, where there was a window. Purely decorative, this was the only window in the Citadel. Perfect greylight was the same in the courtyards and on the greensward as in the chambers and halls.

Booming sounds came through the window and she risked a peek, her feet clamped to the edge of the glass. Yes, the Council was in full swing. Bastien and Hamel were gesticulating but she couldn't understand their words while in bee form.

There was no help for it but to shift back to human, cling and not look down.

The stone ledge was just wide enough for her feet and she could reach the window's lower edge with her fingertips, which gave her the illusion she was holding on to something. Flattened against the wall in a star shape, she imagined her feet had the adhesive qualities of a bee's and she clung on. Then she listened. Not all the debate reached her but she understood the gist.

'They broke the treaty!' Bastien was shouting. '*They* are in exile, banned from the Citadel, supposed to stay in the cursed Forest along with any defectives who leave here to join them.'

Mielitta's heart thumped. *Jannlou. Arven. Herself.*

Hamel's squeaky voice came through the glass like nails scratching. 'They have broken the treaty so that means it's null and void. We need not be bound by it any longer. Chief Mage, this releases you from the blood oath.'

In the silence, Mielitta pictured Bastien's smile. But there was no relief in his voice when he spoke.

'And if the blood oath still binds me whatever they do? We were fools to think such as they are would honour their words, when they can't be bound in our way. But I did sign the blood oath and you won't be the one who pays for breaking it! And you're not the only one who'd wipe dry eyes if I died.'

From the hubbub, Mielitta gathered there were protestations of loyalty from all in the room. Too many protestations, too loud.

Had she and her friends broken the treaty? She hadn't given it a thought beforehand and it was too late now. Surely not, when they were just passing through.

Another voice, one she didn't know. 'One thing's clear. They were told not to return and their lives are forfeit here. Kill them. That's allowed by the treaty and doesn't break the blood oath.'

'Then find them,' roared Bastien. 'Find them all. In the Citadel, in the walls. If they're there, kill them!'

Another hullabaloo, during which, presumably, mages volunteered suggestions.

Then Bastien's voice again. He must be nearest the window and his anger made him loud. 'I'm going into the walls. No doubt that's where my sister has gone, though I don't know how she forced Puggy to help her. We shall have quite a family reunion and deal with the Forest freaks and traitors at the same time.

'Hamel can find the rogue mage in the Citadel and maintain order here with the help of the female Councillors, while I'm gone. I'll need the other men with me…'

Mielitta shrank into her smallest self, having heard enough. She no longer thought Arven would be happy when she reported back. And they had to find a way to get to the portal in the Mages' Tower and into the walls together. Even if she'd wanted to, she wouldn't have gone without him. *No honour.* Bastien's words stung.

CHAPTER TWENTY-SIX

'Can we go into the walls here?' Mielitta asked Arven, indicating the dank stone to their left.

He shook his head. 'I don't think so. There must be a reason the mages use the portal in the tower.'

Only the rush of the stream below and the drip of water down to the slippery paving could be heard in the silence while Mielitta considered her lack of options. No buzzing. The bees had joined in their scout's dance with enthusiasm and, with one accord, flown off to their new home. She hoped they would cross the corridor high up, quietly and quickly.

'I think Bastien will go into the walls straight away with his Councillors, so they'll be out of our way. I can shift and fly there but Hamel will have everyone looking for the rogue mage. I'm not leaving you. And I doubt the walls would let me through without you.'

She shrugged, bitter. 'They might not let me through *with* you.

'They're looking for a suspect mage.' Arven pondered. 'To them that means the cloak and somebody acting furtively.'

He swirled Kermon's cloak off and into his knitting bag, revealing the teardrop armour in all its silvery beauty. Hood down, the pure lines of his face revealed. Slight as he was, every line of his body and garb declared him a warrior.

Mielitta gulped. 'Wouldn't it be safer to disguise yourself with glamour…' Her words withered.

'No more skulking. I am the son of Tannlei and Crimvert, grandson of Qingzhao. I shall behave as such.' His inward gaze suggested he was considering their dangers again and he nodded a concession to her fears. 'The bag looks odd. That could do with a glamour.'

As if there was no hurry, Arven pulled out his knitting needles and worked strands of brown and grey fabric, that shaped themselves into a bow and quiver. He tucked the needles back into the quiver, where they sprouted shafts and then declared himself ready. He no more looked like a typical Citadel knight than Mielitta a lady. Her own weapons were at the ready. But she could shift shape for disguise and must hope that Arven knew what he was doing.

'Past the Great Hall–' she told him.

'And continue along the passage. I know. Jannlou drummed the Citadel's layout into me.'

Jannlou. She couldn't hear his name without her heart jumping, without wanting to say something, *anything*, just to keep him here with them in spirit.

'Jannlou knew all the best hiding-places,' she said, foolishly. 'Once, I'm sure he saw me pressed against the wall but he drew them all past, Bastien and the others. As if he was protecting me, had grown out of their ways.'

She remembered his eyes resting on her, glancing away. As if a bee had alighted on her arm. A touch that changed everything.

'I'll meet you at the portal in the Mages' Tower,' she said, embarrassed at opening up so much. *Personal shelf!* she reminded herself. *Keep it there!* 'The stones be with you.'

'With us both,' she heard Arven say as she focused on the glowing sigil and shifted back into a bee, flying over his head up the passageway and into the most frequented area of the Citadel.

From her vantage point high in the shadows of the rocky ceiling, she saw him bowing his head to two cloaked figures and accepting the respect of ladies and knights, brushing past servants as if they didn't exist. Jannlou had obviously taught him some of the formalities required.

She also saw the people he passed turning back to stare and then talking to each other. But none of them challenged Arven or slowed their pace. He continued walking, his head high, his hand on his bow, as if he had every right to be there. Which he did, as a mage's son and a powerful mage himself.

Whereas she had no right to be there. *No honour,* she thought, as she reached the Mages' Tower ahead of Arven. In the silence and shadows, she shifted back to her human self, stretched, looked a challenge at the untrustworthy walls.

'It is time,' Arven said as he entered.

They joined hands and walked towards the walls.

Mielitta was tentative, remembering the stone rejection of her last attempt, fearing each step would smack her against a barrier.

So it was Arven who gasped as they bounced backwards from some invisible barrier before they'd even reached the walls.

From the deepest shadows underneath the stairwell came the unmistakeable figure of the ungainly green mage.

'Hamel!' exclaimed Mielitta as Arven reached into an amorphous mass that was fast resuming the form of a knitting bag.

'Don't waste your magecraft, boy,' squeaked Hamel. 'I'm not going to stop you or I'd have done so while you were strutting through my Citadel.'

Arven paused but Mielitta was reaching for an arrow. She could fling it or stab with it, if not loose it. One distraction and they could get into the walls. If Arven could break the barrier.

'Don't be ridiculous, girl.' Hamel's upper lip curled with distaste. 'Or whatever you are. I'm not stopping you either. Just listen.' His voice broke as he spoke, spoiling the effect of his sharpness. 'And don't be stupid enough to underestimate me because I don't look or sound like the other mages.'

The irony was not lost on Mielitta. She relaxed her grip on the arrow but stayed vigilant. 'Then you should be more careful with the words you hurl at others,' she pointed out.

Arven had flushed crimson but said nothing. He too was poised, waiting.

'Your kind has no place in my Citadel.' Hamel dismissed them both with an airy gesture of his pointed fingertips. 'The bastard get of two traitor mages and,' he turned from Arven to Mielitta, 'an abomination. You know where you belong so let's not waste the time I've bought you.

'You want to go into the walls. I want you to go into the walls. It would suit me if Bastien, his weakling sister, Lady Puggy and all the mages with them did not return from the walls. And you seem to be the best method of achieving that.'

'We're not your servants,' Mielitta fired back at him.

And received a cynical smile in response. 'No indeed. I don't doubt that Bastien will provoke you and give you just cause to annihilate his party. In case you are insufficiently motivated, you should know that Puggy was the one tasked with suppressing the traitorous Archery Mage. What was her name again?'

Arven didn't rise to the bait but his face was drawn and white in the effort to maintain his self-control.

'Oh yes,' Hamel taunted. 'Tamtam or something like that. In fairness, Shenagra should really get the credit. It took a soul-reader to discover deceit so ingrained and of course Puggy would do anything for her beloved Shenagra so maybe you feel merciful.'

He scrutinised Arven and shook his head. 'No, that doesn't look like your merciful face, I must say. But if – and I say if – you can't bring yourself to do it yourself, Magaram's son would help you out. Puggy said he was *barely* in control of his violence.'

He laughed and repeated his joke, whether because he thought they'd missed it or just to enjoy it a second time. '*Barely.*'

Then his tone grew melancholy. 'I shall miss Puggy. There will be *barely* a worthy opponent left.'

Brisk again, he finished, 'So there you have it. Like an ancient tragedy! Magaram's slut Shenagra discovered another female mage whoring – your best-forgotten mother – and ordered her execution by the beautiful Puggy, who is rotten to the core herself with gender sin. No wonder she puts on a false face. She'd have done anything for Shenagra. Female mages at their best, I must say!'

He waved his pointed nails at the invisible barrier, bowed ironically and wished them good luck. 'May the stones be with you,' he said, walking past them to the entrance. 'I shall now summon the great and the good left in my Citadel so I can inform them that the intruder was seen escaping into the walls and tell them a message to that effect has been sent to our respected Chief Mage. Without doing so of course. 'Bastien was right to hesitate about leaving me in charge. But he had no choice.' His smile dazzled.

'Don't come back,' he told them.

Arven took Mielitta's hand and she had no chance to change her mind about using the arrow. The walls welcomed them without any demur and the mown stripes of park grass beyond greeted them.

Mielitta held Arven's hand much longer than she needed to but she couldn't find the right words and when he gently separated from her, she felt she'd let him down. She'd loved Tannlei too, so much. Why was it so difficult to say *that* word aloud?

CHAPTER TWENTY-SEVEN

Jannlou looked away from Nathan, whose mouth was frothing again as the student struggled to communicate, eyes bulging with the effort.

'It's all right,' Jannlou told him. 'Janette can speak for both of you.'

His reassurance had the opposite effect to that intended and Nathan convulsed, first his head, then his whole body shaking.

Janette turned her attention away from the man in the suit to her companions.

'It's all right, Nathan.' She held his arm as she soothed him. He quieted instantly, slumping to the ground in an open-mouthed stare.

'I'll make sure everything's all right,' she murmured, then turned her attention back to the scene before them. 'We need to watch this.'

She obviously had more technique than Jannlou did. Soul-reading skills, no doubt. She was a strange one. Kermon had given the impression that she was talented and wilful, obsessive about her storytelling, but not that she was so bossy. Had she been an adult he'd have said dictatorial.

What she found of interest in Oliver Dupont he had no idea.

The man was also obsessive and Jannlou was bored with the repetition of his words and action. The only variation was in the other person with Oliver, who was someone different in each scene they visited.

'–to create somebody extraordinary, who will meet the challenge of the future, I need you to donate one hair, of your own free will, without asking any questions.'

The red-bearded warrior towered over the man in a suit, uncertain whether to swing his axe or bury it in the round of tree trunk he was using as a chopping-block. A pile of split logs testified to the amount of work already done.

Ill-matched physically, in garb and historical period, the two men had nothing in common. Boardroom businessman and barbarian.

Jannlou had recognised each of the warriors from the first but he saw no reason to reveal their secrets to two Citadel students. They'd come into the cave in his own time with a message for him and a mission within the walls but seeing them here, in the context of their lives, showed how separate they'd been. In different layers of time, with no more in common than Oliver and Redbeard.

What united them in the cave was some mission but there was no sign in this world of any connection between them. Even the Jewelled King had been busy with his own court, had heard Dupont's plea, granted the boon and dismissed them without further interest. Jannlou was certain that this, the twelfth hair, would be the last one required. Like those asked before him, Redbeard would puzzle a moment over the strange demand, then concede a hair from his head and get on with his business. And then Oliver would no doubt work some magecraft with his strange collection, perhaps create another warrior, some leader who combined all the skills of all these warriors.

'No,' said Redbeard. 'I don't know you. I have no reason to trust you.'

'No, you don't.' Oliver's expression was grim. 'What do you want me to do to prove myself?'

Redbeard did not take the question as rhetorical. He swung his axe in a meditative way then replied, 'Make Tyr's oath to Fenrir. Be brave as a god and catch the wolf.' He bared his teeth in a bestial grin.

Oliver blenched.

'What does it mean?' asked Janette, imperious.

Jannlou shrugged. 'No doubt we'll find out.'

'Well?' sneered Redbeard. 'I thought this was so important you'd give your right hand to accomplish it.'

Oliver nodded, his jaw clenched, and he put his hand on the chopping-block.

As Redbeard swung his axe, Jannlou seized Janette, covered her eyes despite her struggles, and prevented her watching. But he saw and flinched as the steel sliced through the air down towards the splayed hand, palm down on the wood.

Oliver did not move. The blade bit and blood sprayed but still Oliver and his hand stayed in the same position.

Then the half-trunk which had been a chopping-block split in two, falling to the ground.

Oliver straightened, held his hand up high above his head to staunch the bleeding, then fished a handkerchief out of his pocket to bind the cut between thumb and first finger.

Jannlou had counted. All five digits present and correct. One hand, slightly nicked but still attached to one arm. Legendary axemanship.

'Gutless coward!' Janette spat the word with contempt. She'd pushed aside Jannlou's hand and was looking at Redbeard not at the man in the suit. Had she wanted Oliver to lose a hand?

Redbeard grunted approval. 'If you'd moved, you'd be one-handed. And you wouldn't have this.' He pulled a red hair out of his beard and offered it to Oliver, who smiled weakly.

'Would you be so kind as to reach into my pocket, in my… er, britches. If you could place your hair in the pouch with the others, I'd be most obliged.'

With a certain hesitation regarding the 'pocket', Redbeard did as requested.

'You'll want honey on that.' He pointed at the oozing handkerchief. 'And I need a new chopping-block. Go before I change my mind. The wolf is never tame you know, just biding his time.' He bared his teeth in what could have been a smile.

Berserker, thought Jannlou. Were there wolf-warriors just as he was a bear warrior? Was Redbeard like him and had there been others in the past, respected for what they were?

'Follow the man in the suit,' snapped Janette and the scene wavered again.

And continued to whirl, as if in confusion as to destination.

Janette seemed to darken and grow taller in the confusion, more silhouette than person. Jannlou blinked and the illusion cleared. Her curls bounced at the height of his chest. And she was annoyed.

'Follow Oliver Dupont!' she instructed.

More wavering and then two scenes appeared, superimposed. Like each other enough to be nearly visible but with small differences, creating motion which made the watchers feel slightly sick.

Blinking didn't affect the shifting focus as two Olivers walked in slightly different directions. One was walking towards a wall that looked much like the world boundary through which they'd entered from the Citadel. The other Oliver was heading for the back of the cave, through which the warriors had come into Jannlou's time.

In both versions, the man held a parchment scroll. Jannlou squinted and thought he saw spidery green writing. Was that because he hoped to see spidery green writing? A sign from Qingzhao?

He became aware that Janette was watching him, not the double vision in front of them. And she was definitely growing darker and taller.

A whimper came from Nathan. The boy dropped into a crouch, curled up, his arms in front of his face for protection. He exuded abject fear.

Jannlou felt his hackles rise and a growl escaped him as his instincts responded to a threat.

Shadows were creeping out from the vague shape that had been Janette's body but which now writhed in clutching hands, fingertips walking out towards him. Disembodied hands.

What living nightmare was this? Sparked no doubt by Redbeard's handiwork and given form by some trickery of the walls. Mielitta had said the walls could create illusions and were unpredictable.

Then came a voice Jannlou knew well, had heard too often in the Citadel and thought he'd silenced in the Battle of the Forest.

'You know something, mage-crusher,' mocked the voice. 'I can smell it on you. Tell me all and then we can renew our acquaintance more… efficiently. And with a satisfactory outcome.'

Jannlou didn't need to see the face taking over Janette's, the bee sting protruding from a milky eye in ever-shifting depths of blackest evil. He knew who this was, wearing a little girl's body and mind. And he knew what Nathan had been trying to tell him.

CHAPTER TWENTY-EIGHT

Alone was something Drianne only felt with people around her. She sang as she prepared food for the animals, cat first, to acknowledge his status as master of the homestead universe. Her mouth opened and closed in a song of springtime. No matter that others would hear no sound. She sang for herself and the rainbow colours of her mood showed in the garment Arven had knitted for her, currently lying cat-like around her neck.

Hui circled her legs, purring, his eyes smiling in cat, a language which Drianne understood. As she did chicken, goat and horse. Communication in bee was improving, thanks to Qingzhao's journal. She would never get inside a bee's mind as Mielitta could but the journal was teaching her that she had different talents.

The spidery green writing mixed philosophy and farming in a way that seemed exactly right to Drianne. She had so much to learn. Even chickens led complicated lives!

One cock-of-the-walk makes ten hens happy. Two roosters will strut and crow before feathers fly. If the fight be short and one bird dance its wing in a circle around the other, leave them be. The dancer has won and the loser will run, ne'er to crow or mate. If the fight endures and neither will cede, one or both birds will die unless you intervene. Separate lives or a bird for the pot is your choice. Such is the pecking order and fiercer among males.

Places to hide, places to eat and drink and roosts a-plenty will keep the hens laying, not ruffling feathers.

It was just like the Citadel in miniature! Politics, bullying and status obsession, with a strutting male leader while the hens laid the eggs. Drianne listened to the soft clucking outside the door and felt less sentimental towards her chickens than before reading the notebook.

The last observation in the chickens' section caught her eye.

Bad deeds like chickens always come home to roost.

She shivered and shut the book. A gloomy thought.

Her rainbow scarf slithered down her neck and shaped itself into a slip-over top which had a strange bulge not related to her body shape. Her mood changed instantly and she laughed.

Come on out then, she said.

As if the little frog could hear and understand, it pushed its way out from the scarf and hopped onto Drianne's shoulder, puffing out its little voice-box, making no sound. Like her, the frog was female and mute. The creature was also so shy it only appeared when Drianne was without human company and she quite liked having her little secret. Her thoughts shied away from the secrets her friends had kept from her until they could no longer hide them. Her colours flickered, paler, and she reached for Qingzhao's journal again.

She had read one passage so often it was stained with jam and oil from browsing the book and cooking at the same time. Her rainbow colours brightened as she read.

'Disappointment tastes bitter as wormwood and can be just as addictive. You expected more: of others, of the walls, of the world. You are badly done by and misunderstood. Of course you are! That is the nature of relationships between separate beings. Bees are never disappointed.

'You cannot become a bee. But you can destroy the root of the disappointment. Nobody makes your expectations but you. If nothing and nobody lives up to your expectations, change them.

'Worst of all is being disappointed with yourself. You feel a failure—'

Drianne knew the next bit by heart. *'Everybody else is better at whatever you think important, has everything you think is important,* is *more important.'*

Mielitta, Queen of the Warrior Bees, so brave and skilled. Drianne pictured her friend in the archery yard, turning somersaults and defying gravity as she shot arrows into impossible targets. Mielitta calling to Drianne to help her, throwing her head back and laughing in triumph as she achieved something new. So beautiful, so impervious to how Drianne felt about her, so much in love with Jannlou. Who of course felt the same way about Mielitta.

Jannlou with his muscles and maleness, as warrior or bear. Best not to think about Jannlou or her colours would change again.

Kermon, a master smith and a better mage than Drianne would ever be, both in skill and in self-control, so good he could teach magecraft and contribute to the council. So good he could sacrifice himself for his friends and for the Forest. How could Drianne compete with that? Mielitta's eyes would never shine with respect for her, the way they did when Kermon was mentioned. Joined forever by their arrowheads, by smithcraft. Mielitta hadn't even looked back when she'd rushed off to follow Jannlou, never once asked how she'd contact Drianne, whether Drianne would be all right.

Best not to think of that either.

And Arven was too caught up in some notion of destiny to see Drianne as anything other than a loose thread in his knitting. One he'd tried to put back into the pattern.

Yes, everybody else was indeed better at what she thought was important and they *had* let her down.

Drianne glanced at her knitted top and smiled. The rainbow colours glowed, undiminished. She felt the movement of the little frog beside her neck, singing silently, just like her. Hui was licking his paws after what seemed to be an adequate meal from his new servant, to judge by his expression.

So why wasn't she raging any more at the unfairness of life?

What if Qingzhao was right? What if most people feel the same way?

'Learning to be content with who you are and what you have is the hardest journey of any lifetime and the most rewarding. You will find that those who are most successful in the world's eyes have the greatest difficulty in accepting this truth. Wanting more is part of the human way, creating unhappiness.'

Drianne had started her journey but it was indeed hard. She could still feel the hurt from her friends' behaviour but each time she thought about how she'd been treated, she was finding it easier to let it go.

Had they meant to hurt her? No.
Did they care about her? Yes.

Were they following their own paths, their own feelings? Yes.

Had she ever hurt others? She thought of her parents, Perfect citizens who'd feared their own daughter's magecraft as much as her stutter. If they'd known of her other 'difference' they'd have reported her to the authorities. And yes, she'd hurt them. So she understood that people's paths clashed.

But it was a big step to accept that the woman she loved would never love her in return.

There, she'd said it, if only to herself. And she refused to be sorry for who she was. The Citadel alternative was too horrific to contemplate. She would have been some mute wife-servant to Bastien if Mage Puggy hadn't gifted her magecraft to Drianne in the Maturity Barn. The stones be thanked for Puggy's generosity! One day, Drianne hoped to pay her back, to learn from the older woman. She suspected they had more in common than Puggy realised.

Suddenly, Drianne felt sorry for Kermon, imagined how it must be for him. He too loved Mielitta in *that* way, had to watch her and Jannlou. He'd married Puggy to protect her and he must know now that she assumed a false plainness to keep men away. That she didn't have any of those feelings for men.

Drianne put her hand up to her cheek, felt the fine network of scars. She drew her finger down to her mouth, felt the stillness of one half of her face, the mobility of the other. Was that why she had done it? Spoilt the symmetry and drawn a spider's web over her clear skin?

She sighed. All she knew was that she looked more herself like this. And she would like to talk to Puggy about why.

The frog skittered about her neck, blowing rainbow bubbles and tickling her. Then it froze, eyes bulging, startled. As the noise increased in the farmyard, the frog pulled itself into the rainbow yarn and disappeared into the mesh of Drianne's top, part of the pattern again.

The chickens' clucking was louder than when scrapping for

corn. Drianne remembered when she'd first seen them, pecking up roots in the Forest. They'd surrounded her with soft chirrups of encouragement and escorted her to the farmhouse and they were still her companions, however much she learned about their society. That was just their nature.

There was a knock on the door.

So that's what the chickens were telling her! Visitors!

Hui miaowled a warning and jumped up onto the highest bookshelf he could reach, his green eyes glinting, wary.

A little apprehensive, Drianne opened the door; after all, Qingzhao *had* wanted her to make this a haven.

With relief, she saw who it was and welcomed them in with a genuine half-smile and open arms.

She gestured to the chairs but her guests remained awkwardly standing. Never mind, they'd relax once they had a nice cup of tea and some cake.

She picked up two cups from the dresser, waved them at her visitors, who just stared at her.

Never mind. They'd understand soon enough.

Humming silently, which made no odd shapes of her mouth, she headed towards the kitchen to put the kettle on the stove. Qingzhao had believed firmly in the power of a cup of tea.

It was a mystery why Mage Puggy had brought that strange girl with her, Bastien's sister. Verity. That was it. Shouldn't she be with Kermon, seeking the students in the walls?

Drianne peeked at them through the kitchen door. The mage was holding on to her young companion as if the girl might float away if she wasn't anchored.

Anchored. That was the word Kermon had used. Verity was his anchor, to help him return from the walls. And Puggy was Kermon's wife. How complicated people were. Drianne's stomach lurched and for the first time she wondered whether her hospitality would be up to the occasion.

She looked for pen and paper while waiting for the kettle to boil. She had so many questions, so much to say that her hands could not express.

Mielitta would be so pleased if Drianne made these two into allies. And she could. She knew she could. People were all the same underneath the skin and she already knew the common ground between her and Mage Puggy. And Verity was only a young girl. She was sure to be open-minded.

CHAPTER TWENTY-NINE

When Drianne carried the tea-tray back into the cosy family room, her guests were still standing like Citadel statues, staring at her.

And Puggy still clutched Verity by the arm.

Of course! Drianne suddenly realised. They were shocked by her remodelled face. How funny that she should frighten Citadel dwellers.

Drianne pointed to her face, gave her half-smile and mimicked magecraft to show it was her work. Like Puggy's use of glamour to change her from the seductive siren of her natural form to her preferred appearance.

Heedless of wasting magecraft, Drianne demonstrated on the plain wooden table, changing it to a hideously ornate one and then back to a serviceable piece of furniture.

Satisfied that all was now crystal clear, she poured the tea into Qingzhao's best china cups, decorated with roses and gold leaf. She set an example by sitting in the comfy armchair, taking her teacup and a large slab of chocolate cake. One advantage of being mute was that you didn't have to worry about manners regarding talking and eating at the same time.

She put the teacup down and held up the first of the notes she'd written, her handwriting rounded and careful. She turned the words outwards for Puggy to read and she placed her other hand on her heart, seeking the eyes of her benefactor.

Thank you for saving my life.

Puggy glanced at the note. 'That's as may be but I didn't die and I want back what's mine. Let me have my magecraft and we'll call it quits.'

'Where's the Freak?' asked Verity, glaring at Drianne.

Her hands dropped to her lap like lifeless birds and her rainbow knit wriggled down her arm to form a glove on her right hand. A glove that started to glow.

'Stop that, missy,' snapped Puggy, holding Verity so tight there must have been bruises but the girl merely tightened her lips, repeated her question.

'Where is *she*?'

Drianne pointed to the door, let her fingers walk uphill and downhill on the table. She feigned sleep and more walking. She looked defiantly at her visitors.

Long gone. Where you can't touch her. Her glove continued to glow, iridescent.

'Here's what we're going to do,' said Puggy. 'You let me reach into that sweet brain of yours and pluck out the magecraft that doesn't belong to you.'

Her smile was like a jagged row of rocks in a murky sea. 'I'll leave the bit that's yours. Promise. Woman to woman.'

She didn't wait for an answer. Drianne felt Puggy's magecraft poking and prodding at her hairline, pushing through her skin, just like when Rinduran had rendered her mute. She screamed her outrage. Silently.

How could the woman who'd been a victim of such violation, mentally and physically, do this to her? How could Verity just watch?

Let them watch this then!

Drianne gathered all her magecraft – yes, and all Puggy's donated magecraft too – and slammed a block against the invasion of her mind.

This gave her time to think but she'd been provoked beyond thought. She was incandescent with rage. Her glove glowed red then burst into flames as she drew deeply on her power. Arven had been wrong. She needed no warning to know how destructive she was going to be. And it felt good.

The energy whooshed through her body into the room, a life-seeking tornado with one aim.

Destroy Puggy! yelled Drianne in silent fury. The house shook from the force of a spiralling wind and the crash as it struck objects in its way. Furniture was smashed against the walls as the tornado whirled at Puggy and Verity. The girl was white-faced, trembling, unable to move, so tightly did Puggy grip her.

Too bad. She shouldn't have come with Puggy, thought Drianne, watching triumphantly, waiting for her power to smash into these invaders. Qingzhao would be proud of her, defending the homestead.

A comfy armchair lifted and flung itself at Puggy, hung in the air just short of the mage and gently settled on all four castors, back down on the carpet. Qingzhao's rocking-chair was not so lucky but whirled up into the demon wind and met its demise as matchsticks.

Hui yowled his pain, digging into books with his claws to stay on the bookshelf, his fur shocked upright and his eyes like saucers. The books, with Hui on top, slid along the shelf but didn't topple, poised like a sledge at the top of an icy slope.

Too late Drianne felt a pang of guilt and then the tornado hit Puggy.

Eyes shut, Drianne heard death arrive in the silence after the storm. She felt the rush of energy leave; her body now drained, on the point of collapsing.

'All done now, dearie?' asked Puggy.

Drianne's eyes snapped open and the two visitors stood there unharmed, though Verity looked green.

'You can't use my magecraft against me,' Puggy told her smugly.

'But–' Verity began, then bit her lip and said nothing.

'And as you've found out, you haven't got enough magecraft in you to overcome mine so if it's a fight you want, go ahead. Or you can just give up what doesn't belong to you.'

What a fool she was. Arven would be so disappointed that she'd learned nothing, that his gift had been wasted. Her knitted glove clung grey and lacklustre to her hand. She felt shame knock any vestige of fight out of her. What's the point of a fight you can't win?

'She shouldn't be forced,' Verity said in a quiet voice.

'That's up to her – she doesn't have to be,' retorted Puggy. 'But we haven't got all day. The stones know what's happening at the Citadel while we're here messing about and wasting time. I need to get back there sharpish, *with* my full powers.'

'What about me?' asked Verity, her voice so low Drianne had to strain to hear it.

'Well you can see the Freak's not here so there's not a lot you can do about that till she comes back. You can wait here, have a cup of tea.' Puggy sneered at Drianne, who flushed, remembering her naive welcome. She screwed up the rest of the notes she'd written.

'Or,' continued Puggy, 'you can come back to the Citadel with me and take your punishment.'

What punishment? Why? wondered Drianne.

'Let's get this done,' said Puggy. 'Last chance – tell me you are open. Or I'll force you.'

Drianne faced her future. The loss of all that sizzling energy. Once more the invisible little girl. She couldn't trust Puggy to leave her any magecraft at all. She looked at the whey-faced girl who'd been Kermon's anchor and a Chief Councillor. That's what would happen. She'd be like Verity, dispossessed.

Slowly she shook her head. She'd rather die fighting. Her knitted glove struggled back, flashed weak rainbows that strengthened as she focused on her friends. Mielitta's face when she'd thought Verity dead. Arven bringing her back from the brink of her own self-destruction. Kermon and Jannlou trying to give her magecraft lessons. That made her smile. Half-smile.

Her rainbow colours steadied, not blazing but controlled, preparing for battle. She *knew* her friends loved her and she would make them proud.

Puggy dropped her glamour, revealing the sensual physique she preferred to hide. Tall and graceful, with silken blonde hair, arched eyebrows, wide cornflower-blue eyes, symmetry of cheekbones, and full lips.

Good move, thought Drianne dispassionately, *saving all her magecraft for a battle.* Now that she'd regained self-control, she found she could observe both Puggy and herself coldly. She could see how Puggy's beauty would affect others, she knew Puggy was drawn to women and yet she felt no more attraction to this avatar of Puggy than to her pudding-faced plainness.

In her new state of objectivity, Drianne saw the flicker in Puggy's eyes, an inward look, as she gathered force for a strike.

Defence, with all her strength, was Drianne's only plan. If she could keep her shield up long enough, maybe she could turn her opponent's tactics against her, drain her strength. She gritted her teeth, felt the clash and rebound of strike against shield, clash and rebound, until her senses were numb and her colours faded like a rainbow in sunlight.

Her enemy was pulsing strikes, to an irregular rhythm, so that Drianne was using more power in maintaining a shield than Puggy in random attacks. Again and again, beyond human endurance.

Puggy smiled.

At the limit of her strength, Drianne looked to Verity, pleading with her eyes, but the girl was staring at the carpet, motionless, as if only her body were here while her mind travelled in a different world.

The world that could have been, thought Drianne. She would die of exhaustion rather than give up her magecraft. Let Puggy try to take it then!

But she could feel her opponent testing always for weakness, feeling for a way in, and her bravado faltered. Her glove was wearing thin, the strong yarn suddenly fragile and near to breaking-point. The knitted fabric gathered itself into a straggle-ended ball, rolled up her arm to hide against the pulse of her throat.

Drianne's attention reverted to her bared hand, to both her hands. They shook uncontrollably, as if they belonged to somebody else. The veins stood out, blue as rivers through the ridges of her gnarled bones. The canvas of skin stretched across this underlying structure was wrinkled and patchy with brown age spots.

The hands belonged to someone very old, someone so ancient she would soon die; should have died some time ago.

With growing horror, Drianne realised she'd drawn her magecraft from her own future, spending the energy of years to come, to preserve her now. And there was none left. The remaining strands of Arven's gift huddled against the last signs of life in her body, a pulse that weakened with every second.

Then, with an almighty crash, the books on Hui's shelf lost their struggle against gravity and slid off into thin air. The cat scrabbled madly but lost his purchase on flying books. He took an enormous leap in mid-air and landed on Puggy's neck, digging all sixteen claws in.

The mage screamed. Hui howled and attempted to attach himself more securely.

Instinctively, Puggy put both hands up to wrestle the cat off her neck, causing further damage to her skin to judge by her curses and shrieks.

Suddenly released from Puggy's grip, Verity moved out of reach.

'Strike her now,' she said, gliding to Drianne's side and taking her arm. 'I'm the shield. It's nothing to do with whose magecraft you're using. She lied as always. And now I'm *your* shield.'

Drianne didn't need to be told twice.

CHAPTER THIRTY

Through the rheumy eyes of an old woman, Drianne saw Puggy gather her magecraft for the final attack against her weakened shield. Facing the last moments of her life, she let go and dropped her shield completely. Either Verity was telling the truth or she would die anyway.

Clinging to the little life left to her, Drianne ignored her arthritic knees and crippled back, and attacked her enemy. The strike fell short, a damp squib incapable of even singeing Puggy's hair.

Then the full brunt of Puggy's force smacked Drianne – and rebounded. Just as her initial strikes against Puggy had done. The rebuff was tangible.

Unharmed, Drianne felt her waning spirits revive. Her frail colours stretched, limped down her arm, formed a lacy glove like a spider's work on her hand.

Like the network on her face. Another barely perceptible surge in her life force boosted her. While Verity held her arm and the impasse lasted, she could breathe and think.

Puggy kicked Hui out of her way and sidled towards them.

Of course, she planned a physical tussle to get Verity, and Drianne was too weak to stop her.

'Take strength from me,' said Verity. 'I am open.'

Puggy rushed the final yards between them, grabbed Verity and twisted her arm but the girl hung on to Drianne for dear life, lashing out at the mage with her feet and her free hand. She was no match for the curvaceous build of the mage either. Puggy might be seductive but she was also muscular and tall, in her prime, with all the advantages in a physical fight against a girl and an old crone.

But the girl was growing taller, her body filling out, her face becoming an oval with arched eyebrows and cynical mouth.

Hesitant at first, Drianne drew energy from Verity's future, watching the years fly past on the girl's face as she matured.

Enough! she told herself, as much afraid of doing damage as of losing Verity to Puggy's assault. Her glove had gained solidity, enough bright iridescence for her to do this. She would live long enough to tell Arven that his gauge had done good work.

She took a deep breath and hurled at Puggy every extra year she carried in her bones.

Take the arthritis! she screamed and Puggy buckled.

Take my cataracts, bunions and myopia!

Puggy put her hands up to her eyes and whimpered.

My arrhythmic heart and my unreliable digestive system!

Drianne flung every complaint of her ancient body at her opponent and watched Puggy's beautiful face crumple, curves sag and muscles hang loose in bags of skin. No mercy was expected and none asked.

But Verity was shaking and not from exertion.

Enough! Drianne told herself again. She touched Verity's arm gently, motioned her to sit down and this time, the girl – no, the woman – did as bid, picking up some crumpled paper on the chair.

Less gently, Drianne bundled Puggy into sitting position on the sofa and then she too settled into a big armchair, tucked her long, young legs up underneath her with all the flexibility of a young woman. Though still older than she'd been before this battle. As was Verity. If any more years had been passed onto Puggy, she'd have had the death sentence Drianne had narrowly escaped.

In silence, in a parody of the tea party Drianne had planned for her guests, the three of them sat there.

Puggy glanced at Drianne, as if for permission, then cast a glamour over her appearance. The familiar doughy face, dull brown eyes and shapeless body clothed the aged features and limbs. From now on, what was underneath would never attract unwanted attention.

With great deliberation, Drianne held up once more the note she'd prepared.

Thank you for saving my life.

She picked up the pen and wrote on the back of it, then showed it to Puggy.

All debts are paid. Go.

Puggy stared at the note and staggered to her feet. Dianne instinctively put out a helping hand, which was angrily rejected. The broken mage picked up a section of rocking-chair and fashioned it into a walking stick then made slow headway across the room.

Verity had been sitting very still and straight but she rose too.

Drianne pointed at the word *Go* and added a question-mark.

Verity shook her head, spoke to Puggy.

'Kermon and I brought you back to yourself from what they did to you. How could you of all people treat somebody else that way?'

Puggy shrugged. 'Politics,' she said, her voice quavering with age. She adjusted it to sound more like her usual northern bluntness. 'I want back all I had, not just the bits you and the traitor permitted. You'll be sorry when you see what Hamel does to your brother.'

Spite fuelled a little of her former verve. 'But you won't see it.

You can't go back there, can you?' She laughed then. 'Stuck with the freak you want dead and her defective friend.'

She turned to Drianne. 'Don't think that she understands women-lovers. Citadel through and through, she is. You should have some fine discussions. Except, oh dear. You can't speak, can you. Vile man, Rinduran, but he did a nice job on you.'

The door was too solid for Puggy to bang shut and it scraped to a close behind her as she hobbled out.

Verity was ashen, two red spots in her cheeks, and Drianne wasn't sure which words of the parting shot had stung Rinduran's daughter most.

'He even married you from kindness.' Verity choked out the words. 'When he could have married me.'

Only then did Drianne realise that Verity did not have Rinduran on her mind. And that Kermon's wife was now decrepit and even more venomous than before, thanks to her. No time to think about that now. What should she do about Verity?

Mielitta's would-be assassin sat down again, smoothed a piece of crumpled paper she'd been toying with. It was Drianne's turn to redden. Her notes, written for Puggy.

'Do you use glamour to stop men being attracted to you?' Verity read aloud, without expression.

Drianne snatched the note from her but Verity merely opened up another one and read that.

'Could two women live together as a couple and grow old together?' Verity read aloud, without expression.

Then she looked shrewdly at Drianne. 'This is about you, isn't it. You don't have to answer. I can tell you the answers. Puggy only loved Shenagra, who was Magaram's whore. She just used Puggy as an errand girl, to suppress people. Like that Archery Mage.'

Drianne's stomach turned.

'And secondly.' Verity fluttered the second note in the air. 'No. Two women can never be a couple. Not in the Citadel. Not anywhere.'

Deep down Drianne had known that but it hurt to hear the words spoken aloud. It hurt more than arthritis and a crooked back. She just wanted Verity to go but the woman sat there, in control, still speaking.

'But I don't have to like you for us to be allies. And vice versa. I think we've proved that. I want your help.'

Yes, they'd proved that. What would Mielitta want? What would Mielitta ask? *What's the target, Verity?*

Drianne wrote quickly on the blank back of a note and held it up.

Safety for Mielitta. Your word.

'You know I can't make a blood oath.' Verity shrugged. 'And I think we've had enough of those. But all right. Things have changed. I don't need the Freak dead. I won't kill her.'

Drianne glared at her.

'Or have her killed. My word on it as Chief Councillor of the Citadel.'

It would have to do. There was one piece of unfinished business between them before Drianne could find out what this alliance meant for her. She would not keep what she had stolen from Verity. Five future years must be paid back and she would have to age some more, lose that time. She scribbled the question and held it up.

Do you want me to take your extra years?

Verity shook her head vigorously. 'No thank you. We've been through a Maturity Test of our own devising, don't you think?'

Drianne nodded, relieved at not having to become any older than she was. Her glove sneaked over five fingers and rippled its rainbows. Yes, she was five years older than she'd started the day. And so was Verity.

'It suits me,' declared the Citadel's Chief Councillor. 'I shall be seen as a woman, not a little girl.'

Drianne wasn't sure whether she was thinking of the Council or a more personal relationship. If the latter, it was easy to guess who she was hoping to attract. But Puggy had said Kermon was a traitor? So they knew and he was in danger. And what did that mean to Verity? Too difficult to ask such questions in notes!

'And I'll get more respect when I take back my Citadel,' Verity concluded.

CHAPTER THIRTY-ONE

Verity passed through the cave wall into the Citadel, then let go of Drianne's arm so the disfigured mage could return to her homestead. A nod of understanding was an honest farewell between them and all that was needed. Honesty was rare in Verity's world and she would never rely on it.

The familiar echoes of footsteps and voices along stone passageways told her she was home and she sat down in the first niche she came to, before her legs could give way. In delayed reaction, her whole body shook as if freezing, although she knew the Citadel temperature was its usual Perfect ambience. Only the walls and her stone seat leaked cold, reminiscent of the Forest.

She'd done it! Revisited the Forest, the place of every child's nightmares, and come back unscathed. A pity that Mielitta had flown beforehand but killing was not the only way to vanquish an enemy, nor even the best revenge, now she'd had time to think. She'd negotiated an alliance that would give her all she desired and waiting was a payment she could afford.

She'd survived the trek through wing swoops and trees that chirruped, wildness of wind and crackling underfoot like mage-strikes. Noises everywhere and none of them human. Everything loomed or stalked. She'd walked through the striped, growling shadows of the Forest. Past the place where her father had been mauled to death. Now she could contemplate that scene as merely a stage in his passing beyond the wall. A violent stage but she was an adult now and violence was sometimes necessary. Expedient. An accommodating word. One Puggy had used to describe her suppression of Tannlei.

In some imaginary world, how she could crow over her defeat of Puggy; tell Kermon she could reinforce a mage even if she had no magecraft herself; tell Bastien how she'd overcome their Council opponent but no. Perfection *was* her world. She would treat them as they had her. She'd keep her confidences and wield her secrets as weapons. She adjusted the basket of more solid treasures that she hid under her cloak.

Drianne had been right. The path to the cave and crossing through the walls had been far quicker than wandering and backtracking through the Forest to reach the water gate as Puggy was doing now. Unless a tiger had put the old mage out of her misery.

Maybe Puggy had gained wisdom with her extra years but Verity doubted it. She'd mistaken Puggy's nature once and would never give her the benefit of the doubt again or be blinded by pity. Whether Puggy looked like a goddess, a frump or an old crone, she would always be a power-hungry egotist with less empathy than one of her make-up pots.

So ugly in her ageing! Verity shuddered. Thank the stones the Citadel culled those who'd reached an inappropriate age. It would be a blessing to Puggy to denounce her as too old to live. But that would not present Verity in the light she wanted for her next Council appearance, which was imminent. There was sure to be an ongoing meeting, with so much to discuss, and she was keen to present her new self to the Council. After some errands.

No, she wouldn't put Puggy out of her misery. Verity intended to let Puggy create her own misfortunes, as would no doubt be the case. The old mage no longer had the power to do any harm.

Walking through her Citadel, Verity swished her striped cloak, conscious of the way the garments underneath clung to her woman's body. Had there been any changes to her mind to match this maturity? She didn't feel different inside. Outside was another matter and she must see Mage Fabrisse, the seamstress, for some new clothes. Luckily, her cloak hid everything underneath, including her basket.

She nodded curtly to passing knights and ladies, as befitted her rank, then walked into the empty Great Hall and through to the kitchen. She looked under some of the covered trays, which had been prepared for mages who were in meetings or who preferred to eat in the peaceful surroundings of their own chambers rather than in the Great Hall. The nature of Citadel food meant that the mages could determine what it tasted like at their own whim. Hot, cold, meat, vegetable were all the illusions of magecraft and imagination.

She nodded approval at the identical sustenance and drink she saw underneath all the metal domes, then strutted about, snooping in the manner of one inspecting standards. She swirled her Chief Councillor's cloak a little, told the staff to ignore her and carry on with their work. Which they soon did, with only the occasional sideways glance to check her expression.

When she judged that her presence had ceased to be a novelty, she inspected some more of the covered trays, until she found an empty one. Under cover of the swirling cloak, she slipped the precious objects from her basket into the tray and then looked for a suitable messenger.

You could always rely on there being an unemployed servant in the kitchen who blended into the background. And indeed there was, a little boy rubbing his tired eyes and ignored by those bustling around him to prepare the evening meal.

'Boy,' she summoned him and took him into a quiet corner of the Great Hall to give him the tray and his instructions. He picked up a second tray and scurried off, one of the castle's invisible creatures.

Verity continued at a measured, dainty pace along the passageway, past the school and the mages' quarters, to the

Mages' Tower and up the spiral staircase to the Council Chamber. At one point she thought she could hear a strange noise, like buzzing, but when she shook her head, it disappeared. After-effects from being in the Forest and from wall travel, she told herself.

It felt very mature to name such places in a nonchalant way, if only to herself. After what she had been through in that hideously-furnished room, plus contact with wild beasts and a defective, she had every right to speak from experience on such matters. And if, as she predicted, her allergy did not come back, then she had triumphed over more evils than these petty little mages could even imagine. And she would never again be afraid of the Forest or its creatures. They could be useful.

Buoyed up by such thoughts, she opened the door to the Council Chamber without knocking and made her entrance.

'I heard you've been looking for me. I've come to give myself up. But you should hear what I have to say before you lock me up again.'

Her hopes of making an impression were even more successful than she'd hoped. The Councillors gazed at her in stunned silence, goggle-eyed and open-mouthed. Did five years really make such a difference in a girl?

Hamel was first to recover and he spoke to the Council not to her. 'Look at the traitor. The evidence is before your eyes now. She said she had no magecraft. She said she blocks all magecraft. And yet there she is, wearing a glamour that makes her look so different nobody can argue for her innocence.'

Verity doubted that anybody had tried but it was a pleasant thought.

'She lied about the blacksmith and she lied about her magecraft,' Hamel squeaked with anger and thumped the table.

Verity tried out her new, lower voice. 'The traitor is indeed in this room but it's not me. I have not changed at all. The glamour has been on all of you until now. You have seen me as a child when in reality I was a woman. It is not for me to say who placed that indirect curse upon me but I think it was somebody who wanted to discredit me, to keep the Councillors from taking me seriously.'

'This is preposterous!' Hamel barked. 'How did she get out of prison if not by magecraft?'

'It was indeed by magecraft. Mage Puggy kindly rescued me and has used too much strength I fear in lifting the glamour placed on all of you.'

'Where is Puggy anyway?' queried Yacinthe.

Hamel sputtered his innocence. 'But I was as surprised as the others at seeing the changes in you. If I had put a glamour on all, regarding how you appeared to them, I would not see you differently now.'

'I have no idea how glamour works. I'm not a mage.' Verity gave Hamel glare for glare. How satisfying to see the tables turned. 'I make no accusations. I leave it to the Council to consider how they've been duped and who might have a motive. And I do wonder whether a man with Perfect values might find me more suitable – and attractive – as a wife knowing that I'm a woman rather than a little girl.'

There were gasps and red faces around the table. And one face puce with anger and frustration. Hamel could hardly say he preferred a little girl.

Verity smiled. How satisfying to have the body that fitted her mind. They could put all the questions they liked but she could slide out answers that would slip into their suspicions and fill the cracks perfectly. And Puggy had too much at stake to ever contradict Verity's version of truth.

'Puggy too was misled,' Verity said sadly. 'Both as to my appearance and regarding Kermon. As I have tried to tell you, he has been following my instructions throughout. I commanded him to stay in contact with the freaks and they suspect nothing. He has done his work well and will be rewarded.

'I am so fortunate that when Puggy was removing her own glamour, in private, she accidentally took off the layer that included her false vision of me. As soon as she realised, she came to my aid. And she bitterly regrets implicating Kermon and playing into the hands of this scheming mage – whoever he might be.'

They were all listening and she knew Hamel wouldn't dare shut her up. Time to twist the knife.

She looked pensive. 'I wonder whether we could test loyalties, as in the days of Chief Mage Magaram–'

'Shenagra's dead.' Zora could always be trusted to state the obvious.

'Kermon is our soul-reader,' pointed out Fabrisse. 'If we get him back, he could do the job.'

Hamel looked sickly.

Verity merely nodded, not to overdo her act. 'Meanwhile we could allow our chambers to be searched, to prove our private lives are Perfect. I'm happy to go first.'

That should do it. And when Kermon came back, she would reinstate him for the sake of her own reputation, and use him as he'd used her.

CHAPTER THIRTY-TWO

Verity had accompanied the Councillors to give them access to her chamber. Then she excused herself, saying they could search more thoroughly without her there and she wanted to check that Mage Puggy was recovering from her exertions.

'You may wish to check my sickroom too,' she told them, 'but as that is locked from the outside, you don't need my permission.'

'Wait!' snapped Hamel, rifling through the clothes in her chest.

She shuddered. Thank the stones she intended replacing all her clothes as soon as possible.

'What if she warns Puggy?' Hamel said. 'We don't know what plot they'll hatch up together.'

The picture of hurt innocence, Verity suggested, 'Then send a witness with me.'

The relief was palpable as suspicion vied with the need to remain in the good books of whoever proved to be leader at the end of this investigation. Nobody wanted to offend Hamel or Verity until it was clearly their duty to do so.

'I'll go,' said Fabrisse, the seamstress mage. *Perfect*. Verity did not want someone thinking too much about the size of her clothes and the men wouldn't notice.

The two women duly walked along the corridor to Mage

Puggy's chamber, talking about fabrics and Verity's desire to refresh her wardrobe.

'Pastel shades would be just right for your pale skin and blonde hair.' Fabrisse was happily lost in gown designs as they reached the right room.

Verity knocked politely at the door and announced, 'It's Chief Councillor Verity and I've brought Mage Fabrisse. I've told the Council how much you've helped me and how exhausted you were after lifting the glamour the Citizens have been under. I can't tell you how glad I am that they all see me as I am at last, not as a little girl but as a woman. And all thanks to you. Do you feel we could come in for a minute and see how you are?'

The door opened as Puggy lifted the wards locking it. She was sitting at her mirror applying make-up. Whether to beautify or to uglify was not apparent to Verity but the face reflected in triplicate was recognisably the pasty-faced mage. And she did look exhausted.

Verity rushed to kneel at her feet and took her hands. 'Thank you,' she said. 'From the bottom of my heart, thank you. You've lifted the glamour from everyone's sight and they now see me for who I truly am.'

'Is that what I've done?' Puggy stared at Verity. 'Well, well. I certainly feel as tired as if I've worked enough magecraft to open the eyes of every Citizen to what's going on here.'

'You have,' Verity assured her, starry-eyed with hero worship. 'I bet you feel a hundred years older!' She paused to make sure Puggy had received the threat. 'But tomorrow you will be back to normal and able to join us at the Council.'

Puggy nodded grimly, her eyes sharp as Fabrisse's bodkins. 'Business as usual then.'

'Oh yes,' said Verity, releasing Puggy's hands and standing up. 'But you must rest today. Mustn't she, Mage Fabrisse.'

'You don't look well, I must say,' murmured Fabrisse. 'I'll get a potion sent to you to help you sleep and recover.'

'Don't trouble yourself. I just need a sleep and a think.' Puggy didn't look at Verity but she muttered, 'Glad it worked out for you.'

Smooth as glass and dangerous as shards, Verity repeated, 'All thanks to you. And I will always remember what you did.'

Softly, as if to avoid waking a sleeping baby, she added, 'Let's go now, Fabrisse, and let Mage Puggy rest.'

The door swung open in a jerk and they almost tiptoed out into the passageway.

Fabrisse looked in awe at Verity. 'What she did for you really took it out of her. Such a brave woman.'

'Yes,' said Verity, thinking *I am*. 'Let's join the others. I'd like to be there when they search Hamel's chamber as he was so thorough in mine.'

Fabrisse led the way, in a half-hearted attempt to fulfil her role as prison warder, Verity supposed.

'Mage Puggy is indeed looking exhausted,' Fabrisse announced to the mages turning over the few items in Hamel's chamber.

They seemed less interested in his clothing than he'd been in hers, noted Verity. Her own eyes went straight to the two food trays, still covered by metal domes. She hoped somebody else would suggest looking at their contents.

The seamstress mage finished her report, 'And she confirmed everything the Chief Councillor told us regarding the glamour we've been under. I saw with my own eyes how much power Mage Puggy had used.' She shook her head. 'I've never seen a mage so drained and still alive. No wonder Chief Councillor Verity is so grateful.'

Aloof, observing without touching any of Hamel's possessions, Verity waited.

Yacinthe flicked through the library book beside the bed and checked under the pillow. *Time Management for Busy Mages* was hardly seditious. Nor was anything about the regulation nightshirt and bedding. Had she married Hamel as had been arranged, her bed would have been the twin of this, in the married quarters.

She asked helpfully, 'Have you looked under the bed?'

Hamel shot a venomous look at the incredibly grateful Chief Councillor.

But there was nothing under the bed.

Three of the mages had given up looking and there was an atmosphere of relief, an unspoken, 'Thank the stones, we've found nothing,' when Yacinthe, the Library Mage, asked, 'Why are there two food trays?'

Hamel shrugged. 'The kitchens kindly sent me breakfast for tomorrow, as well as tonight's meal, knowing I'm too busy at the moment to waste time in the Great Hall.'

'What a good idea. I might ask for a breakfast. What do they usually send?' Yacinthe asked.

'Much the same as for evening meal,' replied Hamel drily, 'sustenance and a drink. But whatever is provided, any mage worth his salt, will taste only the best quality of produce.' He smiled at his own cleverness. 'I usually favour an apple and some toasted oats to break my fast in the morning.'

Verity looked interested and respectful, as a non-mage would.

Yacinthe lifted the dome from one tray. Underneath was indeed sustenance and a drink labelled 'red wine.'

The other mages had no interest in such trivia and were shuffling impatiently, obviously feeling this was a waste of time.

'Whose chamber next?' asked Fabrisse

'I'll just look at this one too and see if the only difference is how the drink's labelled,' said Yacinthe.

Verity silently congratulated the Library Mage on her curiosity and perseverance.

The dome was duly removed and then dropped on the floor with a loud clatter as Yacinthe shrieked and drew all eyes.

'May the stones be with us and protect us! That's never come from the Citadel kitchens.'

Verity leaned in with the others to try and see what was on the tray but there were too many mages in too small a space. Hamel was trying to fight his way through to the tray but Yacinthe and

Zora held him back, ignoring his protests that he had no idea what was going on.

'For Perfection's sake, woman, tell us what is there!' Fabrisse shouted, trapped behind a view of three heads.

Still restraining Hamel, Yacinthe steadied herself and in a shaky voice itemised: 'Two hens' eggs; two bread rolls that smell–' the shock permeated her voice '–freshly baked; a slab of butter, a bottle containing goat's milk, a little pot of honey and a pot of yoghurt. One mug. One teapot. Wait a minute now, I have to read the labels.'

In the pause, the only sound was the heavy breathing of the mages as they contemplated the crime.

'And four packets of tea-leaves, labelled Broken Orange Pekoe; Earl Grey; Darjeeling and Green Tea. A twist of salt. A twist of sugar. One knife, one plate, one teaspoon.'

Hamel's eyes looked like those of the frog Verity had seen peep out of Drianne's knitted glove before it hid again during the mages' battle: bulging, scared, ranging the room and settling nowhere. Until Hamel fixed his gaze on Verity.

'She did it,' he spluttered. 'It's got to be her.'

Fabrisse shook her head. 'That's a false accusation. There's no way Chief Councillor Verity could have got into your chamber even if she had such objects in her possession. And these come from the Forest.'

The atmosphere in the room darkened and there was no dissent, except from Hamel, pleading desperately.

'Don't you see, it's a glamour. You're all seeing what's not there, just like you did with her. This is just sustenance and drink, as always. It must be.'

'Somebody will have to test it,' declared Yacinthe. 'Glamour has no taste.'

'But a mage will taste what he wants to like Hamel said.'

'I'll taste it,' said Verity.

'No, not her,' screamed Hamel.

'I'll taste it,' said Zora. 'I'm no mage and I am on nobody's side but Zeebo's.'

There was some envy in the mages' eyes as they watched Zora put butter on the roll, then jam.

'I ought to test it all,' she said. 'Could you boil some water?'

Yacinthe used magecraft to boil water in the teapot. Then Fabrisse dropped the eggs into the teapot, asked the water to boil until they were soft but cooked and then evaporate. At this point, the eggs were lifted out and some fresh water boiled, to which Earl Grey tea-leaves were added.

Then two Councillors, salivating, watched Zora eat Hamel's breakfast, while he denied all wrong-doing. Verity watched in silence.

Zora wiped her mouth, remembered to be disgusted.

'That,' she declared, 'was Forest food. No glamour at all! I'm going straight to my room to take a powder in case I'm infected with some vile disease. Deal with him as you must.'

'You were so brave, testing that,' Verity murmured to Zora and squeezed her hand. 'I do hope you'll be all right.'

'I hope so too!' The words were grim but her eyes said, 'It was worth it!'

Verity smiled to herself. It was indeed worth it.

CHAPTER THIRTY-THREE

Kermon missed Verity: the person she was, not just the way her power complemented his. Her trust in him was the most precious thing in his life. Once more he swore that he would do his duty by his students and by Mielitta, then lead an honest life as Verity's Right Hand.

First, he had to find the students. He was sure he was following the story that had called to Janette, the story that would lead to Mielitta's birth. He needed to follow the thread quickly so Verity couldn't interrupt his work when she returned with reinforcements.

He'd followed a man in a suit, Oliver, watched him persuade two warriors to donate a hair each for some mysterious purpose. Dark magecraft, Kermon supposed. Now the same transaction was being negotiated with a third warrior and Kermon could not afford the time. He had to get ahead of Janette and Nathan, wait for them at the story's end, which meant predicting the next few episodes and skipping them.

He was a Mage-Smith, not a storyteller, so how was he supposed to know what happened next? What if Janette had done the same thing and was too far ahead of him? Surely she'd go back to the Citadel after she found the story's ending, if only to reveal to the Council how they could interfere with Mielitta's life. Kermon was sure his students would see the Queen of the Warrior Bees as Perfection had taught them: the enemy, infected with Forest. He had never dared challenge such assumptions directly and his encouragement of critical thinking had shown little result, unless you counted a headstrong girl dashing off on a story-finding mission.

Nathan was sensible, though. Apart from rushing off after Janette. And he *was* trying to protect her, so with any luck the story was in Janette's head and the two youngsters had gone back through the wall to safety. And he would be waiting fruitlessly at the story's end until Verity arrived. At least he would have time to protect Mielitta. If he hurried.

How would the story continue? Oliver would no doubt collect some more hairs from more warriors and Kermon could definitely miss seeing that. At some stage he would do something with the hairs.

'Show me what Oliver does with the hairs,' Kermon ordered. Sure enough, the scene shimmered, then cleared.

Oliver was rolling the hairs into a ball. Then he put them back into his little pouch. Then nothing. He had vanished and there were only misty hints of the different time layers in this place, wherever it might be.

The walls were playing their tricks.

Kermon would have to be more specific. 'Oliver' alone wasn't enough.

The story had started with Qwian and her vision; with bees – but they were long gone. Oliver had visited the village and asked for Mahamauri to come with him but Kermon hadn't seen her with Oliver since that day. Where was she? What if her purpose was linked to the hairs?

He tried again. 'Take me to the place where Oliver uses the warriors' hair and Mahamauri is present.'

The scene wavered again before settling into a view of the walls, stark and solid in contrast to the shifting sands in front of them. Only wind-carved patterns and dunes and patterns gave the illusion of landmarks to the ever-changing desert. Nobody was in sight.

Kermon sighed. So this was the place, anonymous, the sands shifting like time. He needed to be more specific.

'And to the time when Oliver uses the warriors' hair and Mahamauri is present.'

No wavering. Just the sound of voices, then sand swirling around two walkers. Oliver and Mahamauri. Kermon had expected something momentous but the two of them just continued over the sands to the wall and pulled out a stone to reveal a cachette.

They were probably going to leave the pouch of hairs there, guessed Kermon. But why?

Maybe this had nothing to do with Qwian's vision of her descendant. Or maybe Mahamauri was the descendant in the vision and this had nothing to do with Mielitta.

Oliver put his palm on Mahamauri's stomach then curved his hand as if he were pulling a ball from her body.

Kermon winced. Dark magecraft indeed. But the young woman showed no sign of pain or even of irritation. She took back whatever the object was, held it in two hands with reverence, kissed it and placed it in the darkness of the cachette.

As expected, Oliver retrieved the ball of hair from his pouch but then he pulled a hair from his own head, binding the warriors' locks with his own contribution, murmuring as he did so.

Kermon reached out with his mind to hear the words spoken, soft as a kiss.

'We send you like an arrow into the future, with love and hope. May the stones nurture you always.'

The formula made Kermon uneasy and he was even more

convinced that this was dark magecraft, some form of Perfection that was even worse, another evil in the walls.

The strange gift was placed on top of the other object in the cachette.

'Kermon!' His own name jolted him out of his thoughts.

'Verity?' was his instinctive response and he cursed his stupidity when he realised that his arrowhead pendant was thrumming with power.

'Mielitta,' he corrected himself, knowing how irritated she would be, and rushing his words. 'I tried to contact you. I didn't think it worked in the walls. Where are you? What's happening?'

Her voice was brusque. 'I think it works now because I'm in your world. Arven and I came through the walls. Have you found the students? Is Jannlou with you?'

It was obvious which question had more importance for her and he felt less guilty.

'No. I haven't seen Jannlou. I think Janette and Nathan will come here. I'm watching the end of the story she was chasing so they'll follow it to the same place.'

'How are you ahead of them? Oh, never mind. It's easier if we can see each other and talk. I can follow the twinning signal from Perfection Unfinished. Make a mind map, and we'll be with you in a twinkling.'

Typical Mielitta. She didn't stop to ask whether he thought she and Arven *should* come here or what the dangers were. She was on her way and that was that. Brave, impetuous, imperious and beautiful. And Jannlou's. He sighed. But the sigh lacked something it used to express.

Did he still love Mielitta or did he have the habit of thinking he loved Mielitta?

No time for that now. Something very strange was happening by the wall.

The interior of the cachette glowed amber, looking like a cell in one of Mielitta's honeycombs, lighting the two objects within. Unravelling like a ball of wool, the hairs separated, sparkled and burrowed into the ovoid below, which grew brighter and brighter in the fusion.

Mahamauri stood with her head bowed as if in prayer and Oliver's head was flung back in what might be effort or ecstasy.

'What's happening?'

Mielitta was standing beside Kermon, bow on her shoulder and quiver slung around her waist, exactly as he remembered her. Golden skin, red hair straight as a waterfall, down to her waist. Black eyes flashing in impatience. They hadn't seen each other since he'd sacrificed his life in the Forest and returned to the Citadel on *her* mission. And she couldn't even spare him a greeting.

He looked sharply at her, then realised she was clutching Steelwing as if her life depended on it and the other hand was clenched around an arrow. She was hiding her fear behind the casual tone. And he knew what she was afraid of. After all, he was the one who'd warned her that the story had something to do with her parentage.

He prised one hand off the arrow and held it, squeezed and felt the pressure returned.

'I don't have room in my head,' she said, 'or the words for you, for this.' She gestured at the wall.

He accepted the implicit apology and kept hold of her trembling hand while he acknowledged Arven.

The beautiful profile was unreadable. He was one of them because he was Tannlei's son and yet not quite one of them.

'I know it's too much,' Kermon said. 'Arven knows that too. We can talk properly later.'

'Yes.' She clutched his hand as she had the arrow and he understood just how little room she had left for more worries, more responsibilities.

'What's happening?' she repeated.

As they watched, the wall began to breathe, bulging outwards and then curving away from them. The rhythm made a comforting bump, a protective refrain.

I will nurse you, I will nurse you, was what Kermon heard but he wasn't going to tell the others that.

The glowing ovoid began to pulse too, a baby version of the wall's beat.

A baby version.

'I think,' said Kermon, 'we're watching your conception.'

CHAPTER THIRTY-FOUR

Jannlou instinctively began to shift into bear form as the dark mass of a nebulous Rinduran towered over him, with the girl's body still visible at the core.

'I know nothing,' he growled, preparing to fight to the death – his death, undoubtedly. But he would not give his enemy the satisfaction of one word that might endanger Mielitta. He'd unwittingly betrayed Kermon to the Citadel and wouldn't make the same mistake now, whatever Rinduran tried.

The mage threw darkness around them so dense that, even with bear vision, Jannlou could no longer see Nathan huddled on the ground. He desperately tried to remember what Kermon had said about Rinduran's powers in the walls but nothing helpful came to mind. The revenant obviously still had magecraft. And the Mage-Smith had said nothing about the possibility of his students being possessed – or muted. Like Drianne had been.

Crush him! his bear nature urged and he reared up on his hind legs, sniffing out the evil. He charged towards the black stench and then screamed as his fur caught fire. He dropped to the ground and rolled, batting with his paws at the sparks until his palms were raw. The stink of singed pelt told him the flames were out and he let the battle fever course through him, dulling pain that must wait its time.

He charged again, almost ripped into the little human body with teeth and claw but realising just in time what Rinduran was using as a shield. Jannlou swerved, narrowly missing Janette, who was waved in front of him like a rag doll, her eyes glazed.

'You missed,' taunted Rinduran. 'Such a pity. I can use other bodies you know, when I tire of being a shade.'

Jannlou's heart thumped. Not his, surely. His second nature would keep out such an intrusion. Or would it?

If he was in bear form perhaps but what if he were human? He didn't want to find out and he hurled himself at the obscene duo of blackness and lolling girl, trying to snatch Janette out of Rinduran's grasp. The mage just dangled her ever higher, above Jannlou's reach, so high that falling would kill her.

Always a failing of Rinduran's. He toyed with an enemy, enjoyed torturing more than winning. He wasted time. His milky eye was white in the darkness and an army of shadowy hands spread out from his form like debris from a tornado but Jannlou did not look away. If this was to be his sole act of defiance then so be it. He would not look away from approaching death, however it came.

He charged again, leapt towards the girl with claws sheathed. She should know kindness before she died.

'Janette,' he yelled but the sounds came out as grunts and growls. 'We are all here for you. Kermon, Mielitta, Arven, all of us. We will not let you die! There will always be more of us!'

Rinduran made mock growling noises and gathered himself for a strike while Janette flopped around unresponsive in mid-air.

But somebody *had* felt Jannlou's intentions. Nathan hauled himself to his feet, grabbed a handful of singed fur and made the appalling noises that had embarrassed Jannlou before he realised the truth. Now he could cry at the poignancy of what the boy suffered for Janette's sake.

It was true. They were all here for Janette.

Nathan stood tall, faced Rinduran and slobbered his own defiance. He was only half Jannlou's bear height and both of them were tiny beside the howling whirl of blackened sand that blocked out the sky but his courage was beyond measure.

They staggered awkwardly in the sand towards the monster to try again to reach the girl. And to keep trying.

The strike had not come. The towering black cloud was shrinking back into itself, back into Janette, who drifted down, until her feet touched the ground, though her legs did not support her. Rinduran's eyes looked through hers.

The girl's mouth said, 'Bastien! In this world! I must go to him, bring him here. Everything is Perfect now!'

Rinduran brought his attention back to Jannlou. 'I can find this vessel, anywhere, in any time.' He looked with contempt at the crumpled girl. 'I can be inside her whenever I want. But you could get away. If you leave her.'

The creeping shadows withdrew so suddenly that Jannlou blinked in the brightness and Janette slumped to the ground.

Her friend rushed to her side, helped her sit and took a water bottle out of his backpack, dripped some on her lips, waited.

Jannlou grunted something and received a blank stare from the boy.

Stupid! He shifted back into human form, said, 'We have to go, now, while he's away.'

Nathan thumped his own chest and pointed to Janette. If Jannlou had wondered about leaving her, the thought was gone before it took hold.

'No,' he said gruffly. 'We're not leaving her. I'll carry her.' He bent to pick her up and felt his clothes snag on burned skin, catch fire again with pain. He gritted his teeth and took up the burden.

When Janette opened her eyes, he nearly dropped her. She blinked and stared at him. Big brown eyes. No trace of blind hatred or a bee sting, just confusion.

'I can walk, you know,' she told him haughtily.

Jannlou put her down.

'And I think we should watch the end of the story now. I want to see what happens with all the warriors' hair and with that honey hunter and Oliver. I just know it has something to do with the Queen of the Warrior Bees and we'll be able to get rid of her! Oh, and who are you anyway?'

Jannlou exchanged glances with Nathan, who shrugged. Maybe it was for the best that the girl remembered only the story. But they had little time before Rinduran returned with Bastien and his minions. Should he try to explain to Janette what would happen then?

'Kermon sent me to help you,' he said shortly.

'I don't need helping and you should call him Mage-Smith Kermon. You're not a mage. You're not even properly dressed.'

Jannlou wondered what she'd have thought of him in bear form if she considered leather jerkin, britches and a sword improper. His clothes were somewhat weathered by life in the Forest but serviceable.

They had no time for this!

'Take us to story's end,' pronounced Janette imperiously.

They were in the same place but there was a glowing cachette in the wall and Oliver and Mahamauri stood in front of it

And in front of *them* were Mielitta, Kermon and Arven.

CHAPTER THIRTY-FIVE

'Rinduran's coming – with Bastien!'
'Jannlou!' Mielitta dropped Kermon's hand in a guilty reflex but she saw no darkening of the blue eyes she could read so well.

Her warrior strode towards her, grasped her hand and placed it firmly back in Kermon's. 'We all need each other.' He studied her face, grunted, and she wondered what he read there. But it was to Kermon he spoke.

'You don't carry this burden alone now.' He clasped the Mage-Smith in a warrior's embrace and Mielitta took the chance to disentangle her hand again, no longer from fear of being misunderstood but because the priorities had changed. Though many questions remained.

'Arven!' Jannlou greeted the fourth of their company with a gentler embrace. Something about Arven conveyed fragility even when you knew his combat skills were superior to any of the others', even without magecraft.

'Tell him, Mielitta,' Arven insisted. 'This is important too.'
Jannlou looked a question.
The seer's words were not to be taken lightly and she stuttered, 'Kermon thinks–' and she gestured at the pulsing object; the

glowing cell; the walls that breathed steadily, in and out; the man and woman with bowed heads in front of it. No words came. She didn't understand what was happening.

'It's dark magecraft,' explained Kermon. 'The woman has placed an egg in the cell.'

Like brood, Mielitta's bees commented. She wished they'd stay quiet.

'And,' continued Kermon, 'the mage, Oliver, has fertilised the egg with hairs donated by him and the warriors. The baby forming in the walls must be Mielitta. You know how she came into the Citadel.'

'I was in a basket,' objected Mielitta, wincing at Kermon's crude presentation of events. An interpretation she did not accept. 'With my name on a label. In normal baby clothes. With two normal parents. I just don't know who they are, that's all. I was born in the normal way and came through the walls into the Citadel.'

Which warriors? she wondered simultaneously, but she didn't ask. She had a horrible feeling she knew the answer.

Instead, she focused on the two small figures, who'd arrived with Jannlou and who were staggering with fatigue. Could they be…?

'Janette! Nathan!' Kermon rushed over to his students, Jannlou at his side.

'Be careful, Kermon,' Jannlou cautioned, taking a deep breath before telling them. 'When Rinduran comes, he will be in the girl's body.'

The Mage-Smith flinched as if he'd been struck, more horrified and less surprised than Mielitta would have expected.

Jannlou must have seen the reaction too. 'You know, don't you,' he said, searching Kermon's face. 'You knew that Rinduran could possess somebody. You knew because–'

'Yes,' said Kermon quietly. 'He held my mind subject to his.' He looked at them wild-eyed. 'But not now. Not since Verity shielded me.'

Arven insinuated his slight presence between Kermon and the two students. 'I took your place with the students. I know how you feel about them and how they feel about you. Nobody could have done better work than you in the Citadel. Let me share your burden now. You shall never face the evil in the walls on your own, never again. I promise.'

Jannlou reached out and clasped Kermon's arm. 'And I.'

Mielitta spoke for her bees, for the Forest, for herself. 'We all swear to it!'

Slowly, Nathan drew himself up, not leaning on the wall nor on the warrior beside him. He grunted and slobbered, his eyes filling with tears of frustration.

'Nathan gives his oath too,' said Jannlou, clasping the boy's arm in the same warrior's grip he'd given to all. 'Rinduran took his voice, fouled his best friend and he stands with us.'

The boy stood taller.

Arven dug into his cloak and pulled out two knitted bracelets, each in different colour-weaves. He put one on Nathan's wrist, where it tightened into a perfect fit.

'Your fellow students made these in class for you,' he said. 'To show you we care, to bring you home safely.'

Then he turned to Janette, stooped to put the other bracelet on her wrist. But there was something wrong. Mielitta could see the change in the girl's expression, from confusion to cunning, from true to feigned.

Arven seemed oblivious to the change, was reaching down towards Janette with a multi-coloured knitted bracelet as shadows sloped out of the girl's body, sneaking their smoky fingers around behind the seer.

'Arven!' Mielitta yelled. 'He's here.'

Janette jumped to her feet, blank-eyed, a swirl of darkness at her core and emanating outwards, encircling Arven. He'd been moving so softly and slowly that his sudden vertical leap was unexpected, drawing all eyes up to an impossible height, giving pause even to the darkness. Janette pointed upwards and the shadows surged in pursuit of the seer like hounds scenting blood.

Flipping as quickly as a page in a book, Arven dived down, placing the bracelet exactly over Janette's outstretched hand and somersaulting to land on his feet, as if he'd slowed time to allow such gymnastics. Mielitta had perfected trick shots and acrobatic turns but she could not imagine how any human could defy gravity like this. Or even have the temerity to try.

For a second, Arven was on his feet, so close to Janette he could barely be seen in the obscurity spreading from her core. Her hand was still outstretched, the rainbow bracelet adjusting its fit, tighter than a handcuff.

Then she screamed, shaking her wrist. The knitted circlet caught fire, burned like rubber in oil, emitting a foul stench and black smoke above the melding colours.

The scream started at a man's pitch, rose higher as the shadows writhed in agony, pulling at the bracelet, which clung like a second skin.

As if Rinduran had the same thought, he blasted the wrist with magecraft until Janette's arm was peppered with burns. Still the bracelet held, though Janette's arm was charring and the odour of burned flesh made Mielitta want to gag.

Just when it seemed her ears would burst, the screaming changed. From demonic to human. A girl's anguished cry, then sobs, as the darkness left Janette, slithering across the sands out of reach, stirring up clouds of dust.

Arven dropped to the girl's side, inspected her arm, said, 'I'm so sorry. Mielitta?'

She already knew what was needed but how?

Call them, urged her bees. *They will come.*

Mielitta focused on her sigil until the queen bee glowed golden and she could hear industrious buzzing. She pictured the bee swarm, building their hive high up in their cleft outside the Mages' Tower.

'I need honey!' she told them, dancing the extreme hunger of winter and making mind maps that showed the route in the Citadel and through the wall. If the walls permitted such a traverse.

'Fly high and fly safe!' she bade them, then turned her attention to present dangers.

Kermon was holding the semi-conscious girl while Nathan looked on, bubbling and frothing his own hurt.

'We have no magecraft here,' Kermon explained to his students, 'but some artefacts seem to work. Our arrowheads still communicate.' He showed them Perfection Unfinished and pointed to its twin around Mielitta's neck.

'And it seems these have power too, thanks to Mage Arven and your friends,' said Kermon. He gently touched the blackened scrap of fabric embedded in Janette's skin.

'You're safe now, from… him. In *that* way. I know Janette is in pain but the arm will heal.' He hesitated, looked at Mielitta and she shook her head. She didn't know whether the bees could come. The walls had denied her often enough. She glanced at them now, a cocoon around a fertilised egg. She looked away.

'I can still reach somebody's mind.' Kermon spoke slowly. 'Share the pain, make it easier for you. If you want me to, Janette? I know what it's like. Somebody in your mind. It's your choice.'

Her words came faint as a bird's breath. 'I am open.'

Kermon nodded. 'Mielitta, all of you, Rinduran has changed since he… since I… during these last few months. Then, he looked as he did in the Citadel. Now, he's amorphous. As if he's gathered others like him, dark forces here in the walls. I don't know what this means for his powers.'

Janette tried to suppress a groan and Kermon murmured something to her.

'My duty is to my students,' he said. 'May the stones be with you.'

'And with you,' Mielitta replied automatically. She remembered Kermon speaking for Drianne when the girl had returned mute from the walls, knew the strain it was for him to merge with another in this way, even before he'd been violated. But each of them must do what she or he could, whatever the personal cost.

'They will try to kill you at birth.' Jannlou's words merely stated what they all knew was coming.

'You may return to your tribe.' Oliver's voice was startling, too loud in the silence of waiting.

Mielitta had to remind herself that these people were of another time and would be unaffected by anything that happened now. Unlike the baby in the wall, between worlds. For she was starting to accept that there was a baby.

She shivered as Mahamauri stepped through her as if she were an open wall.

Mother, she thought, painfully aware of the honey hunter's muscular frame, long straight hair, graceful poise and bare feet. She walked with a tribal sway. Her back view would be etched in Mielitta's mind forever, a swathe of her robe wrapped over her head against the dust. The pattern of her feet in the sand. Walking away.

Mielitta did not move. Her place was here, with her comrades.

As Mahamauri disappeared through the sandstorm, the air began to clear, revealing thirteen figures, all cloaked, all Citadel mages. Around them lay swirls of darkness, emanating from a black tower of twisting, transformed sand. The revenant's new form.

'Bastien is come,' breathed the voice they all knew too well. 'And I shall be master of two worlds now.'

CHAPTER THIRTY-SIX

Black grit flew into Mielitta's eyes, blinding her. She doubled up, shielding her face with her hands, desperately seeking some way of covering her head, as the honey hunter had done.

'Use this.' Arven's disembodied voice was followed by a ripped fragment of his cloak, big enough to wrap around her head and face. She sheltered her eyes with a band round her forehead.

'He's out there, stirring up dust devils,' Arven shouted above the grinding sand. 'But I don't think he can do anything more. His magecraft is weak when disembodied. Just hold firm.'

Mielitta shut her eyes, feeling the scrape of sand against any bare skin, battered by the screeching tornado, but not bowed. She was no longer the girl whose doubts gave the darkness a way in. Her inner light shone like the glowing cell in the wall. She was Jannlou's life partner as he was hers. She had loyal comrades, friends, her bees. If she had to stand here patiently waiting for Rinduran to wear himself out, then she could even do that, trusting the others to do their part.

After a lifetime of swirling abrasion, the noise diminished enough for Mielitta to hear the clash of swords, the shouts and grunts of men fighting. Gradually the sand particles dropped to the ground. The black shadows gathered themselves, left her so they could add their might to Bastien's forces. She was already nocking an arrow as she took stock of their battle position. Hopeless was an optimistic assessment. Jannlou, Arven and herself against thirteen mages and Rinduran.

Kermon was out of action, holding Janette, sitting in a huddle beside the wall, with Nathan standing in front of them, his bare fists clenched, ready to punch an attacker.

The last line of defence, thought Mielitta, a sour taste in her mouth. She should have sent the children back through the walls.

Bastien watched from the rear, probably not from cowardice. Like her, he was assessing the situation. The amorphous black shadow that was Rinduran and his appendages spread over the sands, inching towards the combat. Arven and Jannlou were impossibly outnumbered but none of the Citadel mages was prepared to risk coming within the lethal and unpredictable sweep of their blades. Jannlou held his position by skill and reach with a sword while Arven somersaulted, stabbed with both needles and reappeared behind or beside a bemused enemy. But they could only postpone the inevitable.

What then? Mielitta wondered. Only Rinduran had magecraft. If he wasn't using it, maybe he couldn't. Or, as Arven thought, not in this shapeless state. Could he occupy one of theirs? The students and Arven were protected by their wristbands. The warriors were not of this world so maybe they were inviolate but what about Kermon and Jannlou? If Rinduran could have blasted into *her* mind, he would have done so with the sandstorm.

What's the target? she asked herself. She couldn't risk hitting one of her own and firing at the blackness would waste an arrow.

In the timeless calm before action, she suddenly knew the target.

Focus on the target not on the arrow. Line up the two by pointing not aiming. Use your finger to point until you can do it in your mind's eye. See the arrow in your peripheral vision, see the line between the two, let your body make the trajectory. How she missed Tannlei!

She'd tried to explain her teacher's words to Jannlou in the

Forest, skipping stones into a pool. 'You don't look at the stone, do you. It's the same!' But he always looked at the arrow. And missed.

Mielitta pointed to the target in her mind's eye, let fly the arrow that would kill Bastien.

Then yowled a war cry of rage and frustration as Jannlou stood between her and his boyhood friend, her arrow protruding from the shield he'd taken from a defeated mage.

'I swore an oath to him,' Jannlou shouted at her as he whirled around, avoiding a knife in the back from Bastien. 'We'll find another way.'

No honour, thought Mielitta bitterly. If only that were true, her life would be easier.

She loosed an arrow into a mage who presented an easy target now Jannlou had moved. He fell instantly, as Bastien should have. One arrow should have ended this. Her harsh thoughts were echoed by an unlikely source.

'It's a weakness, son,' rasped a voice dry as the sands from which it emerged. 'Use it. Kill the bear. You can get near to him.'

Jannlou had indeed shifted shape. The two mages nearest him barely had time to cower before they were gouged to death. Roaring, Jannlou attacked three more mages, who had no chance against the blood madness that had swept over the warrior. As if he were compensating for blocking Mielitta's attack but still avoiding Bastien.

Mielitta nocked another arrow, starting to hope. The bear had reduced the odds, given them a chance, and was still throwing his might against the enemy, indefatigable.

Then the first dead mage filled with a creeping hand of darkness and rose up to fight again. And the second. And the third. Until all were marching against Mielitta's forces, regardless of missing limbs or slit throats. Their blood no longer flowed and their eyes were as dead as their smoky bodies but still they walked towards the wall, slashing at anyone in their way.

Jannlou stood on his hind legs and roared three times. The

sound, raw and brassy, rang across the vast sands, as challenging and insistent as a hunting horn.

And the enemy rose to the challenge. The walls flickered with shadows that had human form. Reinforcements from the Citadel! Each one of whom could be killed once and undead forever, taken by the darkness. Usually dread numbed or petrified one: Mielitta just felt an invisible weight crushing her, every pore screaming, 'Enough!'

The first figure burst through the wall, brandishing an axe, his fiery hair and beard reminding Mielitta of something, somebody.

'We come, Berserker,' he yelled at the unheeding bear.

Then more charged from the walls to attack the mages. A giant, whirling broken chains as weapons. A man in a plumed helm. Another in a leather skirt, carrying a shield with an eagle on it. One wearing a king's jewelled crown around his black helm. Twelve of them.

Jannlou's warriors! Tears in her eyes, Mielitta named them softly to herself as she watched them form two defensive lines. Five stayed back beside Nathan to protect the youngsters and the glowing cell in the wall. They ranged themselves either side of the lad, as if he were one of them, and Redbeard handed him a dagger, said something in his ear that made him stand taller, before the warrior moved past with six comrades.

Seven warriors joined the fray. Mielitta forgave Jannlou his fascination with their weapons as she watched the flash of a curved sword, the cut and thrust of straight ones. Redbeard's axe and his comrade's hammer would have terrorised Citadel mortals but Rinduran's manifestations merely fell, stood up and fought again. Those who took a dart from a blow-pipe knew nothing of their poison deaths but they too rose and fought on.

She was so bemused by the turn in events that she'd forgotten her own vulnerability. If Arven hadn't leaped from nowhere and pushed her out of the way, a swipe from a mage's sword would have given the enemy their first victory.

'Get behind our deathless warriors!' yelled Arven, setting an example.

Mielitta did so with alacrity, the bear with reluctance, but there was no haste in the revenants' progress. Slowly but inexorably, they advanced. Twelve of them against the twelve warriors. Matched one against one, the combat was a dance with no meaning and no wounds. Stalemate. One more revenant would tip the balance and reach the wall, via whichever human bodies tried to prevent it.

Rinduran had clearly reached the same decision. The amorphous black swirl reared up beside his son, flung words like sand into the desert air. 'We need to share our assets, finish this,' he told Bastien.

'Don't–' said Bastien but whatever he was about to say was forestalled by the rush of darkness into his body, which grew tall, invincible. One milky eye spiked with a bee sting seemed to fix on Mielitta.

She nocked an arrow. This time she would stop Bastien's breath even if the malignant power kept him walking towards her. Rinduran would know what it felt like to lose his son. As she focused on the cloaked figure, tried to distinguish between the swirl of the garment and the torso beneath it, decide on head or heart, she felt the beat of a million wings.

They come, buzzed her bees, showing themselves and flying to the wall, where they were integrated into hordes of their relatives. The glowing cell was black with bees coming from the Citadel through the wall, past the baby and into the battle.

'Take honey to the wounded girl,' Mielitta directed her hive, unable to focus on hitting Bastien, who plodded ever nearer, as slow in the sand as if he wore boots too big. She would save Janette before she died. She pictured the girl as an injured bee, mind mapped the place where honey must be spread.

The first bees to grasp the principle led the way and explained clearly to the others. Soon, Janette was covered in bees, each smearing a little drop of regurgitated honey on the burnt arm.

Kermon lifted a weary head, disengaged from his student and staggered to his feet, his hand on the sword he wore under his cloak. He lurched towards Bastien.

'Where's Verity?' he yelled. 'Why isn't she here?'

Bastien's voice answered, not his father's.

'Your friend betrayed you,' he mocked, 'as he betrays all his friends. Your *young* girlfriend is locked in her sickroom until sentence is passed. The same sentence as on you, traitor. But we'll dispense with formalities and put you out of your misery here.'

'No!' yelled Kermon, waving his sword above his head in a futile attempt to charge at Bastien.

A shaft of power stopped him in mid-stride, lifted him in a twist of darkness and dashed him onto the sand. He lay there as if broken and Mielitta felt something inside herself die with him. Jannlou had betrayed Kermon?

The bear was on hind legs, roaring. An apology? Rage? She didn't care any more.

Nobody would stop her this time. At least she'd take Bastien with her as she died. She nocked the arrow calmly, as she'd been taught, banishing emotion. His head, she decided. More difficult but a clear target, unlike the torso masked in a swirling cloak.

The blackness was growing, filling the air around Bastien, dividing, buzzing.

The wild bees are come. Her own hive exulted like drones scenting a queen.

Bastien was flapping madly at the swarms surrounding him, covering the milky eye that seemed to draw the bees. Still they came, settling in layers on the revenant until the very mass of bees brought the Chief Mage to a halt.

The voice screaming across the desert from within the coat of bees was Rinduran's. 'They can't hurt me or Bastien. They're of this world.'

'But *these* are Citadel bees and they can kill your son,' Mielitta shouted back as she sent her swarm to sting Bastien to death; her heart was sore at the cost to the hive but she couldn't find her target now with an arrow. Like Death-Pipe, she must use poison darts.

'You can't kill *me* and I will set fire to the Forest, root out every defective in the Citadel and show Perfection what we do with infected citizens. They will wish they were dead long before they are, from the youngest child to the oldest rebel hiding her abhorrent ways. Puggy will pay for her gender crimes, those students will pay for their treason and Perfection will return to its proper ways.'

'No!' the word came faintly in Bastien's voice but it was too late.

The wild bees zoomed off in a black tornado of their own making, as suddenly as they'd arrived, and Mielitta could see Bastien's body cracking like parched earth.

The blood oath! Bastien had sworn on his own life and magecraft that he would never take the lives of gifted citizens and his own mouth had broken the treaty.

'No!' This time the howl was Rinduran's as the body encasing him imploded, trapping the revenant in the doom of the broken oath. Hundreds of black fingers swept back from the undead mages, withdrawing into Bastien's crumbling body.

The bear became Jannlou and dashed over to the dead body of his childhood friend but he did not touch the greying remains of Bastien and his father. He bowed his head, waited with his sword at the ready.

Nothing moved.

Arven walked over to join Jannlou, moved his hand through the clean air around what was now a pile of ashes. 'They're gone,' he said.

'May the walls take them,' said Jannlou, set-faced, and he walked over to where Kermon's body lay sprawled on the sands. He knelt beside the Mage-Smith, murmured something that Mielitta couldn't hear.

How she would miss him. She automatically reached for Steelwing, remembered their shared love of Declan and the forge, Kermon's courage and sacrifice.

'No monument could be big enough to show respect for what Kermon has done.' She dashed a hand across her wet face, angry that she couldn't at least speak well for him, and then she felt the tiny movement in the steel.

'He's alive,' she whispered, then yelled, 'Jannlou, carry him back through the wall. We need help in the Citadel and we will get it, whatever I have to do.'

CHAPTER THIRTY-SEVEN

Drianne had always thought she was a kind person. So many times she'd restrained Mielitta, preached kindness. Her gentleness with all living creatures was surely why Qingzhao had chosen her as heir. If the wise old lady knew what Drianne had done, she'd disinherit her on the spot!

She had been violent in thought and deed, abused her magecraft and left a mage worse than dead – so old as to be antique. Worst of all, Puggy was in the right and Drianne *should* have given her magecraft back, accepted that she was a very minor mage, instead of hogging power generously given to her under false pretences. Puggy had saved her life in the Citadel and *this* was how Drianne had repaid her.

And yet, although she felt guilty, she wasn't sorry. If she had to do it again, she would. In truth, she was so selfish that the details which troubled her were the horrors of being old herself. Would she really be so ugly and suffer so much? Maybe she could go back to the Citadel and be suppressed when she reached that time. But how would she know? Did it creep up on you gradually so you couldn't see how vile you were?

Then she remembered Qingzhao. As wrinkled as a human

could be, with eyes bright as a sparrow's and compassion for all. Full of warmth and life. Could she choose to grow old like that?

Drianne, you are callow, callous and… and.. she couldn't think of another word beginning with 'c' that fitted so she gave up on her introspection. Judgement was easy but sentencing was impossible.

She sipped her cup of tea, wondered what mischief Verity had caused with a basket of homestead provisions. The Chief Councillor had been most insistent on green tea.

As was her custom now, Drianne flicked through the pages of Qingzhao's notebook to check on her chores for the day and the season. A note fell out, which was strange, as the journal had been read from cover to cover.

Hurt exists. I have been hurt and caused hurt. If I can forgive those who've hurt me, I can forgive myself too.

Drianne couldn't imagine Qingzhao hurting anybody who didn't thoroughly deserve it and certainly not doing anything as terrible as what Drianne had done to Puggy. Maybe her alliance with Verity would result in something equally horrible. How could you know what the consequences of any action would be? And yet at least in helping Verity she'd meant well. She wasn't sure the same could be said about how she'd dealt with Puggy.

Calamitous! She'd found the third 'c' word to fit her perfectly.

She read Qingzhao's words again. The sentence they delivered fitted her own crime and she knew her duty. She had some forgiving to do and a walk in the Forest would help.

The chickens accompanied her through the boundary from the farmyard into the green shadows and birdsong. Clucks and squawks disappeared as Drianne walked deeper into the Forest, her footfall as natural a part of the environment as the slithers and slinks.

The wind gave voice to the trees. Their conversation surrounded Drianne with creaks and groans from the heavy branches and soughing amid the fluttering leaves above her. She opened her mouth and sang with them, a silent air that played its part in the susurration, like the bees' ultraviolet in the spectrum of light. As if summoned by the thought, her rainbow scarf ballooned out and the little frog joined her in a voiceless duet.

At one with her world, she felt lighter as she returned to the homestead, her rainbow colours glowing with health. Until she saw she had visitors. Her heart thumped wildly. She no longer assumed that a welcome and a cup of tea would meet the needs of strangers.

A covered wagon was stationary to the side of the farmhouse, near the field where the beehives stood. Two large drayhorses had been unhitched and were grazing, tied to the fence. Whoever it was had come from the opposite direction to the Citadel, where Qingzhao said there was a town, a market and trading. None of which held any attraction for Drianne.

If they thought she was a pushover, they had another think coming. She felt the tingle of her magecraft, readied herself and walked over to peer into the wagon. Sacks and boxes.

The horses whickered a greeting.

'Easy there, boys,' she told them.

Nobody was in sight.

She cursed herself for leaving the front door unlocked. She really must change her habits and add wards to the physical locks so nobody could surprise her. Qingzhao had been too trusting.

She marched up the steps and past the new rocker on the veranda, where Hui was enjoying a shaft of sunlight on the windowsill. He blinked sleepily. Everything was normal as far as he was concerned but who would believe anything a cat said?

Drianne flung the door open and stopped short. Whatever she'd been expecting, it was not a welcome, a smile and a cup of tea.

'I hope you don't mind but Qingzhao always told me to walk right in and make myself at home. I thought you'd be back soon so I made a pot for two.'

Eyes green-gold as the Forest canopy, alight with mischief, and a sun-browned face with freckled cheeks. The woman must have been about Drianne's age – her new age. Male clothing, leather jerkin and britches, made a sensual contrast with the soft white chambray blouse underneath, its opening tied casually below a shadow of cleavage.

Drianne quickly looked up at the woman's face again. The mouth quirked upwards. She was clearly aware of the attention being given, and enjoying it.

'I'm Ariadne,' she said, pouring Drianne's tea and passing her the cup. 'But everybody calls me Raider. It's a sort of joke because I turn up and take stuff away but it's not very funny. Not true either because we trade. That's what I do. I've brought all Qingzhao's usual spring supplies but you only have to say what you want and I shall endeavour to provide it.'

Her eyes laughed at Drianne and that softest of mouths asked, 'Biscuits?'

For a moment, Drianne thought the biscuits were in the wagon and then she realised she was being offered a plate of her own biscuits. The impudence struck her as funny.

This stranger was taking over Drianne's home and instead of irritation she felt a growing excitement. Like the stirring of the wind before a storm broke.

'Qingzhao sent me a message.' Sadness changed the light in the eyes, the set of the mouth, as beautiful as the changing seasons in the Forest. 'She knew she didn't have long and she told me all about you. I've been longing to meet you all winter but had to wait till the snows cleared and then there were folk who needed supplies.

'And then there's the problem of bees dying over winter and I knew just who to visit, to see if you could trade some hives, not just honey, this year. Between ourselves, I'm hoping you'll say you can but not for a month or two, as then I'll have every excuse to come back. Qingzhao said we'd get along like a house on fire and she was always right. But here I am, talking too much as usual.'

She reddened, paused. 'I know you can't speak but that doesn't matter. Shall I make more tea?'

They both stood up at the same time and bumped into each other, brushed hands. Drianne's turn to blush and give an apologetic shrug.

'Exquisite,' said Raider, touching Drianne's face, tracing the silvery web of scars as if they were precious metal repairing a broken vessel. The finger continued its delicate journey to the still half of Drianne's mouth. 'I've never seen anyone who looks like you. Who did this for you?'

For you, not to you.

Drianne pointed to herself.

'Oh my, you're every bit as extraordinary as Qingzhao said. Mage, artist, farmer.' Suddenly Raider's face seemed very close, the freckles inviting.

'You can tell me anything,' the trader whispered, 'with or without words.'

Drianne's rainbow scarf bulged and out popped her frog, puffing out her cheeks in soundless song.

Raider jumped and so did the frog, retreating back into dark safety and peeping out between Drianne's clasped hands.

'He's cute,' said the trader, reaching out to touch the frog's head and stroking the back of Drianne's hand.

'She,' croaked Drianne, her voice rusty with disuse.

Sometimes it was as easy as that.

A look and a touch broke the locks as surely as the tendrils had forced the water gate in the Citadel. Words came like a soreness in her throat, but they came all the same and whispered their way into the outside world. The hopes that had been crumpled in sheets of discarded paper filled her mind as gold-flecked eyes met hers, open to all possibilities.

'Is this allowed?' She cleared her throat and spoke again, rusty raw but without a stutter. She had found her voice. 'In your world.'

Raider took hold of both Drianne's hands and the contact sparked rainbows.

'It's your world too. What we both want is like speaking. It just takes someone who lets you express yourself, who listens. You've been quiet long enough.'

'Yes,' whispered Drianne, in agreement and consent.

And then a kiss changed Drianne's world, broke all the barriers.

CHAPTER THIRTY-EIGHT

Mielitta's knees were shaking so she didn't try to move. Jannlou's warriors had left their posts protecting the wall and gone to his side

'We will take turns in carrying your burden, Berserker,' the king said, lifting Kermon onto his shoulder. 'You have brought honour to your name and will one day lie with the sleepers.'

Mielitta felt a stab of jealousy, dismissed it as ridiculous. The warriors had nothing to do with her personally and the last thing she wanted to consider was where she would be when dead. She needed time to accept not only that she wasn't dead but that just over there, in a glowing cell in a wall, she was being born. Or would be in a few hundred years.

As if the walls had heard her, their breathing stopped. She walked right up to the glowing cell and looked into it, saw the egg pulsing with life, the vari-coloured fibres, hairs, threaded through its contents.

The warriors' hairs. She reached out to touch the egg but Arven caught her arm, drew her back.

He pulled something out of his knitting bag, turned back to the wall and slipped a note into the cell. In spidery green handwriting the name 'Mielitta' was written on it, a label for a foundling.

'Qingzhao's gift to you,' Arven said softly. 'And mine. We must let him finish doing what he came for.' She'd almost forgotten about Oliver, a shadow-man from the past, from her past. Supposedly, one of her fathers. It was all ridiculous.

The man in a suit drew his hand across the front of the cell, creating a thin screen which thickened until the cachette was hidden behind solid wall. There was no sign that anything odd lay within the wall. Or beyond it.

Without a backward look, Oliver walked through the wall, into whatever and whenever lay beyond it.

Mielitta shook off Arven's restraining hand and tried to follow, cautiously, but she recognised the rebuff. The walls had blocked her again. The walls that could be considered her birth mother, that were growing her at this very minute.

She shook her head to clear it of too many impossible thoughts.

Around her on the sand were the corpses of twelve mages, whoever they were. Standing, waiting for her, were Arven, Nathan, Janette, Jannlou and his warriors. Redbeard bore Kermon over his shoulder. It was time to go.

'The Mages' Tower?' she asked Arven.

'I think so.' He articulated clearly. 'The park at the boundary of the worlds.'

As the setting shimmered, Mielitta did not look back across the sands to the wall where a new life was being nurtured.

Like brood, her bees reminded her. She didn't want to be reminded.

Then she could see rectangles of grass in mown stripes, a dog chasing its tail. People in clothes that no longer seemed strange were running together, in family groups, in pairs, friends, all of them belonging to someone, to somewhere. Past people in their past world.

She counted her people, checked they were all present and led them across the park, ignoring the signs to keep off the grass, ignoring the inhabitants of this world, who walked through them and past them. The evil within the walls was gone. Kermon's students would be safe from now on. She looked at the two youngsters; Janette's good arm linked with Nathan's, the girl as silent as the boy.

At the park entrance, she stopped. Jannlou took Kermon's unconscious body from Redbeard and heaved him across one shoulder. He reached out for Mielitta's hand and she felt the calloused strength of his grasp. Arven took her other hand. Nathan and Janette stood by Arven, all linked by hand except for the warriors.

They formed a line behind the king, bowed formally to Mielitta and Jannlou.

'Fare well, Berserker and his woman.' Each spoke in turn.

Mielitta felt no desire to respond to such an uncouth parting speech but clearly nothing was expected from her. Only their berserker held their respect and Jannlou duly expressed his gratitude to them. The stones knew the warriors merited thanks but they didn't have to be so… patriarchal. Especially in the circumstances.

The drones who made you, her bees cheerfully pointed out

'No,' she insisted but without conviction.

The warriors marched one behind the other through the walls as if there were no barrier at all.

'Now,' said Arven and Mielitta felt the usual apprehension as she stepped towards the stone face.

And through it into the dark stairwell of the Mages' Tower.

The warriors continued through the open doorway, loping with the pace of men who could march for days if need be. As the last broad back disappeared from view, Mielitta felt their loss, forsaken. Refusing to say the word that linked them to her.

'The sleepers must return to their barrows and caves, under

lake and mountain, until they should be called again.' Arven too was watching the once and future warriors leave. 'I don't think anybody will block their path.'

'I don't think they'd notice if somebody tried!' Jannlou's admiration was evident.

The shadows in the darkest corner of the stairwell stirred and Mielitta reached instinctively for an arrow, though her fears knew the weapon to be futile.

But it was a lady who emerged, the greylight picking out the black and white of her cloak, striped like the lawns in the park. She was taller, older, but her blonde hair and pale face were familiar. As was the haughty tone of voice. Did Verity have an older sister?

'Kermon!' The young woman rounded on Jannlou. 'What have you done to him? Lay him down while I call our physician to attend.'

With a glance at Mielitta, Jannlou obeyed and they waited, prepared to defend themselves. Arven's hand dipped casually into his knitting bag.

But the woman in the striped cloak showed no interest in them. She went to the doorway, hailed a messenger, instructed him to fetch a doctor at once.

'Yes, Supreme Councillor Verity,' the boy's high voice shrilled in reply.

How long have we been away? wondered Mielitta.

This new, assured Verity returned to Kermon's recumbent form and sat beside him, resting his head on her lap, heedless of the dirt and damage to her fine garments.

'I called you home and I've been waiting here so long,' she said to the unconscious mage-smith. 'You are such a stupid man, incapable of looking after yourself.'

She looked up at Mielitta and Jannlou, repeated her question. 'What have you done to him?'

It was Arven who answered. 'The shade who held sway in the walls landed a strike on him and he suffered a fall when he was so tired he lost himself. I think his spirit recovers even now.'

'Of course it does,' Verity snapped. 'That's what I've been doing.'

Kermon's eyes fluttered open, widened, closed again. Then he tried again, his face screwed up in confusion.

'Verity?' he asked.

'For the stones' sake. Does an extra five years make such a difference? You can stand up on your own now.' She pushed him gently into a sitting position, her actions kinder than her words and then she stood up, brushing the dirt from her cloak. 'You can't go off into the walls and expect things to be the same here.'

More coldly, she spoke to Mielitta. 'All you need to know for now is that my Citadel has an agreement with your person in the Forest. During our negotiations we both aged five years, which is irrelevant but answers your surprise at seeing me changed.'

Drianne? Agreement? Aged five years? Mielitta opened her mouth to ask a hundred questions but Verity — Supreme Councillor Verity – cut her off smoothly, addressing Arven.

'You said the shade held sway, past tense. Let's not mince words. If no vestige of my father remains, you should say so. But first: does my brother live?'

'No,' said Arven. 'Your brother is dead and nothing remains of your father. Neither deed is by our hand.'

'What happened?'

Mielitta recognised the tight control in Verity's voice as a sign of how close she was to losing it and pitied the girl. Woman, she corrected herself. How would she get used to Verity and Drianne being her own age?

'Rinduran occupied Bastien's body and broke the treaty by his words and deeds. The blood oath killed them both.' Arven's words were carefully chosen and true – and yet they left out everything, thought Mielitta.

Verity nodded, swallowed. 'Did my brother give permission? Did he say he was open?'

'No.'

A stillness enveloped Verity and the silence waited for more questions.

When they came, her words were also carefully chosen. 'I used to wish my father held me in the same esteem as Bastien. I suppose I must count myself lucky.'

Jannlou's gruff voice came as a shock. 'Bastien was never allowed to be himself.'

'No, not even in dying,' she said. 'Even that was stolen from him.'

She fixed Mielitta in a brown-eyed stare as stony as any bear's. 'Some would say you broke the treaty first, returning to the Citadel when you'd agreed to exile, according to the terms.'

Mielitta's face heated up. *No honour*. 'We merely passed through,' she said.

'As you took no blood oath, you can't be judged by it. Perhaps you should count yourself lucky too.' Verity's voice was as stony as her eyes. Then shifted back to smooth diplomacy. 'Doubly lucky as your *passing through* now is timely. You will be there when I announce our alliance to my citizens.'

Silence seemed the safest response as Mielitta pondered the chance of them all leaving the Citadel alive.

Verity's last questions came without inflection. 'The other mages?'

'Dead in battle,' answered Arven.

'And the warriors who came before you?'

'Were also passing through. They are not of this world and return to whence they came.'

The physician arrived and a fluster of heart and temperature checks ensued until Kermon was pronounced in need of rest but otherwise not at risk of any dangerous consequences to his ordeal. In a disarray equal to that of his appearance, the doctor left.

Kermon immediately turned to his students, who'd been lurking, transfixed by the inside story of power politics. Janette had a faraway look, as if she was already writing an exclusive account for her next assignment.

'Janette, how's your arm?' he asked.

She blinked, frowned, looked at her arm as if it belonged to somebody else. 'It doesn't hurt any more.'

'Let the honey finish its work,' Mielitta told her. 'Just rest for a day. It's best if you stay in your room.'

Janette's mouth turned down in silent rebellion and Kermon shook his head at both his students. 'To your rooms, now, and stay there until I've talked to you both!' their tutor ordered. 'Quick, before I clean your minds so you remember nothing. Which I will do if you speak or write to anybody without thinking of the consequences.' He rather spoilt the effect by adding, 'I'll have some food and drink sent to you.'

Like rabbits released from the wolf's glare, they shot off through the doorway.

'Verity?' Kermon queried, staring at the Supreme Councillor. 'You waited for me. I thought I… we… were denounced as traitors.'

She spoke as to a child. 'Really Kermon, there's no point us continuing this farce so I'm telling your friends the truth.'

If Mielitta thought she'd seen honesty in a person's eyes before, she thought again. Never had a gaze shown the transparency and innocence of Verity's clear gaze.

'He's been working for me,' the young woman said. 'And for the Citadel. I knew he was contacting you so I got him to report every conversation to me. To spy on you. And the moment I revealed this to the Council, along with the duplicity of the substitute Chief Mage, the Citadel was mine. The Council had already judged my loyalty and Kermon's to be indivisible so once they realised how well he'd done his work for us, I was given the appropriate respect.'

Kermon looked completely befuddled but said nothing.

'I don't believe it!' said Jannlou.

Verity accepted the compliment gracefully. 'We did hide it well.'

'And now we're allies.' Mielitta was struggling to keep up with the subtleties of Citadel politics but she was sure of Kermon's loyalty and friendship.

His love however might have turned elsewhere. If so, she was glad for him. She touched Steelwing in her usual gesture of comfort and she glanced at the Mage-Smith. He mirrored her gesture and she felt the warmth reach her own hand from his touch on Perfection Unfinished. They understood one another. She only had to call off the bear, give Jannlou time to read beneath the surface.

'Yes, allies. We should go to the greensward by the forge and I'll tell you what I want.'

Mielitta held Jannlou's arm, a warning, said, 'And we'll discuss it all with Drianne as soon as we're home.'

'Don't worry,' sad Verity airily, 'you'll be allowed to leave.' She put an arm through Kermon's, a lady with her knight, a Supreme Councillor with her Right Hand. 'For love of the stones, Kermon, stop looking at me as if you've been hit by an anvil! I'm still me, just a bit older on the outside.'

'Anvils are too heavy to lift,' he objected.

'Don't say that in Council or we'll have every mage in the Citadel proving their magecraft in a game of hurl-the-anvil.' She raised a warning finger. 'Don't speak. Like your students, you need time to think. It would be appropriate to notify your wife that you are still alive and of course vice versa.'

'Puggy.' Kermon's tone held no enthusiasm.

'She was the one who called you traitor,' Jannlou recalled. 'I thought she might care about you and then she realised that I did. I betrayed you.' He stopped short, continued slowly. 'But she was a fool wasn't she, not realising that *we* were the ones being duped.'

Good, thought Mielitta. Jannlou was catching on. Let's hope they could all keep up with the intrigues here.

'I'm well aware of all the things Puggy has done and I'm sure you're keen to see her again.' Verity's air of innocence was as natural as the grassette of the greensward.

Arven followed in silence, his hand never leaving his knitting bag.

Puggy, thought Mielitta. Kermon's wife. Tannlei's murderer.

CHAPTER THIRTY-NINE

Verity stalked along the passageway with Kermon at her side and the Forest dwellers in their wake. Citizens made way before her as if she was a battering-ram. Behind her, they turned to stare and follow the bizarre entourage.

'Tell every servant in the hall to bustle about the Citadel and pass on the message that I have news to announce. They must come to the greensward in front of the forge.' Verity didn't even stop walking as she instructed the little messenger, who promptly scurried away as he was bidden.

'Are we safe?' asked Mielitta.

Verity heard her and threw a reply back over her shoulder. 'You are with me and the Citadel is mine.'

That would have to suffice but Mielitta kept a hand on her quiver all the same. Memories assaulted her.

Here, she'd hidden from Jannlou. But that was true of many places. She glanced at him and his eyes flashed brighter blue as he smiled at her. He remembered too.

This was where she'd appeared from the wall as a baby, landed at Declan's feet. Her foster-father had told her the story so many times that she could picture the propulsion of a crib through the wall, the baby all in white clothing and the label with a name. Mielitta.

And that strangely textured part of the wall was where she'd sent her memories for safe-keeping when Shenagra had tried to wipe her mind clean. Where she'd retrieved the Council's secrets the next day and known how to get to the forbidden Forest. One of the times when the walls had protected her.

So many enemies and so much betrayal. What did Verity really want?

They walked through the door to the greensward and across to the forge. Verity had a word with Kermon, who nodded and, with the help of the nearest citizens, brought a heavy table out from the forge.

He took Verity around the waist and lifted her onto the table then jumped up beside her, facing the growing crowd.

Mielitta told herself she was Verity's equal and had every right to be here. She walked with a confidence she didn't feel to stand beside the table, where Jannlou and Arven joined her. She had no intention of making a speech but she remembered how the grassette had clamped her legs, taking her prisoner so she jumped up alongside Verity and Kermon, feeling very exposed.

Arven caught her eye. 'If this is a ruse, we won't let them take you,' he told her. He dipped into his knitting bag and extracted his needles and a length of fine silvery yarn. As relaxed as if he were alone in his living-room he stood there knitting. The yarn glinted as it ran loose from the bag to the stitches being worked.

More armour? wondered Mielitta.

'Citizens and mages,' began Verity. She had no magecraft to project her words but she didn't need it. The populace hung on her words.

'I bring you news of a great victory.'

Mielitta felt public attention switch to her and made sure she did not look like a defeated enemy being paraded for ridicule. She swung her bow a little, just to show she was bearing weapons.

'But every great victory has its price and I have sad news of the cost. Thanks to my knight, Mage-Smith Kermon, as loyal to Perfection as he is to me, the evil within the walls has been defeated and our plans for students to learn from visiting the walls can now go ahead without danger!'

Verity paused for the expected cheers and was not disappointed. Kermon's face was a study in impassivity. No doubt he'd had practice, Mielitta realised, suddenly appreciating just how complicated all those Council meetings he'd attended must have been.

Under cover of the noise, she heard him ask, 'What about getting the students back safely? That's a victory too.'

'Their infringement of the laws sets a bad example. We'll pretend it didn't happen,' Verity told him quickly. Then she returned to her speech-making.

'Mage-Smith Kermon led our valiant mages and our allies,' here she waved an arm towards Mielitta, 'against the common foe and thanks to his expertise within the walls, they triumphed.

'Sadly, the cost was great. I have lost a brother.'

Another pause and a chance for everyone to look at his feet, as was proper at news of a death. 'My grief is only assuaged by knowing he did not die in vain. And I hope this will comfort those who, like me, have lost somebody. Their courage will never be forgotten. I offer my sincere sympathy to Councillor Zeta, for the loss of her husband Zeebo.'

A woman screamed, was comforted and led away from the gathering. Then Verity named each of the dead mages with due solemnity and praise.

'Had it not been for Mage-Smith Kermon, evil would have won the day. He had to be carried back to the Citadel and were it not for the skills of our physicians, he too would have left us.'

And will leave you yet, thought Mielitta, her face grim. But she had little option other than to play the part scripted for her, of the noble ally. She'd been called worse the last time she had stood on the greensward.

'Thanks to the courage of those we've lost, we have a brighter future than ever before. Some changes will make Perfection the society we all want it to be.'

Here we go, thought Mielitta. *This is where we find out what Verity really wants.*

'I am not a mage but my powers have proved equal to those of the mages. There are many among you with skills that have not been recognised because in the past we only valued magecraft. From now on, our school will nurture and respect all talents.'

Kermon was nodding. Mielitta waited for the catch.

'We no longer need to fear the Forest or those who dwell there.'

There was a collective gasp at the unmentionable word being uttered so easily.

Mielitta told her bees to keep out of sight. Now was not the moment to test Perfect tolerance.

'We offered a magnanimous treaty after our victory in the Battle of the Forest.'

Mielitta smiled between gritted teeth, comforted by the clack of knitting needles beside her. *Good.* Arven was up to something.

'Now we can take the next step: work together as neighbour states. I welcome future discussions on border controls, freedom of movement and mutually beneficial trade. I ask you to show the same respect for the Queen of the Warrior Bees as you do for me.' Verity inclined her head graciously towards Mielitta, an invitation to speak.

She swallowed. Her words sounded as rough to her ears as chewed wood, compared with Verity's practised fluency but they came from the heart. 'Chief Councillor Verity spoke the truth about Mage-Smith Kermon.' She would *not* add Supreme to Verity's title. 'I have never seen courage such as his nor greater evil than he faced. If he speaks for the Citadel, I must listen. I want peace between us. I want every man, woman and child born in the Citadel to feel they belong, here and in the Forest. My world is open to you.'

She swallowed hard, knowing the meaning of the formula in Perfect society. '*I* am open.'

Kermon's eyes were full of tears as he looked at her. But Verity stood between them and Mielitta couldn't reach for his hand this time. She stood alone on the table in front of a thousand of Perfect citizens.

Not alone, objected her bees.

The knitting needles were silent and Arven added his words to hers, his voice cool and silvery as his teardrop armour, shining with truth. 'And the Citadel will be open in return,' he declared.

The seer's eyes turned upwards and everyone present followed his example, looking up at the grey expanse of the canopy protecting the Citadel.

'It is time,' murmured Arven, stooping to bring something out of his bag. A broken arrow.

Mielitta watched him press the silvery knit fabric to the arrow, where it melded to the metal head, repaired the shaft, made the weapon almost whole. The tip had been blunted and bent, was not fit for purpose.

Arven's black eyes still gleamed in trance state as he passed the arrow to Mielitta, said, 'Ask Kermon. It must be his choice.'

With no idea what she was asking, Mielitta held up the arrow and looked a question at Kermon. Then she saw the pendant around the soul-reader's neck begin to glow, the same silvery blue as Arven's arrow.

She reached up to touch Steelwing but her own arrowhead was as cold as the icy fear she felt. But it was Kermon's choice.

His eyes never left hers as he took off his arrowhead, no longer twinned to hers. He gave it to Verity, who held it a moment, thoughtful, then passed it to Mielitta.

The moment Arven's arrowhead touched Kermon's it flamed white hot and the two fused.

Arven's words carried the weight of spidery green writing, of all prophecy. 'Unfinish Perfection so that it may be re-made, differently, by Tannlei's arrow and Kermon's courage.'

Mielitta pulled her bow, nocked the arrow and focused.

What's the target, Mielitta?

Open the Citadel. To the sky, to the weather, to the wilderness, to the Forest.

She pointed in her mind's eye to a meadow beyond the walls, to a better future. Then she loosed Arven's arrow, not into the canopy but straight through it and far beyond.

As the world cracked open, grey shards of canopy exploded into the upper atmosphere and golden shafts of sunlight hit the grassette like strikes of magecraft.

Mielitta thought she heard the clickety-click of knitting-needles, smiled at the thought of Arven working weather magecraft in the Citadel.

But something was bothering her. She felt a predator watching her, waiting its chance. She scanned the crowd, following her instinct to the source of her unease. A cloaked figure. Malevolent raisin eyes in a dumpy face. An arm raised to strike. Unnoticed in all the hullabaloo.

'Perfection will always win!' Puggy yelled but it seemed only Mielitta heard her or saw the lethal magecraft loosed.

Fly! buzzed her bees.

Mielitta shifted shape and flew, high above the lifeless woman collapsed on a table, her quiver spilling arrows in a pattern that made no sense.

Had Verity planned this?

CHAPTER FORTY

Mielitta wasn't aware she'd summoned the swarm but she was surrounded by enraged bees, roaring. Or was it the bear roaring? So many human shapes below her, so much confusion.

Caught up in the purpose of the hive mind she dived down with the swarm, which showed no interest in the tableau where Kermon had pushed Verity aside and was leaning over the dead woman. Arven was knitting the sky an intense blue. His needles stabbed, worked and stabbed again.

Mapped in her mind was the direction for the bees and one instruction.

Kill.

The murder of that woman – her mind shied away from acknowledging whose dead body that was – had caused chaos. As if the canopy ripping apart wasn't enough for Perfect citizens. Now they had a rampaging bear and bees in their midst.

They ran for shelter in the building, fighting to get through the only door and blocking each other's way, screaming, until Verity deployed her mages and their craft to calm the crowd.

But the Supreme Councillor offered no protection to the only person targeted by the bear and the bees: allies as unlikely as

Forest and Citadel, brought together by their common love and loss.

They pursued Puggy through the open forge door, to the back exit, out onto the greensward where Maturity Ceremonies had been held. They caught up with her against the Maturity Barn, where she'd sent so many children to their forging. Where she'd saved Drianne and lost her own mind. Where Kermon and Verity had given her the chance of a new life.

Which she did not deserve.

It killed our queen. Kill it.

Mielitta held herself distant from the sense of outrage and loss flooding her mind from the other bees. Better not get involved. But the scent of bee venom was all around her, arousing her battle fury and she *could* sting. She did so, feeling the flesh yield as her dart pierced it. The scent released maddened her and, unlike the worker bees all around her, she could sting again. And again.

Clumsy in their midst, the bear ignored the frenzy of bees. He delivered his own lethal judgment on the mage, whose feeble attempts at defence had long since changed into a drug-induced euphoria. Puggy's face was swelling up in reaction to the venom but she was trying to dance with the bear, ducking his unsheathed claws as if in a game, apparently oblivious to the wounds he'd inflicted.

Allergy, thought Mielitta as Puggy's ballooning face reddened, and she gasped for breath. She was suffocating.

And then it was over. The mage's body slumped to the ground and as the glamour faded all that was left was a wizened corpse. Desiccated skin and wisps of white hair. A faint scent of roses evaporated with Puggy's essence.

The bear roared and his eyes regained their human blue, deep wells of suffering. He held out his shaggy arms and the remaining bees went to him, crawled all over him, shared comfort and loss. Mielitta joined them, aware of the warmth, the smell of wet fur and earth beds. She should have been afraid but she wasn't. His roar held the war cry of twelve warriors, who'd taught him how to unleash the berserker and how to restrain himself. This bear would never hurt bees.

But they *were* hurt and so was she. Love and loss. A light-headedness came over her and immediately a cadre of workers came to her side, prodded her. One stuck its tongue down her throat and fed her. She felt a small injection of energy, enough to get her to the hive.

The bear was returning to human form and she crawled onto his lips, touched him once with her antennae, then accepted the insistence of her guardian bees.

Home, they told her. *Healing*.

She flew back over the forge, saw the table in front of it. Jannlou was lifting the woman's limp body onto his shoulders as he'd done Kermon's. He shook his head angrily at offers of help and walked heavily into the Citadel, out of sight.

None of my business, thought Mielitta. *So tired.*

The sky lightened her weary flight but the breeze made her wings heavy as guilt.

Keep going, insisted her bees, surrounding her so closely on all sides that their bodies held her up. Bobbing along, lopsided, she could see the cleft in the wall and she made a final effort.

Entrance guards hauled her into the darkness of comb, worked unevenly in the shape allowed by the hole. She was escorted into the safety of the warm, throbbing centre of the colony and told, *Sleep*.

When she awoke, Mielitta felt hollow. No amount of honey could revive her spirits so she went back to sleep.

Five times she slept, woke, ate, felt no better and sought oblivion again. The sixth time, she felt different. She asked herself why she was lazing around doing nothing, like a drone.

Work, she demanded.

Work, agreed the bees.

She was prescribed light duties and she set to the first tasks of any newborn worker bee: cleaning and polishing the cells for food production and egg-laying; feeding the older larvae.

Quickly bored, she asked to try the jobs of an older worker bee.

At one week old, we make royal jelly and wax to build honeycomb.

When Mielitta found out that this meant processing substances in her gut and regurgitating them all day, she said she'd skip this stage, as she was a special Queen Mother, sampling life as a worker bee rather than enjoying the full experience.

Bee laughter suggested they knew she wasn't up to the task.

At two weeks we collect pollen. At three weeks, nectar.

Mielitta had collected pollen in the past and she wistfully remembered falling asleep in a flower with Pollen Bee but she couldn't face the inevitable flight through the Citadel and out into the meadow beyond its walls. To see the Forest, knowing her other life was over, would break her.

Carrying out the dead bodies.

Repairing leaks and holes with propolis.

Guarding and feeding the queen.

With every suggestion, she grew more and more gloomy. The hive was thriving, full of brood and honey stores. The queen was still young and laying well. Mielitta wasn't needed.

She longed for a role that suited her and nothing in bee life fitted. She should be part of the changes in the Citadel or celebrating in the Forest with her friends.

Friends? queried her bees.

'My other hive,' she told them. 'I can't stay here. But I don't think I can go back.'

What could she do as a bee to make her feel useful in the

human world? She'd had such grand ideas for the children in the Citadel and Kermon had worked so hard here. She wanted to be part of it all.

What were those children doing now? They'd be in school, no doubt. Kermon would be tutoring his young magecraft students. Janette and Nathan would be plotting some new misadventure.

What if she led the bees to the school, took the children a taste of honey, a reminder of the Forest. She could say goodbye to Kermon and then. Her mind blanked.

And after that– Her mind blanked. She couldn't stay a bee forever and nobody was immortal. She'd already proved that in one life. In Mielitta's life.

Her heart started pounding. Mielitta. She named the corpse on the table. Jannlou had been carrying *her* dead body away from the table. *Her* friends were grieving for her. Love and loss hit her like a tidal wave. She was drowning in emotions she didn't want to feel. Hers, other people's. She saw the colour red. Bees couldn't see red. Bees didn't have all these terrible feelings. The awfulness of being human flooded her, carried her away from the hive, back to another way of life.

She was not a bee and she wasn't dead. She was back in her own human body. Two arms, two legs and a stomach that heaved. She was lying on a bed in an empty chamber in the Citadel and the knock at the door could only be one person. Her gaoler.

CHAPTER FORTY-ONE

Mielitta steeled herself and sat up. She would not give them the satisfaction of seeing her flinch and she no longer feared her own death. She'd been through it.

The door opened fully and Jannlou came in, alone. The raw animal noise he made smashed her brittle control and she put her head between her knees to hide her tears.

'You've been in some kind of coma for days. I just kept hoping you'd come back, like Kermon did. At first, I thought you were dead,' he accused her, holding her so tightly she couldn't breathe.

'I will be if you keep squeezing.' Her attempt at humour was spoiled by the quaver in her voice and her wretched body's continuous shaking.

He let go of her but only so he could jump on the bed to sit behind her and cradle her body with his own. He folded his legs around hers and hugged her, nuzzling her neck. She leaned back against him. Shelter.

They sat this way in silence. When had they last been just the two of them? With time for the Personal Shelf.

As her body stilled and her mind stopped doubting that this was real, she took in her surroundings. Yes, a chamber in the Citadel, but which one?

'The first time you were here, I found you sleepwalking in the library and brought you to my room so nobody would ask questions.'

Her laugh sounded broken but at least it was a laugh.

'I thought you were hoping to have your wicked way with me.'

He rolled her over to face him and traced the lines of her face with his finger.

'I was but I hid it well.'

She remembered so much. 'You asked me to the Maturity Ball.'

'Only after you'd beaten me in an unfair fight.'

'You shouldn't have followed me into the Forest. It was forbidden. Jannlou,' she hesitated. 'When they tried to forge me, gave me the drugs, I imagined us here, a Citadel life, us married…' She whispered, 'Children.'

His face changed and she wished the words unsaid.

He put his hands either side of her face so she couldn't escape his gaze without shutting her eyes. And she didn't want to shut out the blue. There had always been a glimpse of sky in the Citadel, an awareness that life could be more. She'd seen it in his eyes.

'I wonder what the sea's like,' she murmured.

'We married in the Forest,' he told her fiercely, the blue deepening by fathoms. 'I don't know whether I'd trust you to look after ordinary children. But bear cubs and bee grubs should cope.'

Her heart clenched.

Tell him, urged her bees. *When your gut is wrong, you have to get the poison out or it will spread.*

'I wanted to find two normal parents, in the walls. Not a mother who laid me like an egg.'

Like a baby bee. And that's how it should be.

Mielitta ignored the bees, struggled to find the words. 'Not multiple fathers who don't even know I exist. Donors, not parents. And then growing in the walls for hundreds of years. I suppose the walls are the closest thing I have to a birth mother. I *am* a freak. I just wanted normal parents like you and everybody else have. How could I ever *be* a parent now, with what I know about my background?'

The more drones mate the queen, the stronger the eggs.

'That's not helpful!' Mielitta blurted out.

Jannlou looked quizzical. 'The bees?' he guessed.

'They're telling me it's all normal for a bee. And that babies grow in comb. I am not a bee!'

'I can tell.' He kissed her gently. 'What I saw in the walls was a lineage to be proud of. The stuff of legends. A mother from whom you inherit your link with bees and your beauty. All but the red hair.' He stroked the long mane that flowed down her back. 'And mythical warriors who each gave some quality to make you who you are. If the walls looked after you, then they had their reasons.'

'I don't want to think about which of my qualities came from *those* men – or *things*, whatever they were.' She shuddered. *Red beard, black eyes, golden skin, skill with a bow, link with bees.* When she took each of her characteristics and traced it back to a parent, she felt her skin crawl. It was like being forged. As if others determined who she was. Too difficult to talk about.

She ignored the bees and tried to lighten the tone. 'You *would* think mythical warriors better than one real father,' she teased.

'Yes.' But his reply was serious. 'So would you if you'd listened to me and Bastien, comforting each other after a lashing. From tongue or strap didn't matter. They hurt the same.'

'I'm sorry. And I'm being thoughtless, as Drianne always tells me. I know your mother died when you were young. Do you think she made you a berserker?' She tested the new word on her tongue and liked its flavour.

'I hope so. She made me a better man. She even made my father a better man. And a worse one when she died.'

'I remember you telling me what she said, about the difference between living and existing.'

Jannlou's eyes were inkwells. 'That's what we should pass on. That's what's important.'

The children. 'I should say goodbye to Kermon. I know he's staying.' She still half-hoped Jannlou would deny it.

Instead he said, 'He won't be alone. Arven told Verity that Kermon has too much to do, in the forge and in Council, that he would stay and tutor the young mages.'

'Oh.' Mielitta felt winded by yet another body blow.

'But no goodbyes are needed. They will come to us in the Forest, often, especially when they know they can see you.'

Mielitta thought about the gap between what she'd hoped and what had happened. Maybe it wasn't so bad.

'Do you think Verity planned it all? Puggy and everything. She won Kermon.'

Jannlou considered the idea. 'She looked as shocked as everyone else when it happened. I don't think she felt much grief over Puggy though.'

'I'm sure she didn't.' Kermon was free now.

Mielitta looked at the bare walls in the greylight, the chair that looked ready for an interrogation, the no-nonsense chest in which to store clothing. Cottonette sheets and woodette floor. She had spent eighteen years existing in Perfection.

'Let's go home,' she said, trying to disentangle her limbs from Jannlou's. He winced and she remembered the wounds he'd received fighting Rinduran, but he made light of them. He tensed his muscles, kept her close to him. She recognised the dangerous spark in his eyes, caught the dark brown scent of earth dens and her pulse raced.

'Not before we've realised my boyhood dream, in this room,' he murmured. 'Wherever you are is my home.'

His touch made her response a certainty.

MATURITY ASSIGNMENT

THE HONEY HUNTER

By Apprentice Storymage Janette
Witness and Anchor: Apprentice Mage Nathan
Tutor: Mage-Smith Kermon
Sources: Wall location: Sub-layer 15, tribal

He wasn't there. Qwian scanned the gathered villagers again while the Headman spoke the words of blessing for the honey hunt. The familiar ritual brought her no comfort and she barely listened until mention of her own name burst into her self-doubts.

'Qwian was chosen by her father, whose passing we grieve. And she has been visited by the dream so she must lead the honey hunt in his place. Her shoulders are slight, with much resting on them. Today the bees will make their own choice, confirming or rejecting.' Gurratan's voice was clear and sharp as the diamond he was named after.

Qwian shivered in the dawn chill and her heart hammered like a war drum. Where was he? Surely, he would not let her go on the hunt without one gesture to wish her well? He knew she might die this day, falling like her father had, one year ago, to death below the cliffs. What if the bees slashed the bamboo ties of her rope ladder, as they had done to his?

When they argued last night, she'd told Tau that she must walk her own path and if she died hunting honey, then this was her fate, like her father's. Of course he retorted that death would find her more easily halfway down a cliff, attacked by giant bees, than if she sat cross-legged, weaving in her family hut, like the other women.

'I am not like other women,' she'd told him and his eyes gleamed like stones wet with river-water but he had not kissed her to make up. He'd turned away, stoking his fears to a blaze of resentment. He could not even come with her. The Headman's son was too precious to the tribe's future to be allowed to hunt honey. He could only wait to know if all who set out returned and waiting was a humiliation fit for women, not warriors. So he'd told her.

What if she did die today? Her thumping heart told her that she would. Her father had said she must have the honey hunter's dream to follow in his footsteps so she'd told the Shaman of the one where she climbed down a rainbow in pursuit of a dark red monkey. This satisfied everybody although Qwian was sceptical about the way men's interpretations of dreams suited their plans.

Maybe she had never had the honey hunter's dream. Tau was not here because all the omens were bad and she would die. Gurratan would be forced to buy a honey hunter from another tribe and the bees would be angry at such disrespect. She did indeed carry a heavy burden on her slight shoulders.

Gurratan brought the rite of well-wishing to an end but it meant nothing to her if Tau was not here. The Headman handed her the two long bamboo spears with square wooden ends that she would need for her work. Her father's spears, recovered undamaged from the shrubs around his broken body, by the bees' will. She had been there, his apprentice, when he fell to his death and now the spears were hers. In such a manner did a child become an adult. She bowed her head in acceptance as she took them.

'Do not taste the honey,' hissed Gurratan, for her ears only. 'You are still only a woman even if the bees accept you as our honey hunter. If your father had been blessed with sons, we would not have come to *this*.'

As she raised her head, she felt some shift in the scene, the presence of the newcomer, before she saw him, coming out of the shadows at the back of the gathering. Dawn sunlight bronzed hair that hung straight as weighted threads on a loom. Tau. His face granted her no smile but he raised one arm slowly, put his hand on his heart and offered it to her in mime.

Qwian's open palm caught his invisible heart and placed it on her own, in a gesture that could have been acceptance of Gurratan's words. But was not. Her heartbeat steadied and now she was ready. She would not die this day because she was born for bees.

Now she could smile and so she did. 'The day begins well,' she told her team of twelve hunters and she turned her back on the village to lead the way with her spears through the surrounding jungle to the place of preparation.

On the previous day, the honey hunters had carried bamboo ropes, slats of wood and a wicker basket to the sacred clearing above the high cliffs. They'd braved the freezing river, helping each other across on the slippery stones. Leeches had latched onto two of the men; their wounds were still bleeding. This time they knew all the danger spots and could move more quickly without their burdens, chanting songs to bring courage.

When they reached the place of preparation, they needed no word from Qwian to set about their tasks. The ropes and slats were assembled as ladders and the bamboo-shoot joints were double-checked. Nobody spoke of the death of Qwian's father but she knew they all carried the blackness of it, like the rage of bees. This day's harvest would be in homage to him.

With nods and whistles, their work at the top of the cliff was done and the group split in two as the May sunshine grew stronger. One team took the pathway down to the base of the cliffs, avoiding the bees.

Last year, Qwian had been among them. She'd gathered wood and saplings for the fires, secured the rope sent down from the top. She'd shinned up the rope, carrying leafy brushwood and lodged it in crevices, just below the huge scallops of honeycomb, so that the smoke would reach the bees without hurting them. The roar of the giant bees drew her, spoke to her in a language she did not yet understand.

'Be patient,' her father had said, before he fell to his death.

She'd been fanning flames upwards, proud of her work with the brushwood, when he reached out with his spear to dislodge more comb. The cliff was black with giant bees, clouded with smoke, but she saw him stretch, saw the ladder tilt impossibly as a slat gave way. He should have been held by two security ropes.

Had he slipped them to reach that tempting honeycomb, just out of reach? Had the jerk on the two security ropes been too much for the trees they were attached to, on the top of the cliff? Had the knots come loose? In the confusion of smoke and fire, fall and death, cause was irrelevant. The bees had decided.

When the first whistle came from below, Qwian looked over the edge. She saw the first wisps of smoke and the first black clouds of bees swarming in panic two hundred ladder-steps below. She could glimpse the team of fire-starters, like ants scurrying in and out of flames another hundred ladder-steps or so further down the cliff.

Her stomach filled with wings. Tau was right. A woman could be safe weaving in her hut.

The men beside her gestured, whistled back to those below. All was ready. It was time.

She donned the honey hunter's veil, her only protection.

Anything more would show disrespect to the bees, deny the bond they shared. She murmured the words due to the gods, attached the two security ropes and started to climb down the ladder into the smoke and black buzz, into the heart of bees.

Then Qwian was lost, choking in fumes, her entire body vibrating in the wrath of bees that bounced off her veil, her arms. They were almost weightless but there were so many she was suffocating in bees. Thousands of them in contagious panic. She must fly! She pulled on one of the security ropes, the signal to lift her up again, get her to safety. She could not do this!

Nothing changed. Was this how her father died? Wondering why he'd been abandoned?

A rope whistled down beside her, snaking through the blinding white, dangling an empty basket that stopped close enough for her to hook it with a spear. The men were good at their jobs. They'd interpreted her jerk of panic as a sign to send down the basket and they'd guessed where she was on the cliff face. They'd guessed well.

Already she was adapting to short breaths, closed mouth, listening to bees and echoes, marking the position of the honeycomb each time she had a clear view of the glistening hives. She made a tentative stab, swung a little on the ladder, stabbed again. She *would* do this. She grew used to the swing of the ladder as she stretched more, became braver, determined to dislodge the first comb.

Nearly severed, Qwian thought. She used one spear to position the basket and then gave a last jab with the other. Stretching the last sticky dollop of dark red honey as it ripped free, the comb dropped into the waiting basket, which jerked with the weight. Immediately, the basket was lowered by the top team to those on the ground.

Qwian swung on her ladder, waiting for the empty basket to come back up, so she could fill it again. She was a honey hunter surrounded by her bees. Her mouth opened in laughter and at that moment a breeze of bees lifted her veil and smacked her mouth with a morsel of honeycomb. She licked it instinctively, the mad honey made from rhododendron nectar. Aphrodisiac honey, that made men crazy or healed them. Forbidden honey that she should not taste.

Fly, the bees told her. *Fire! Dangerous!*

She understood them in their language but it did not seem strange. Their voices were in her head.

'We are not robbers but guests in your home. Thank you for the gift of honey,' she told them politely, licking the last bit from a corner of her mouth as blackness zoomed around her, too fast to be more than fuzzy shapes.

We will need you, they told her. *Your hive and ours. Never forget our gifts and your promise.*

Her head swimming, Qwian saw the smoke curl into the image of a girl's face surrounded by bees. Then the girl was running through a forest. A bee tattoo glittered on her thigh, came to life, took flight. The smoke blanked white and the vision was gone, broken by an empty basket, returning from below.

Remember, the bees buzzed. Then they stung her so she would not forget but she just laughed. The stings did not hurt her. Qwian shook her head to clear her thoughts of honey madness.

She heard the bees say, *We must protect our queen. We must protect you…* and then all she heard was humming. She set to work once more, careful to take only outer honeycomb, leave the heart of the beehive safe, where the new brood was in capped wax cells. Where the queen was at work, laying eggs. *Protect the queen.*

After four heaped basketfuls of comb, Qwian's work was done and she jerked on both ropes to show she was coming up. The ascent was slow, her limbs suddenly stiff with fatigue, and she let the men help her onto firm ground. Her legs shook as if she was still swaying on the ladder and she disguised her weakness by sitting.

Someone passed her the leather bottle and she eased her throat with freezing river-water. *Waiting is women's work,* she thought. On the ground below, the men were mashing comb and straining the precious honey into their containers. On the top, ropes and ladders were untethered and dismantled. Qwian had earned her moment resting.

When the honey harvest arrived on the cliff top, each man saluted Qwian, kissing her spears in reverence.

'The bees have recognised your father's daughter,' they said.

More could not be said without transgressing the mystery of bees and Qwian had no desire to ask questions. She too was reluctant to talk about her experience. And of course she could not say she had tasted the honey. She merely looked on, indulgent, while each man took his allotted gulp of honey and became talkative, foolish or quarrelsome, as was his nature.

Although each felt the urge, nobody returned to the honeypot for more. Nobody wished to go home in the shame of drunken sickness, remembered only in jokes. This harvest was their triumph, worth a fat year for the village.

The trek homeward was lighter in spirit than the outward journey, not just because of the honey's effect. Now the men could tell stories of past hunts and talk of Qwian's father. She felt his approval like a warm blanket on a cold night.

They called out as they approached the village, to let all know they were returning. This time, Qwian did not need to search for the one person who mattered. Tau, in front of the other villagers, did not wait for her to reach him but rushed towards her, heedless of custom.

'You came back,' he said.

'I will always come back,' she replied, losing words in a kiss that tasted of mad honey. 'For the honey,' she murmured, kissing him again. 'And you.'

If you enjoyed this book, please share your thoughts in a review, however short. Reviews help other readers find my books.

Anyone who reviews one of my books can have his/her dog featured in the Readers' Dogs Hall of Fame on my website

Contact me at jeangill.com

I love to hear from readers.

Acknowledgments

Many thanks to:
my editor Lorna Fergusson of *Fictionfire Literary Consultancy* for believing in my bees;

Babs, Claire, Jane and Kristin for your invaluable critiques and support;

Writer friends in The Sanctuary, which lives up to its name;

Jessica Bell Cover Design for the amazing covers for all my books.

Tannlei's archery teaching owes much to the most famous philosopher-archer: Confucius

Selected reference works:
Collins Beekeeper's Bible
Geoponika, a 10th C Byzantine Greek farming manual, translated by Andrew Dalby
The Buzz About Bees – Jürgen Tautz
Honeybee Democracy – Thomas D. Seeley
Grizzly Heart – Charlie Russell and Maureen Enns
When Bears Whisper, Do You Listen? – Stephen F. Stringham
Great Bear Almanac – Gary Brown
Buddhism for Busy People – David Michie

L'Apiculteur – a monthly French journal for beekeepers

ABOUT THE AUTHOR

I'm a Welsh writer and photographer living in the south of France with two scruffy dogs, a beehive named 'Endeavour', a Nikon D750 and a man. I taught English in Wales for many years and my claim to fame is that I was the first woman to be a secondary headteacher in Carmarthenshire. I'm mother or stepmother to five children so life has been pretty hectic.

I've published all kinds of books, both with traditional publishers and self-published. You'll find everything under my name from prize-winning poetry and novels, military history, translated books on dog training, to a cookery book on goat cheese. My work with top dog-trainer Michel Hasbrouck has taken me deep into the world of dogs with problems, and inspired one of my novels. With Scottish parents, an English birthplace and French residence, I can usually support the winning team on most sporting occasions.

www.jeangill.com

facebook.com/writerjeangill
twitter.com/writerjeangill
instagram.com/writerjeangill
goodreads.com/JeanGill

If you enjoyed this book, I can recommend
SOMEONE TO LOOK UP TO

Written from a dog's point of view.

Top Pick Award from Litpick Student Reviews. By IPPY and Global Ebook Award Winning author. For all dog-lovers!

'Jean Gill has captured the innermost thoughts of this magnificent animal.' Les Ingham, *Pyr International*

A dog's life in the south of France. From puppyhood, Sirius the Pyrenean Mountain Dog has been trying to understand his humans and train them with kindness.

How this led to their divorce he has no idea. More misunderstandings take Sirius to Death Row in an animal shelter, as a so-called dangerous dog learning survival tricks from the other inmates. During the twilight barking, he is shocked to hear his brother's voice but the bitter-sweet reunion is short-lived. Doggedly, Sirius keeps the faith.

One day, his human will come.

SAMPLE CHAPTER
SOMEONE TO LOOK UP TO

Let me show you where I was born. Shut your eyes and imagine skies so blue they dazzle, snow so white the glitter bursts against your closed eyelids, mountains dancing in the winter sunshine, dancing all the year round. In summer, the high peaks swirl their veils of heat-haze and tease with sudden nakedness to catch your breath, the chain of summits stretching beyond the horizon, whispering the ancient southern names, Pic de Viscos, Pic de Néouvielle, Pic du Midi de Bigorre, Pic de Macaupera. The shadow of a cloud drifts on the wind, lazy as a grand raptor surveying its domain, darkening an entire valley, the Val du Lavadon. I was born in the Pyrenees, with my two sisters and four brothers, seven little white rat-sausages jostling blindly to reach our mother's teats. I've seen a few pups born in this long life of mine, so what I can't remember, I can imagine. The warmth and smell of mother, the sleepy pleasure of a milk-full tummy and the newness of an outside world on this body after nine weeks growing to a curled-up ball inside my mother's baby-sac.

So much to learn… stretching, wobbling on four legs, squeaking for food, pushing Stratos off the teat I wanted (if you'd known Stratos, you'd have pushed him too), cuddling up to Snow, Sancho and Septimus to sleep in a pile of puppy fluff. The first thing I really remember was when I was about six weeks. You know how it feels when someone niggles you and niggles you; a push here, a little nip there and then one of those sideways looks just to make sure you knew it was deliberate? One sideways look too many, big brother! I can still feel that rush of power into my brains, paws and, most importantly, teeth, which sank into that plump cushion of flesh like a claw into mud. I've tried again and again to explain the pleasure of biting but words just don't do it. The first time, there's the slight hesitation as the points of your little teeth puncture the skin and then you're in! And he's squirming and squealing … and then it all goes wrong. He's spoiling it by asking for help, real help, and he's your brother so it hurts you to hurt him and you have to stop – and you hate him for making you stop. So you've discovered how complicated life is for a dog. You can't just do what you want because the want splits in two and fights itself, confusing you.

When Stratos and I met up again, years later, and were telling our stories by the light of the moon, that was something we shared. First bite. One good thing about the animal refuge was that you did get to see the moon. If I think of anything else that was good about the refuge, I'll be sure to let you know, when the time comes. But each bit of the story has its place, time and smell, and the moment for extra-strong disinfectant, ears oozing pus and dog-breath sweet with worms, has not yet come. What Stratos and I did agree on was that the second bite was more dangerous, sweeter with the knowledge of breaking the taboo, knowing you had to be strong enough to follow through. I'm talking about biting dogs of course, not about – whisper the very words! – biting Humans. Though Stratos and I had to talk about that too, given his situation. He's my hero, you know? But as I said, everything in its own time.

So, there we were, puppy-fighting and of course Stratos bit me back as soon as I let up on him. And if you don't forget the first bite you've given, boy do you remember the first time you got bitten, which is usually the reply to your own attempt! I was so shocked, I screamed before it hurt and then the pain flooded me with rage and I turned right back on him once more. He was shocked in his turn, and stopped biting me, with just that little shake he always gives. From then on we worked out that it was safer to stop at the squealing stage but Stratos' extra power was already starting to weigh in for him, even as a pup.

Dominant? Stratos? Maybe when he was little. When he was grown up, he didn't need to do anything. He'd just walk. And when Stratos walked you felt this urge to roll over in front of him, wag your tail, look at some far-distant imagined mountain, look anywhere but at Stratos himself. You'd want to say, 'Hey Stratos, did you skip breakfast? Here have my throat. I don't really need it.' You'd know that once you'd cleared up the niceties of status, you'd follow him to the ends of the earth and that same big brother would protect you to the death. We were pack.

Our talents were very different and I could hold my own in some ways. Not always the brightest puppy in the pack, my brother, and he didn't get the chance to learn like some of us did. 'University of Life,' he told me later. 'Some of us learned the hard way, Sirius, and some of us ARE hard.' But even then, I wondered. What if things had gone differently for Stratos?

But that's me, Sirius, the sort of dog who wonders 'what if?' The sort of dog who started as a little rat-sausage, jostling his siblings to reach a teat, unaware that there could ever be more to life than Mother. That's something else that Stratos and I talked about – Mother, otherwise known as Morgana de Soum de Gaia. She'd been a beauty queen and even though we were dragging her down, 'draining her haggard,' she complained, there was something about the way she carried herself that said 'Princess'. She knew it and she made sure that we knew it too. 'A Soum de Gaia never does *that*,' Mother would sniff contemptuously at some puppy pee or worse fouling the straw, 'in its own den!' and then the offender would be picked up by the scruff of his neck and tossed into the yard, where the rest of us would mock and nip whoever was suffering Mother's discipline, just to show her our support. And because it was fun, of course. And doubly fun if it was Stratos in trouble and not allowed to answer us back. Not so much fun when it was your own wrinkled rolls of neck fat gripped firmly between forty-two maternal teeth and your own four waddle-paddles pedaling in mid-air, not as keen on flying as you'd thought.

'A Soum de Gaia stands like this,' she told us and made us practise standing very still, head high and stretched out a bit, front legs straight and parallel, back legs uncomfortably far back, as if you were having a stretch and then someone said, 'Hold it there!' and kept you like that. Still, practising 'the position' with Mother made it easier when Alpha Human took us one by one, put us up on a table and did 'grooming' and 'the position'. Mother had not prepared us for 'Show me your little ears,' when our Human flicked them back and rubbed them clean with olive oil. You can imagine how much fun we had afterwards licking oily ears. I reckon we were the puppies with the cleanest ears in the whole Pyrenees. Nor were we prepared for 'Show me your little teeth'. In fact Mother tended to be averse to seeing too much of our little teeth and had shown her own once or twice when someone really caught her teat on the raw. We didn't have much option about showing our little teeth to our Human as she put her fingers to our mouths and curled our lips back. If you'd seen the expression on Stratos' face you'd have bust a gut laughing. I wasn't convinced he'd be a Beauty winner, even at that age; no-one checking Stratos' little teeth could look in his eyes and think how cute he was. And 'little teeth' was not the worst for the boys although at that age we weren't too fussed really. But when I look back, I do wonder now whether Humans ought to be quite so free and easy in checking out our masculinity. But at the time I just thought that it was part of being a Soum de Gaia to have that tickly feeling you get when a Human puts her hands down there and checks there are two. Perhaps I was right, because I've met a few dogs since then who feel strongly enough about their rights to consider the very idea sufficient provocation to justify the B-word.

I don't know. I think you have to take their intentions into account with Humans and they mean well, you know, in their own strange way. And Stratos surprised me there. He always got that slightly glazed look in his eyes that meant he liked it. No accounting for tastes. Anyway both of us achieved the 'one, two!' tally without any trouble at all. No surprise there.

Not only was Mother a Princess, but she knew her realm from puppyhood and had grown up with most of the other dogs, the Soum de Gaia aunts, uncle and sisters. But Father was from Away and at twilight, the hour for wolf-tales before dark and real work, Mother would tell us the story of how they met and a slightly abridged version of how they mated. Amados de los Bandidos, my father. The very name was enough to make you want to run off into the mountains and howl with him, according to my mother, and she'd heard enough about him from our Human to make any bitch salivate. Amados this and Amados that and more importantly Amados for THE marriage. Even a Soum de Gaia can look at a rottweiler swaggering along the street, or the local hero with half an ear, mange and fleas, and wonder what he might be like… or so we heard during the twilight stories. But youthful fancies are only that and dynasties are founded on parents like ours, so Morgana accepted her destiny (and so should we, was the maternal message).

They met at the annual gathering, the Great Show at Argelès-Gazost, with snow sparkling on the mountains and dogs everywhere, not just the Pyreneans, but the little Pyrenean and Catalan Shepherds, and the great Matins with their bleary, bloodshot eyes. There were music, dancing, cafés overflowing with dogs and their owners, festive with horse-drawn tour-carts. Pennants were strung between the houses, the horses were wearing garlands, and even some of the dogs were wearing Béarnaise red and yellow kerchiefs round their necks. Apparently this was all to celebrate the meeting of my parents. And where did The Event take place? Where else but in the Show Ring of course. While she was strutting her stuff with the girls, he was leaning casually against the fence-post, starting one of those competition drools that can reach tail-length if you're lucky.

Stratos and I have discussed drool technique and he admits that he loses from impatience. At about half-tail length, the urge to shake your drool is just so strong that he can't resist it, the way the dewlaps vibrate, the ears flap, and the cool slobber sprays your scent as far as a good head-shake will send it. I have told him that if, like me, you hold out, stay very still, focus your mind on the longest stalactite of drool in history, the satisfaction of the shake is even greater but he just can't do it. Still, both of us have elicited squeals of pleasure from our masters at the quality of our drool-sprays – I've even seen mine rushing round to add some water to what I've already provided on his clothes and body. All very satisfying.

So there was Dad, starting a drool but, as I say, you need a bit of luck, and it wasn't to be. His Human had the towel clamped to Father's mouth before he'd even reached a respectable drop and, when Mother sent a flirty look in his direction, what she saw was the sheepish and sullen upper face of her fiancé, his fine head cut in two by the pink towel wiping his jaw. She says it made her laugh so much the judge awarded her 'best expression' and commented on how lively and spirited she was in the Ring. She won of course. That goes without saying. I have no intention of boring you with all the Shows and the prizes, and anyway that wasn't how my life went.

Then it was her turn to watch him and this time his Human was more of an asset. He knew she was watching and every prance, the lift of his head, every sparkle in his eye was for her and when he took his static pose, he was looking right at her with melt-your-heart-brown eyes and she was won. The judge commented on his fine aroundera and his 'star quality' as if he were performing for a special audience. You bet. For those of you new to my world, the aroundera is what we in the Pyrenees call the wheel, that high circle we make with our tails when we're happy or excited or just saying, 'Hey, world look at me'. Human words are so limited compared with what a dog can say with just its tail alone, but the gist of it is, aroundera=good mood. And the better the tail, the better the aroundera. Father's tail was perfect, a feathered curve cascading in perfect proportion but his masterstroke was to stand with his tail in repose – down, relaxed with the little hook in the end ready to rise – then when the judge looked at him, up went that tail and like the great seducer he was, my father timed the moment impeccably. He won of course. That goes without saying. I think that by this stage he was already Champion of France, Spain, the World, the Universe and Everything, so it's difficult not to be blasé about shows.

The two of them had a chance for some more personal, nose to bottom, contact while their Humans talked travel and transport, then two months later my mother headed over the mountains. Just because he had 'won her' at the show didn't mean she made it easy for him. Oh no. She enjoyed the chase as much as the next girl and the chase used every gallop of ground she could run round, every bush she could turn behind, and every insult she could hurl at him when he caught up with her. No-one would have given them beauty prizes, or dared to check their little teeth, as Mother finally stopped running away and succumbed to the oldest instinct in the world. And though she hadn't seen him or heard of him since, she left us in no doubt that his name was on our birth certificates. And what a name. What a dog. Someone for us to live up to.

'No pressure there then,' I told Stratos. Some of the others drank it all in, the shows, the father from away, the romance of a name – and nothing more than a name and your imagination – but Stratos and I, we always wanted something else. We had no idea whatsoever *what* we wanted but we were already sure we wanted something else. And we'd reached eight weeks, the age of the Choosing, when our chance for Something Else might come knocking on the door.

You might also like

SONG AT DAWN

Book 1 in the award-winning *Troubadours Quartet*.

FREE *to members of Jean Gill's Special Readers' Group. Sign up at jeangill.com*

'Historical Fiction at its best.' Karen Charlton, *the Detective Lavender Mysteries*

Four Discovered Diamonds Awards

Historical Novel Society Editor's Choice

Winner of the Global Ebooks Award for Best Historical Fiction

Finalist in the Wishing Shelf Awards and the Chaucer Awards

Set in the period following the Second Crusade, Jean Gill's spellbinding romantic thrillers evoke medieval France with breathtaking accuracy. The characters leap off the page and include amazing women like Eleanor of Aquitaine and Ermengarda of Narbonne, who shaped history in battles and in bedchambers.

LEFT OUT

If you like Young Adult books that are enjoyed by adults too; if you're left-handed or know a leftie, try *Left Out*

"A compelling story about friendship, its strength, and the unusual ways it develops." Rebecca P. McCray, The Journey of the Marked

Being different isn't easy but it can be exciting!

How well do you know your friends? Are they left-handed or right-handed? Are they left-brained or right-brained? And what difference does it make?

Shocked at discovering how left-handers are persecuted, Jamie ties her hand behind her back for a public protest in school. This does not go down well with the teachers. Her best friend Ryan joins in but just when their campaign is working, Ryan's mother drops a bombshell. She's whisking him off from Wales UK to live back in America.

There he faces bullying at its most deadly.

FORTUNE KOOKIE

Can dreams take over your life? Although it is Book 2 of the series *Looking for Normal*, the book stands alone.

Shortlisted for the Cinnamon Press Novella Award

"Jean Gill brings her magical storytelling skills to teens, to weave compelling and thought-provoking stories that will linger on in their minds well after the last page is read."

Kristin Gleeson, author and children's librarian

Jamie's mother is hooked on fortune-tellers, and running the family into debt. To cure her, Jamie decides to investigate the psychic world. Their research causes havoc in school and they are drawn deeper into the very world they are investigating.

Jamie's dreams of walking a medieval battlefield are so vivid that she feels compelled to resolve a historical mystery that starts at Kidwelly Castle in South Wales, where Princess Gwenllian once lived.

Jean Gill's Publications

Novels
Natural Forces
Book 3 The World Beyond the Walls *(The 13th Sign)* 2021

Book 2 Arrows Tipped with Honey *(The 13th Sign)* 2020

Book 1 Queen of the Warrior Bees *(The 13th Sign)* 2019

The Troubadours Quartet
Book 5 Nici's Christmas Tale: A Troubadours Short Story *(The 13th Sign)* 2018

Book 4 Song Hereafter *(The 13th Sign)* 2017

Book 3 Plaint for Provence *(The 13th Sign)* 2015

Book 2 Bladesong *(The 13th Sign)* 2015

Book 1 Song at Dawn *(The 13th Sign)* 2015

Someone to Look Up To: a dog's search for love and understanding *(The 13th Sign)* 2016

Love Heals
Book 2 More Than One Kind *(The 13th Sign)* 2016

Book 1 No Bed of Roses (*The 13th Sign)* 2016

Looking for Normal (teen fiction/fact)
Book 1 Left Out *(The 13th Sign)* 2017

Book 2 Fortune Kookie *(The 13th Sign)* 2017

Non-fiction/Memoir/Travel
How Blue is my Valley *(The 13th Sign)* 2016

A Small Cheese in Provence *(The 13th Sign)* 2016

Faithful through Hard Times *(The 13th Sign)* 2018

4.5 Years – war memoir by David Taylor *(The 13th Sign)* 2017

Short Stories and Poetry

One Sixth of a Gill *(The 13th Sign)* 2014

From Bedtime On *(The 13th Sign)* 2018 (2nd edition)

With Double Blade *(The 13th Sign)* 2018 (2nd edition)

Translation (from French)

The Last Love of Edith Piaf – Christie Laume *(Archipel)* 2014

A Pup in Your Life – Michel Hasbrouck 2008

Gentle Dog Training – Michel Hasbrouck *(Souvenir Press)* 2008

Printed in Great Britain
by Amazon